The Lasso Springs Series

Book One

Callie's Heart

The Lasso Springs Series

Book One

Callie's Heart

By

Kathleen Ball

The Lasso Springs Series

Book One: Callie's Heart
Book Two: Lone Star Joy
Book Three: Stetson's Storm

Desert Breeze Publishing, Inc.
27305 W. Live Oak Rd #424
Castaic, CA 91384

http://www.DesertBreezePublishing.com

Copyright © 2012 by Kathleen Ball
ISBN 10: 1-61252-988-7
ISBN 13: 978-1-61252-988-2

Published in the United States of America
eBook Publish Date: April 1, 2012
Print Publish Date: November 2012

Editor-In-Chief: Gail R. Delaney
Editor: Theresa Stillwagon
Marketing Director: Jenifer Ranieri
Cover Artist: Gwen Phifer

Cover Art Copyright by Desert Breeze Publishing, Inc © 2011

All rights reserved. No portion of this book may be reproduced or transmitted in any form or by any electronic or mechanical means, including photocopying, recording or by any information retrieval and storage system without permission of the publisher.

Names, characters and incidents depicted in this book are products of the author's imagination, or are used in a fictitious situation. Any resemblances to actual events, locations, organizations, incidents or persons – living or dead – are coincidental and beyond the intent of the author.

Dedication

I dedicate Callie's Heart to my parents James and Rosemary Tighe for their unyielding love and never ending support. Mom I wish you were here but I know you're proud.

I also dedicate Callie's Heart to my sister, Tricia Tighe who encouraged me and supported me every step of the way. There wouldn't have been a novel if it weren't for her.

Thanks to Ryan Foss, my nephew, who calls me amazing and gave me the Japanese Cherry Blossom scent that Callie wears.

A very special thank you to my new daughter in law, Brittany who brought horses and fun into my life.

I have made so many good friends through my writing journey and I thank you all especially Charliann Roberts, Jean Joachim, my friends from Textnovel and Facebook.

And of course I dedicate my novel to my three guys, Bruce, Steven and Colt because I love them.

Chapter One

Callie Daniels was home.

Her heart fluttered as she stepped on the porch of the achingly familiar ranch house. Each lonely night as she finished college, she'd longed for this ranch, the sounds, the smells, the feel of the earth under her feet. Yet her longing didn't stop there. She longed for the man inside the house. The man she'd fallen in love with as a tiny girl, shadowing his every move. She'd finally come home to him.

Now her real life could begin. Inhaling, she smelled the sweet Texas grass as excitement filled her. Yet she hesitated. Would he have changed? She hadn't seen him in months. They hadn't spent last Christmas together, he'd forgotten her birthday, and most puzzling, he hadn't attended her graduation. Not knowing what to think, Callie gave him the benefit of the doubt. Ranching always came first, but he'd been missed.

Admiring the improvements made to his house made her smile. They'd decided that keeping one house open was more economical. It looked grand with its new coat of white paint, and new green shutters. The door was still red. His mother had insisted a red door brought good luck. Anticipation filled her as she opened the door and walked in. It always seemed such a cheery house, with lots of windows to invite in the bright Texas sun. A sense of peace came over her as she walked down the hall, until she walked into the living room. Speechless, she froze at the door.

He sat on the couch with a black haired beauty in his arms. They didn't notice her as they kissed, his hands moving through her hair. Callie watched the woman unbutton his shirt. She gasped, they looked at her and jumped up off the couch.

The dark haired woman seemed confused, but Garrett O'Neill's expression changed from surprise to guilt. He quickly buttoned up his western shirt and tried to give her a smile. "I didn't know you were coming home."

"I guess not," Callie replied, woodenly. How could he? She had thought... hell, it didn't matter what she thought. He was her husband. In name only but they had exchanged vows.

Callie could see why Garrett had the woman in his arms. Her long, dark, hair glistened in the light, hanging to her waist resembling a beautiful curtain. Her tanned complexion enhanced her blue eyes. Jealousy wasn't something she'd experienced before. It didn't feel good.

"This is Sylvie, my new housekeeper." Garrett's explanation sounded lame.

Callie wanted to throw up but good manners prevailed. "Hi," she said, looking at Garrett. He was still the most handsome man she'd ever seen. Tall, dark, and handsome hardly covered it. He wore his hair short; the color always reminded her of rich Texas dirt with gold sprinkled on it. His sky blue eyes looked clouded with confusion. It killed her she wasn't the one who had been in his brawny arms. She had no right to be upset, he never made her any promises, but she couldn't turn off her feelings.

He still viewed her as the little seventeen year old he had married. When would he look at her with a man's appreciation? Even in her new dress, she couldn't entice him.

"I'll just go to my room. I had hoped to surprise you for lunch."

"I wish we'd known you were coming," Sylvie said. "I've been storing my clothes and stuff in your room. The sheets are clean, I sleep with..."

Callie didn't wait to hear the rest. She couldn't bear it. She had made excuse after excuse for his lack of attention these last few months. Somehow, she never guessed another woman.

With slouched shoulders, she climbed the old wooden stairs to her room. Sitting on her bed, she could see Sylvie's stuff everywhere. It brought home what she just witnessed. Garrett never made her any promises except to keep her land safe. They'd never even kissed except for a quick peck at the wedding ceremony. Still it hurt.

She had always enjoyed a certain closeness with him she could never find with any other person. Her mother's health had deteriorated and she wished for them to marry. She knew her greedy sister would try to wrestle the ranch away from Callie, so she begged Garrett for a favor. Callie had been all of seventeen and just about ready to graduate from high school.

In the end, her mother had been right. Her Aunt Abigail arrived for the funeral and the ranch. Her shock at Callie and Garrett's wedding made it all seem worthwhile. Garrett's part of the deal was to keep the land profitable and safe while Callie's part was to finish college.

Even though it wasn't a real marriage, somehow, her heart got involved. The truth cut painfully. Callie walked over to the full-length mirror and gazed at her reflection. Her skin appeared too white and her blond hair too dark. A few weeks in the Texas sun would take care of that. Sadness reflected back in her violet eyes. She shook her head in disgust, went to her closet, and found a pair of her old jeans and a faded red tee shirt. She couldn't believe she had worn a dress and left her hair down for her supposed husband. No more pretending to be anything other than what she was, a rancher. Dressed in her normal clothes, she pulled on her old scuffed boots and tried to smile.

Looking in the mirror again, Callie braided her hair down her back. Her heart still broke, but she refused to cry. Putting on her black Stetson, she walked out of her room and out of the house. It wasn't her house anymore. It never was. They'd decided to close up her homestead and have her move into Garrett's farmhouse. It had all been an illusion, the same as her marriage.

The newly painted barn looked good. Callie's step lightened as she made her way to her horse, Pirate. Pirate had been her horse since forever. He'd been a gift from her father. From the first time she sat on Pirate's shiny black back, the two had become inseparable. Laughing as Pirate nickered at her; she opened the stall and walked in. Immediately she hugged her best friend, wishing she could just cry against his neck.

Garrett stood on his porch when she led Pirate out of the barn. Callie looked away and jumped onto the saddle. She knew he wanted to say something but she just couldn't. Turning Pirate, she headed out toward open land.

*****

Garrett watched her ride away, his heart heavy. Knowing he'd hurt her weighed profoundly on him. He had no business being married to her, she was just a kid. She deserved more than him. She was so sweet and young, not old and jaded like he'd become. He purposely put distance between them at Christmas, but he would've been at her graduation if he'd known. He'd been a fool getting involved with Sylvie, but if it deterred Callie and made her find someone else, he'd continue. Their relationship hadn't gone past the heavy petting stage and it surprised him Sylvie had suggested she slept in his bed. It served his purpose so he didn't correct her.

He had to admit Callie looked good, almost too good. The last time he'd seen her in a dress was at her mother's funeral more than four years ago. She looked damn good in her jeans too. He wished he could go after her. She'd go to her own house, probably planning to stay.

Guilt and concern made him seek out Old Henry. He had been a ranch hand on Callie's land since before she was born. Garrett found him walking out of the barn shaking his gray haired head.

"Old Henry, hold up. I need you to bring Callie's things over to her house."

Old Henry gave him a look of disdain. "Why would that be? I bet seeing Sylvie here really cut her up. It's bad enough that you always date a new gal every time Callie comes home but to have one living with ya. She's heard the men talk about your revolving bedroom door."

"I pretend to date. Callie's too young. If she thinks I'm dating several women, maybe she'll set her heart on someone her own age."

"Pretend dating? Could have fooled me but hey who am I to be judging you? Marriage must be different now than in my day. In my day when you shared vows with a filly you stayed true to her."

"Just bring her stuff over. Make sure you bring her some supplies too. That old house has been closed up for years."

"Sure thing, boss." Old Henry's voice sounded hard and unyielding.

Walking back to his house, his conscious got the better of him. If looks could kill, he'd be dead. Seeing Sylvie leaning against the front door made him want to turn and walk the other way. He needed to be alone.

His scowl must have been fierce since it made Sylvie back away. "I'll be in my office and I don't want to be disturbed." Her look of doubt didn't faze him. He knew he was doing the right thing for Callie's sake. She didn't know about love. What she was feeling had to be infatuation, pure and simple.

Garrett poured himself a glass of whiskey and drank it down in one smooth move. He'd made a deal with the Devil, by making her mother's wishes come to fruition. He'd had to watch Callie grow up into a lovely young woman. She filled out in the right places and he couldn't help but look. Staring out the window, he knew he was right. He couldn't let his feelings get in the way of her future. If he had to make her hate him, he would. It really was for the best but somehow his heart didn't want to agree.

*****

Riding Pirate was a balm to her soul but just a small band-aide to her heart. Even her childhood home didn't perk her up, at least it wasn't Garrett's house. Pirate immediately went into the barn, it made her happy to see the fresh hay and feed. She grabbed a currycomb intending to brush Pirate, when a strange noise startled her. Callie peered out of Pirate's stall and laughed. Nanny had come to visit. Nanny was one of Garrett's horses, a beautiful grey. Soon after she had stopped foaling, she became Houdini. There wasn't a stall or barn that could keep her in. In the vein of a social butterfly, she wandered from ranch to ranch visiting the other horses. Usually she let herself into the barn and made her way into a comfortable stall.

The other ranchers took her in stride and called Garrett to let him know where she could be located. Callie just loved her. "Well, come on in Nanny. You're looking good girl. Where have you been? I know you weren't at Garrett's this afternoon."

"Talking to the horses still?" Old Henry teased, his voice filled with love..

Callie moved out of Pirate's stall and ran to her old friend giving him a big hug and kiss. "It's good to see a friendly face."

"Yeah, I can imagine. Hear tell you met up with Sylvie."

"Yes, I did. I guess I interrupted them."

Old Henry gave her a sympathetic smile. Callie loved the way his green eyes crinkled when he smiled. His hair was gray and his face had a leathered tan look. "I think I'm going to stay here at my homestead."

"Don't blame you. I don't care for her either. Good news is I'm staying here too."

Callie smiled. "Good, I could use a friend."

Old Henry took her into his arms and held her close. "I know, darlin', I know. Garrett had me bring a few supplies for you. The utilities have been turned off at the house for a while."

Callie sighed. "Well, at least we won't starve."

They both turned at the sound of an approaching horse. She walked out of the barn, surprised to see a cowboy she didn't know. "Who's that?"

"A new hand. He showed up around Christmas. He's a good guy and a hard worker."

Nodding absently, Callie looked her fill at the good looking man with straight black hair hanging below his collar. He had that chiseled angular look that she found attractive. As he rode closer, she could see his copper skin and deep dark eyes. She wished she could say he made her heart beat faster but he didn't. He wasn't Garrett and unfortunately her heart beat only for Garrett. He sat tall in the saddle and seemed even taller as he dismounted and reached out to shake her hand.

"Howdy, ma'am. I'm Stamos. Garrett sent me over to give you a hand around the place."

His handshake was firm and he exuded confidence. Callie nodded at him. "Great to meet you. Stamos, is it?"

"Yes, ma'am."

"Call me Callie. I assume you know Henry?"

"Sure do."

The fact that he looked her in the eye and didn't look her up and down impressed her. His expression didn't show a lack of respect for a woman boss and Callie liked him immediately. "We have some sandwiches for tonight and I'll get supplies as soon as the utilities are turned on. Tomorrow we ride the fences. I've been gone way too long and I need to ride my land again."

"Sounds like a plan," Henry responded, looking down the driveway.

Callie looked too and saw Garrett's truck and her car. She'd wanted her things brought over but she wasn't happy to see Sylvie driving her vehicle. Callie clenched her teeth, trying to stem her jealousy.

"Wow, I haven't been over to this part of the ranch before. No wonder you live at the other house," Sylvie said, wrinkling her nose at Callie's house.

Callie ignored the slight. She only had eyes for Garrett and before she realized it, she stood, staring at him. He held her gaze for a minute and then turned away. "Well, I just wanted you to have your car," he explained, looking uncomfortable.

"Thank you. I appreciate it."

"Wow, what a letdown from the other bunkhouse, Stamos," Sylvie commented, smiling at him.

Perturbed Callie turned toward her. "I'm sorry if my home doesn't meet your standards. I've been living on a shoestring budget for a long time now and I haven't been able to afford extras."

Garrett grabbed Sylvie by the hand. "If you need anything..."

"I'll be fine," Callie said, softly. She wore her heart on her sleeve, but she couldn't help it.

*****

Callie, Old Henry, and Stamos just finished their morning coffee when they heard a truck horn blowing. All three headed outside. Garrett had brought the horse trailer and it had two horses in it. Callie wondered what he was up to. She'd hoped for a little time away from him. He'd been all she could think about last night. All of her assumptions, everything she thought she knew had been turned upside down. It had shaken her foundation to its core and she didn't know how to regroup.

He filled out wranglers like no one else. His blue western shirt wasn't as tight as some cowboys wore theirs, but Callie knew he was buff with six-pack abs. He'd taken his shirt off a lot last summer and she never shied away from looking. Her expression must have shown her sorrow, the look of sympathy Garrett gave her made her stomach turn. Somehow, she had to get him out of her system.

How she planned to accomplish it, she had no idea. She never dated before and she didn't have any female friends to ask. Callie was on her own with this one.

Pasting on a smile, she went to the horse trailer and looked inside.

Garrett's roan, Tiger, stood at one end but she didn't recognize the beautiful silver filly. Pleased, Callie jumped in the trailer and talked to the silver horse, forming an instant connection with her.

"Whose horse is this?"

Garrett helped back the filly out of the trailer before answering. He looked right into Callie's eyes. "She's all yours, honey."

"I don't understand," she said, not looking away from him.

"It's your graduation present."

"Oh."

She didn't want a horse because he had a guilty conscious. He didn't know how hurt she'd been. All through graduation, she kept scanning the crowd for his handsome face and she never found it. The worst part was the pity in her roommate, Gretchen's, eyes. Gretchen's parents had offered to take Callie out to dinner, but she couldn't celebrate. His absence devastated her. She spent the night packing and crying her eyes out. She should've known he had someone else. That it hadn't occurred to her only emphasized how stupid she'd been.

Feeling her eyes begin to tear, Callie walked back into her house. She couldn't do this.

"Cal?" Garrett stood behind her. "Are you all right?"

Callie didn't want him to see her tears; she simply nodded her head, hoping he would go away. She could feel him coming closer, when he turned her around she lost it. It was as though a dam broke. Shame and heart ache washed over her.

She grabbed a tissue. "I have some unpacking to do..."

"I'm sorry, so sorry. I never got the invitation, honey. You know I wouldn't have missed your graduation for the world."

Damn him! He looked so sincere. "I'm sorry too." She walked away.

An hour later Callie heard the men saddle up and ride away. They were probably going to ride the fences. Callie couldn't stay in her room forever. She wasn't one to hide, but she knew Garrett could read her and she didn't want him to know she loved him. How could she learn to hide her feelings?

Walking through the house, she smiled and touched the worn furniture. It might be old but it belonged to her. Her mother's glass angel collection hung near the window. The sun radiated through the glass hitting each piece just right to give each angel a glowing, rainbow effect. It gave her the comfort she'd been seeking; her mother was watching over her, she knew it.

She grabbed three apples and headed out to the barn. She wasn't a fool. What was that old saying -- don't look a gift horse in the mouth? It sounded stupid but true in her case. The silver filly in the corral made a remarkable sight. Nanny stood just outside the fenced in area watching the new horse. Callie wondered if Nanny had made a new friend.

Callie headed into the barn and moved toward Pirate's stall. He sniffed at the apples in her hand before grabbing one.

"So what am I going to do?"

He put his head next to her face as if he understood her turmoil. She sighed and moved to unlock his stall when she heard a commotion outside the barn. She ran out and watched Nanny chasing the silver filly inside the corral. From the new filly's agitation, Callie figured Nanny hadn't made a new friend after all. She walked into the corral, and locked the gate after her. Giving Nanny an apple, she stepped past her and slowly approached the new horse. 'Hey, beautiful," she said, in a soothing voice. "I'm going to call you, Misty. A beautiful name for a beautiful horse," she murmured, getting closer to her.

Callie edged forward holding out another apple. Misty seemed receptive and Callie smiled with relief. Suddenly Nanny came trotting up and Misty reared up on her hind legs, her front hoof hitting Callie on the temple. Callie fell to the ground and the filly reared again, glancing Callie in the ribs.

Nanny bit Misty on the neck and immediately stood over Callie. The last thing she saw was Nanny's underside. Then everything went black.

Chapter Two

Callie woke to the sound of Doc Baker's voice. She reached up to touch her head. It hurt tremendously. He took her hand in his and held it. "I still need to bandage it, young lady, your ribs too," he explained, in a gruff voice.

"Did I fall off a horse?"

"You don't remember what happened?" He looked concerned.

Callie closed her eyes trying to remember. Suddenly her eyes flew open. "My filly! Is she okay? They didn't try to put her down, did they?" She struggled to sit up. Not even the pain in her ribs was going to stop her.

"Whoa, little lady, lay back down. The filly is fine; it's you everyone is worried about."

Callie closed her eyes in relief.

"I'm just going to get some help so I can bandage your ribs, lay back, and try to relax."

Callie nodded. It had just occurred to her she was in Garrett's bedroom. She wanted to jump off the bed. These sheets weren't clean, and it freaked her out Sylvie had slept here. Shuddering, Callie struggled to sit up again.

"Lay down, Callie," Doc Baker ordered.

Reluctantly Callie did as instructed. Her eyes widened as Sylvie walked into the bedroom behind the doctor. Callie balled the covers in her hands. It was incomprehensible Sylvie had the nerve to come near her. "What's she doing here?"

"She's here to help me."

This time Callie did manage to sit up. The pain didn't even compare to her rage. "Get her out of here. Get out. Get out."

"You need to calm down. I need her to help me."

"No! Get Garrett. I want Garrett," Callie cried.

*****

Garrett ran into his room needing to get to Callie. Her voice, full of tears, sounded on the border of hysteria. Garrett observed Doc Baker trying to calm Callie while Sylvie leaned against the wall smirking. "What in God's name is going on?" he asked, making his way to Callie's side.

"She doesn't want Sylvie to help," Doc Baker said, shrugging his shoulders.

Garrett turned to Sylvie. "You'd better leave, you're upsetting Cal."

"Well, we can't have that, can we?" she said, walking out of the bedroom.

Garrett shook his head; seeing a different side of Sylvie. Kneeling on the floor next to Callie, Garrett touched her tear stained cheek. "I'm here Callie."

Callie nodded and took the tissue he offered. "I need you."

"I'm here," he reassured her as he stood. He looked at Doc Baker. "What needs to be done?"

"This isn't proper. I need to take her shirt off and frankly, Garrett, you shouldn't be here."

"Whatever it takes. I know from experience just how painful bruised ribs can be, so let's just get on with it."

Doc Baker began to cut off Callie's tee shirt. He peeled the shirt off revealing Callie's very transparent bra.

Garrett gulped when he saw her pink nipples. God she looked beautiful. He never appreciated the size of her breasts. He didn't stop staring until Doc Baker called his name.

"What are you staring at?" Callie asked.

Garrett didn't meet her gaze. "You're pretty bruised, honey. Let's get these ribs bound."

Garrett tried to think of anything else besides her perfect, delectable breasts. He didn't want anyone to see the evidence of his yearnings. He stared at her bruised ribs with complete attention, trying to keep his eyes away from her chest. He helped the Doc to sit her up and wrap the bandages around her. As soon as that was done, Garrett grabbed one of his chambray shirts and buttoned her into it.

Doc Baker put a bandage on her head. "I don't want her sleeping. Keep her quiet and entertained. Anything happens call me. She can sleep after twelve hours."

Garrett shook the Doc's hand. "Thanks, Doc."

Doc Baker nodded. "When I got the call to come out here, I was expecting to fix up one of your men. I didn't know Callie was home." He turned and left, closing the door behind him.

Callie's wide eyes told him something was on her mind. He knew her that well. "Out with it, what's wrong?"

"I can't be on this bed where you sleep with..."

It was painful to see Callie so upset. "We don't sleep together."

Callie threw him a dirty look. "I don't suppose it's sleeping the two of you do in here."

Garrett sat on the side of the bed and kissed Callie on the forehead. "We don't do that, either. I don't know why she said it. Jealousy, maybe?"

Callie's violet eyes filled with pain. "You let me think..."

"I know, honey, and I'm sorry. It's just that you're so sweet and innocent. I married you to keep your land safe, not to take advantage of you. It just wouldn't be right," he explained, looking deep into her eyes.

Callie looked away from him. "What if I said I wanted it?"

Garrett got off the bed. "I can't allow it to happen. Let's talk about something else. Suppose you tell me why Nanny played guard dog when I rode in. She nearly took my head off when I tried to get to you."

Callie finally smiled. "Misty reared and hit me, and Nanny stood over me protecting me."

"You named her Misty?"

Nodding Callie went on to explain how Nanny spooked Misty and how it wasn't anyone's fault.

*****

Screaming was on her mind. Callie couldn't take it anymore. She had to do something. The hell with Doctor's orders, she needed to get out of this damn bed. She didn't believe for a minute Sylvie hadn't been in it. Hadn't she seen them on the couch only yesterday? Garrett had lied to her, it was the first lie he'd ever told her, that she knew of. There was bound to be more, she thought, as she gingerly edged off the bed.

One of the cows was having a hard time birthing so Garrett left Callie in the viper's hands. If Sylvie opened the bedroom door as if she owned the place one more time, she'd just have to hit her. Callie grew up on a ranch and hung around cowboys most of her life. She'd learned to fight, and she itched for one now.

Sighing, the pain in her ribs hit her full force. She'd have to wait and slap that... that... Hell, she didn't even know what to call her. Sylvie would get hers. Who did she think she was smirking at her all the time?

Callie decided she had to move her things back into Garrett's house. She wasn't going to leave the field wide open for that hussy. There, she found something to call her. It lifted her spirits to have a private name for Sylvie.

"What are you doing out of bed?" Sylvie put her hands on her hips.

"You don't dictate my life, got it? I am half owner of this ranch so you work for me. Get your ass out of here and do your job. This house is not very clean, so do a better job."

Sylvie stood there with her mouth hanging open. She turned and fled out of the room.

Good. Now she wanted to check on the horses. Garrett had told her he was bringing them here while she recuperated. Won't he be surprised when she didn't leave?

It had been a private ceremony. Money being tight, she didn't even have a new dress to wear. The only people who knew were the Preacher, her mother, and Old Henry. She planned to go to college and Garrett planned to work the ranches and merge them into one. Callie had always known deep down it was a temporary marriage, but even on her wedding day, she said yes with loved-filled eyes.

Eyes wide open, she vowed. She would keep her eyes wide open. Garrett said he didn't sleep with Sylvie. Yeah right. She wasn't here for her cleaning skills. Her cooking was passable; Callie was a better cook. Well, one good thing, it would give her more time for ranch work. She wouldn't be stuck doing housework.

Still wearing Garrett's chambray shirt and her jeans, Callie looked in the mirror. Her temple was turning a deep shade of purple, the color of a world of hurt. She imagined her ribs looked the same. She smiled, noticing just how big Garrett's shirt was on her but she just rolled up the sleeves. The shirt smelled of him and she wanted to wear it. Braiding her hair Callie remembered a time when Garrett would try to braid her hair when it came undone.

Ignoring Sylvie, she gathered her apples and sugar cubes. The other woman's dislike was palpable and it made Callie smile. She wasn't going to make living here fun for that witch. If Garrett hadn't lied, then Sylvie had. There was something about her, something not quite right.

Breathing in the fresh country air was pure heaven to Callie. All through finals, she dreamt of coming home to the ranch. It was the end of May and already the Texas sun was blazing in all its glory. Not a cloud dotted the sky, making it seem even bigger and bluer. Reaching the barn, Callie looked into each stall and talked to each horse. She knew them all. Misty was the only new one.

Finding Pirate, she fed him an apple, complaining to him all the while. He seemed to agree with her assessment of Sylvie, at least he nodded his head. She loved him best but she didn't tell any of the other horses that. Next, she found Misty and talked very softly to her as she walked closer to her stall. Misty nickered at her and took the apple. Callie patted her on the neck and the filly rubbed her head against her.

Callie knew she and Misty would be good friends. Looking around she didn't see Nanny. She was probably off visiting her other equine friends; though she did have a Billy goat she was fond of. The scent of a barn was not for everyone but Callie enjoyed it. She loved all the animals. She walked down further into the dim darkness and spotted a calf penned up.

She knelt down to mother it and experienced excruciating pain. She wasn't going to get back up, not by herself. Thankfully, she didn't have to wait long. Stamos arrived.

He looked good; his black hair hung loose giving him a sexy look. Callie could make out a good deal of his shape through his tight shirt. His biceps alone would have made any woman swoon. He hurried toward her.

"You okay? What are you doing out here?" he asked, kneeling down beside her.

Trying to smile, she failed miserably. "I wasn't thinking. I wanted to hug the motherless calf and before I knew it I was unable to get back up."

"Well, I'd better get you back to the house before Garrett sees you." Stamos stood up and swung Callie into his brawny arms.

"Garrett isn't the boss of me. I'm my own woman."

Her violet eyes grew wider when Stamos moved his head closer to her. Making a small sound of protest, she turned her head away.

"Put her down," Garrett demanded. She heard the anger in his voice.

"Don't you dare let go of me, Stamos." Callie sent Garrett a disgruntled look. "He's helping me. I tried to hug the calf, and I couldn't get back up."

Garrett's face softened a bit. "You always were an old softy when it came to animals."

Before she could answer, Garrett stomped over and took her from Stamos' arms. She winced at all the jostling. She wasn't happy with his high-handedness but she didn't say anything.

"Well, come on Stamos, I need you to open the front door for us."

Callie looked over Garrett's shoulder and saw the look of disappointment on Stamos' face. She wondered if maybe Garrett could be jealous. It was something to think about.

Stamos opened the door and Sylvie came quickly to see who entered the house. Her look of annoyance made the pain worth it as far as Callie was concerned.

"Where shall I put you? In the living room?" Garrett asked, holding her a bit closer.

Callie wanted to put her arms around his neck but the pain in her ribs wouldn't allow it. "No, I think I'll take a nap. Take me back to your bedroom, that bed is comfy."

Looking over Garrett's shoulder once again, she met the look of fury on Sylvie's face and she smiled at her. She wanted to stick out her tongue but she didn't want Garrett to think of her as a juvenile.

Garrett carried her into his bedroom. Gently he put her down on the bed and helped her arrange the pillow until she seemed comfortable.

"You know you should have stayed in bed, don't you?"

"What's the fun of that?" Callie smiled into his eyes. "I ended up in the arms of two very handsome cowboys so maybe it was worth it."

Garrett didn't smile. "I know you're up to something." He leaned over, kissed her forehead, and walked out the room.

Chapter Three

Breakfast became a trial. Sylvie took every opportunity to rub against Garrett. Callie kept eyeing her but Sylvie ignored her for the most part. The older woman gave her breakfast but she made it clear she was here for Garrett, and only Garrett.

Callie started growing disgusted by the whole thing until she noticed Garrett wasn't paying Sylvie any attention. In fact, he looked disgruntled about something. He also looked tired. She hoped he hadn't slept with Sylvie since there was only a twin-sized bed in the other room.

Although the outside of the house had been spruced up, the inside looked much the same. Callie noticed the same handmade cabinets and avocado-colored appliances. The faded yellow checked curtains were still there as was the colorful rag rug his mother had made. As a little girl, she had spent a lot of time in this kitchen with Garrett and his mom. His mom always seemed to have a wooden spoon in her hand, always cooking. Callie remembered a certain sadness about her.

Garrett scowled at her, interrupting her musings. "What?"

"I asked you what you were planning to do today?" He sounded annoyed. "I know you won't rest like you should."

"I do want to spend time with the calf. Maybe I could sit on a bale of hay and it won't bother my ribs." She smiled widely at Garrett.

The look of tenderness he gave her warmed her heart. "All right, honey, I'll see what I can do. You can play mama to the calf."

Callie gingerly got up from the table and walked to Garrett's chair. She leaned both hands on the table in front of him and gave him a hard look. "I'm not a little girl anymore. I don't intend to play at anything. I plan to help with the ranch."

Garrett's smile spread across his face. "Believe me, honey, I'm just beginning to realize you're growing up."

Flustered, she watched him walk out the door. It had been so much easier when they were young and best friends.

"Honey, honey, honey," Sylvie mocked, giving Callie a look of loathing.

"Not your business," Callie responded, staring down the other woman.

Breaking the stare, Sylvie walked out of the room.

Callie walked to the far end of the kitchen, and opened the door. The room had a few boxes in it but it could be remade into the housekeeper's room. It really was where Sylvie should be sleeping. Callie wanted her room back and she hoped that Garrett wouldn't feel obligated to invite Sylvie into his room.

Walking toward the barn, Callie looked down at her clothes. Her green tee shirt had seen better days and her jeans had holes in them. The only new clothing she'd had in about three years was the dress she wore out here. What a waste! She knew times were hard around here. It didn't matter, she didn't need new clothes. Seeing Sylvie dressed in a pretty pink blouse made her give it a second thought. She kicked up some of the Texas dirt that reminded her of Garrett's hair and laughed. This was where she wanted to be, on her ranch and that was all that mattered. She couldn't keep pounding her head against the wall Garrett had built between them. It hurt, a lot, too much but as she told Garrett, she wasn't a little girl anymore. Maybe she should take his advice and date other men. It just didn't seem right being married and all.

She spotted Garrett at the calf's pen and made her way to him. Seeing the bale of hay with a few blankets on top made her smile. "Thanks."

Garrett looked up at her. "No problem. Anything to keep you out of trouble," he said, gruffly.

A lash of pain hit her, making her heart twist. "I'll keep out of your way."

Garrett studied her for a moment and shrugged his shoulder. "Let me help you down onto the bale."

"I can do it myself. I don't need your help, never did, never will." She walked into the pen and started to ease her way down onto the bale of hay.

She grit her teeth at the pain, not wanting Garrett to know. Before she knew it, he had his large tanned hands on her hips, easing her down with care. She resented the way his hands made her sizzle. "I'm fine, now you can go."

"What's your problem? You're as prickly as a cactus today."

Callie grew indignant. "My problem? Really? My problem. I see you're not wearing your college ring on your ring finger like you used to. Fine, if that's what you want," she said, taking his high school ring off her ring finger. "Here take this back."

"You're jealous."

"You know, just take the ring and go. I knew it wasn't a real marriage. I do thank you for all you've done for the ranch and me. But I can take it alone from here."

Garrett stared at the ring in the palm of her hand. Callie trembled trying to contain her tears. He took the ring from her hand and walked away.

Her heart grew heavy. She remembered how unhappy his mother had been in her marriage. She always blamed it on the age difference between her and Garrett's father. They were twenty-three years apart in age. Somehow, he must have gotten it in his mind that the age difference between them was too wide. Fifteen years wasn't so much, was it? She had hoped he'd change his mind, but now, she just didn't know.

She had better things to do. She had a calf to feed.

"What shall I call you?" Callie asked the calf. "You have such a pretty face. I'm going to call you, Maggie Mae after one of my favorite songs. I know it's an old song but my mother loved it," she explained to the calf as she hand fed it using a bigger version of a baby bottle.

"She sure did like that song didn't she, Cal girl?" Old Henry sounded wistful. He stood at the barn door watching her.

Callie smiled. "That she did," she responded, loving the way Henry always called her Cal girl. It was, as close to Cowgirl her mother would allow for her tomboy daughter. Her smile faded and a lone tear slid down her face.

"Awe, Cal girl, are you in pain? Is there somethin' I could be doin' for ya?" He walked to her side.

Shaking her head, Callie tried to compose herself. "I gave Garrett his ring back."

Henry's eyebrows rose in surprise, then they furrowed as though he was trying to figure something out. "I wish I knew what to tell you. He had me fooled. You should see the way he looks at you when you're not lookin'. If I was a bettin' man, I'd say he was carryin' a torch for ya."

Sighing, she just shook her head. "He took his ring off first. He didn't have it on today."

Sitting down on the bale of hay, Henry put a comforting arm around her. "You wear your heart for all the world to see, Cal girl. You'll end up wearin' your heart plum out on him. He doesn't deserve you. Plenty of men here about would love to take a chance with ya."

Callie rested her head on his shoulder. It comforted her to have someone besides Pirate to confide in. "You're my only friend, Henry."

"Tell ya what. Let's stop this old pity party and make things happen. Find yourself a new sweetheart."

"Do you really think I should date other people? I am married."

"Only on paper, darlin'."

"You're right the next handsome man that asks me out I'm going to say yes."

"Glad to hear it," Stamos said, his eyes shining with mischief. "I'm asking."

Callie could feel her face turn red. How much did he just hear?

Did he hear about the marriage? He didn't act like he knew. "Well, then I'm accepting."

"Accepting what?" Garrett entered the barn, sporting a big frown.

"Stamos asked me out and I accepted," she said, giving him her best innocent look. "You even said it's time for me to date. I can't wait."

"Stamos, has night guard duty tonight," Garrett announced.

Stamos looked surprised but he didn't say anything.

Throwing Garrett a defiant look Callie asked, "Will this guard duty last until I say no?"

Garrett gave her a superior smile. "Something like that."

*****

Three long days later, Stamos was finally off night duty. Looking at her reflection, Callie was pleased. She didn't wear makeup very much; it surprised her just how a little blush, mascara, and lipstick could light up her face. Her blond hair was loose, hanging down her back. She had always worn it long; it made it easier to braid. She glimpsed a ghost of a smile in the mirror remembering the one time she had cut her hair. She wanted to look identical to Garrett and be a cowboy. Those were better days.

Taking a quick glance to check her one dress, Callie experienced confidence. She left her room and walked into the family room. She dreaded seeing Sylvie. Ever since Callie fixed up the housekeeper's room for her, she'd been pouting. It made her even madder when Callie gave her a list of chores to be done. The look on Sylvie's face had been priceless. Surprisingly, Garrett didn't take Sylvie's side when she showed him the list and the room. All he said was this was a working ranch and Callie, being a half owner, had every right to do as she pleased.

He added within reason, but Callie decided to ignore that part. Somehow, they had managed to avoid each other for the last three days, except for mealtime. Callie missed the lighthearted banter they used to have. She was moving on with her life.

Feeling Garrett's perusal, Callie patted her hair making sure it was in place. She peeked over at him and was surprised to see him scowling, yet again. "Okay out with it. What did I do wrong this time?"

Garrett's eyebrows rose. "I was just wondering if that was the only dress you have. It's a bit too sophisticated for you, is all."

"I happen to adore it. You just don't like that it shows my cleavage. Besides I'd appreciate it if you wouldn't criticize my only clothing purchase in three years."

"What's that supposed to mean? I sent you more than enough money every semester."

Callie looked at his reddened face. She didn't want him to know and now with her big mouth the cat was out of the bag. "Look, I knew costs were up and profits were down. I'm a rancher. I kept my fingers on the pulse of the ranching world. I knew the money you sent was all you had. Don't think I don't realize the sacrifices you had to make to send me the money but tuition kept going up and so did housing. A single textbook cost over a hundred bucks. I had to take a job waitressing to get the bills paid."

Garrett looked pole-axed. He walked over to her and hugged her. "It wasn't a sacrifice, Cal. I wish you had told me, I could have sent more..."

"I appreciate the sentiment but we both know you can't take all the profits out of a ranch. I know you have to put back in as much as you can.'

Garrett held her tighter. "You're amazing."

The sound of the doorbell jarred them apart. They stood in the middle of the room, staring at each other.

"Hey, Callie," Stamos greeted, letting himself in. "All ready for a night on the town?" He looked her up and down. "Nice dress!" he said, giving her an appreciative grin.

"Am I interrupting something?" Stamos asked, looking from Garrett to Callie.

Callie went to him and took his arm. "No, not at all. I'm glad you like my dress, Stamos. Shall we get going?" Not waiting for an answer, Callie whisked him out the front door.

Smiling as Stamos opened the car door for her, she wondered what was wrong with Garrett. Would she ever get him off her mind? "So, where are we going?" Callie asked, watching Stamos put his seat belt on.

"I thought we'd have some dinner at The Whiskey Barrel. They're having a country western band play an..." His smile faded. "I guess you expected to go somewhere nicer, the way you're dressed and all."

"Oh no, I've always wanted to go to The Whiskey Barrel. I was never old enough before." She tried to reassure him.

He looked relieved and grinned at her. His laugh lines went deep. His dark eyes sparkled, causing her to feel special. "Good, The Whiskey Barrel it is."

They walked in holding hands and everyone turned to look. Callie deemed herself very overdressed. Most people went back to their conversations but a few cowboys stared at her. Stamos squeezed her hand, giving her the confidence to walk over to an empty table.

It was a much bigger place than she'd imagined. Round wooden tables dotted the eating area and at the far end stood a stage with a big wooden dance floor in front of it. She loved the hand-honed paneling on the walls. The wooden floors were original as were the exposed wooden beams. The Whiskey Barrel was an apt name. It certainly looked barrel-like with all the wood. The bar sported the color of fine Kentucky Whiskey, polished to a fine sheen. Behind it hung a huge vintage mirror framed in ornately carved wood with a slight hint of gold gilding here and there. It looked wonderful. It was one of the oldest buildings in the small town of Lasso Springs. The whole place awed her.

"Why are people staring?" she whispered, as he pulled her chair out for her.

"Because you're beautiful." He sat down.

A blush swept her face and she wasn't sure what to do. She'd received few compliments. She thanked him, and pretended to study the menu.   The server appeared happy to see Stamos. She gave him a secretive sexy grin and it made Callie wonder. Maybe Stamos was a player. He had the looks with his shoulder length black hair. It was easy to understand why the server paid him special attention.

The special attention ended up getting downright embarrassing by the time they had finished their meal. The server, Stacey, did everything but sit on Stamos' lap. She brushed her breasts against him when she served the food and drinks. She touched him when she asked if everything was okay. Callie had had enough of Stacey.

"Sorry about her," Stamos said. "We dated for a short time."

"Oh."

"Listen I can see she upset you. She probably planned it that way. Callie, you wear your emotions well. I can usually tell what you're feeling by the look on your face."

"Sorry..."

Stamos reached across the table and took her hand in his. "There is no reason to be sorry. It's a trait of yours I find enchanting."

Callie found herself getting lost in his eyes. There was no denying his charm. "Good, I'm glad you enjoy it because try as I might I can't manage to keep a poker face." She chuckled.

"Looks like the band is getting ready to play. Do you dance, pretty Cal?" Stamos looked at her. "I can see you don't like me calling you, Cal. Am I right?"

"Yes, only Garrett calls me that and..."

Stamos stood up and took her by the hand, leading her to the dance floor. "I don't want you to think about him when you're with me."

Gasping in delight as he pulled her into his arms, Callie didn't get a chance to answer him. He had a point, she shouldn't be thinking about Garrett when she danced with him. She laughed as Stamos led them in a lively Texas two-step. "You are a great dancer! Just remember my ribs."

"Am I hurting you?"

"No, I just want to keep it that way. You make my dancing better."

"It's all in the partner." A sexy smile spread across his face.

Stamos swept her across the dance floor. Callie was having such fun. She didn't stop smiling until she caught a glimpse of Sylvie in the crowd. She could feel herself frown and she almost tripped when she saw Garrett with her.

"Damn," Stamos said, as he turned Callie and spotted the couple.

"I need to use the restroom," she told Stamos when the song ended.

"I'll be at our table."

*****

Garrett knew his eyes revealed the rage he harbored while he watched Stamos cross the dance floor. Stamos looked surprised to see them sitting at his table. Garrett smiled, noticing the discomfort of the other man. "I can't believe we ended up at the same place," he said smoothly, watching his every move.

Stamos nodded at them both and sat down. "I didn't know you two were going out tonight."

"Why would you know what my plans are?" Garrett challenged.

Stamos gave Garrett his usual cocky grin. "I wouldn't, Boss."

"Hi, Stamos," Sylvie purred at him.

Stamos nodded at her and looked away but not before Garrett could see the sharp irritated look he flashed her.

"Do you want to dance, Garrett?" Sylvie asked, hopefully.

"No, you two go ahead." Damn, all he could think about was Callie and just how sexy she looked in her black dress.

Watching the other two walk on to the dance floor, Garrett was surprised at how close Stamos held Sylvie. They were looking into each other's eyes. Sylvie then pushed him away so they weren't so close.

Garrett wondered what they were talking about, they seemed awfully chummy. Maybe there was a romance he didn't know about, going on at the ranch.

Callie walked out of the restroom and scanned the crowded bar. With a purposeful stride, Garrett walked toward her.

Garrett stopped just short of her. Stepping around him, Callie started for the table. His arm snaked out and grabbed her around the waist before she got far. He hauled her back against him.

She immediately turned in his arms, her breasts grazed his chest making her nipples harden. "Let me go," she ordered tersely.

Giving her a slow sexy grin, Garrett simply shook his head. He was enjoying himself too much.

"I said let me go," she whispered to him.

"Are you going to sleep with him?"

Callie pushed at him, this time he let her go. She was hopping mad. "Not that it's any of your business but I don't jump into bed on the first date." Not waiting for his reply, she whirled away from him and found the table.

Garrett watched her backside sway as she hurried away. God she was sexy in that black dress. He was jealous. He was a fool. The age difference didn't matter. He'd planned to do paperwork but here he was with Sylvie on his arm. He couldn't stand the fact that Callie might be with another man. Now, he recognized his mistake. Between Sylvie crawling all over him and then seeing her rub up against Stamos, he knew she wasn't for him.

Callie was the woman for him. Now, how was he going to convince her of that when all he'd done was push her away? Rubbing the back of his neck, he couldn't think of a plan of action. He was too irritated she was with Stamos. He needed to get out of here and cool off. He'd talked Stamos into driving Sylvie home but Sylvie caught him before he made it out the door. He didn't want to make a scene so he decided to take her home.

Garrett raced to the barn and quickly saddled up Tiger. He needed a moonlight ride. Riding at night could be dangerous for the horse but he planned to take it slow. He just needed to be under the wide-open Texas sky. The plentiful stars shimmered and the moon was aglow.

He'd had to fend off Sylvie the whole ride home. She tried everything short of unzipping his pants. Hell, she had the arms of an octopus. Shuddering as he remembered it, he hoisted himself onto the saddle and rode into the pasture, where he knew there weren't any gopher holes for Tiger to step in.

Callie had hardly looked at him when he left the bar. He could see in her eyes she loved him, but he could also see her determination to put a wall between them. He patted Tiger's neck and sighed. "We've been through thick and thin, old boy. What should I do?"

He knew he wasn't the only one to talk to their horse, Callie did the same thing. She always had, ever since she was a little girl and once she had Pirate, there was no stopping the conversations. He laughed, realizing he had learned it from her.

Turning Tiger back toward home, Garrett decided he couldn't push Cal but he would find many opportunities for them to be together.

*****

Every time Callie turned there was Garrett, constantly underfoot. Ever since her one date with Stamos, Garrett had been dogging her heels. She'd been halfway hoping Stamos would ask her out again. He'd been a lot of fun but they didn't even get a chance for a kiss goodnight. Garrett sat on the porch swing when she returned from her date. Stamos kissed her on the cheek, which was very brave considering Garrett's glare. Now it seemed as though Stamos had been sent to Siberia. Garrett always had him working out on the range.

Meanwhile Sylvie kept sending her daggers with her eyes. Screaming wouldn't even be enough to get all of her frustration out. Sitting at a computer with Garrett made her antsy. They were going over the accounting system so she could take over the books. Garrett insisted on going over every little detail even though she had an accounting degree.

Feeling claustrophobic, she pushed back from the desk and walked out of the room. She could feel Garrett's glare burning holes in her back but she didn't care. She needed some alone time before she hit someone. She grabbed a few apples and ran to the barn. Here she could breathe.

After feeding both Misty and Pirate apples, she haltered them so she could lead them out to the pasture. She couldn't ride yet due to her ribs but she could watch the horses frolic for a while. Her horses had taken a shine to each other. Maybe that's what made Nanny act the way she had a few weeks ago.

She watched the horses run together and started to feel better. An arm around her shoulder startled her. "Stamos. Where have you been?"

He hugged her against his strong hard side and kissed her on the cheek. "Working, you?"

Callie pulled away and sat on the top rung of the fence. "Same here. No time for fun it seems."

Stamos laughed and joined her on the fence. "I have a feeling it'll stay that way until we declare to Garrett we're not going out again."

Turning her head abruptly, Callie stared at him. "Is that what you want?"

Stamos took her hand and caressed the back of it with his thumb. "No, I want to go out with you again and soon." He let go of her hand. "Here comes the Boss. I'd better go. We'll make plans soon."

Callie beamed at him. "Yes! Let's make it soon."

Tipping his hat to her, he turned and left.

"Flirting with your boyfriend?" Garrett searched Callie's face. "The silver filly is a beauty," Garrett said, when Callie didn't answer him.

He leaped up to the top rung of the fence, touching shoulders with her.

"Her name is Misty."

"Yes, I know. Still a beauty though."

Callie glanced at him and looked away. "I never did thank you for her. It's a thoughtful gift and an expensive one I bet."

"I traded stud services for her."

"You make it sound like it was nothing but we could have used that money."

He touched the side of her cheek, turning her head to face him. He stared into her eyes as he tucked a strand of blond hair behind her ear. "You're worth it," he said. He jumped down from the fence and walked away.

Callie was bewildered. She could never figure him out. He didn't want her but he didn't want her to date either. Her brow furrowed as she tried to puzzle it out. As much as she enjoyed Stamos, he wasn't Garrett. Garrett made her feel things she didn't quite understand but she knew she loved him. Stamos was fun but it just wasn't the same. She probably shouldn't go out with him again. She didn't need her life more complicated.

The sun dipped below the horizon showing a colorful display of reds and oranges. Reluctantly she slid off the fence and went into the house. She could hear Sylvie laughing about something Garrett had said and she sighed. Dinner was going to be a long one.

Callie tried to ignore the jovial banter between Garrett and Sylvie during dinner. It seemed they had a few private jokes between them and it irritated her to no end. Feeling his gaze on her, Callie looked at Garrett. He gave her a slow easy grin. The leech. He enjoyed her discomfort. She was tempted to pour her sweet tea over his head. At least the food tasted edible. Looking up from her bowl of beef stew, Callie could see a change in Garrett's expression. He looked both shocked and uncomfortable. Did she miss something? His baby blues weren't taunting her anymore.

Sylvie looked like she was enjoying herself. She wore another low cut blouse and she seemed to be moving her legs under the table. Slowly, Callie slid her sneaker off. She had an idea what was going on and she wanted to catch them in the act. Pretending to stretch, she lifted her bare foot toward Garrett's legs and she got her answer. Her foot met Sylvie's on Garrett's lap.

All three gasped at once. Sylvie quickly removed her foot, Garrett sat up straighter, and Callie was just plain disgusted. After slipping her shoe back on, she rose from the table. "You two make me sick. At the kitchen table, really? With me here? What is wrong with you?" she ranted, looking at Garrett the whole time. His look of guilt said it all.

*****

Garrett stared at the closed door leading to the office. Callie had been in there for two hours. When she marched in there and slammed the door, it'd been deafening. He could hear her banging things around. Garrett didn't know what to say to her. She looked madder than a wet hen and he was responsible. Somehow, Sylvie had done it again.

It was just as much his fault, he could have discouraged Sylvie. Taking a deep breath, Garrett opened the office door. He spotted Cal behind the desk, typing away. She typed so hard that each key she touched echoed in the big room. She didn't look at him, but he wasn't surprised. She always avoided him when she was mad.

"Callie? Are you all right?" he asked, tentatively.

"Fine and dandy," she replied, not missing a beat in her typing. Still, she wouldn't look at him.

"Callie, listen it was my entire fault."

Callie finally looked at him, her eyes spitting fire. "Don't you dare take the blame for that little hussy. She takes every opportunity to rub up against you. But hey, if that's what you want I can move back to my house. I don't want to be in the way."

Garrett crossed the room in two long strides. He pulled the chair out from the desk and spun it around so that she faced him. He could see the hurt and pain in her eyes. It killed him to know he'd caused it. He grabbed her by the shoulders and lifted her to a standing position. Her lips quivered and he simply couldn't help himself. Garrett leaned down and took her lips with his.

She tasted of sweet tea mixed with heaven. Her lips were so soft, just as he had imagined a thousand times. Her gasp encouraged him to deepen the kiss. He could feel her open her mouth to him and to his surprise, she buried her fingers in his hair. He pulled her closer, feeling aroused. God, he wanted her. Her body, while well-toned from ranch work, had a delightful woman's softness. Feeling her hands move to his chest caused him to become hard. They felt warm and loving through his plaid shirt. It took a few more seconds for him to realize she was trying to push him away.

He let her go. Her lips were swollen from his kisses and her face had a becoming glow to it. The accusation in her eyes startled him.

"Callie?"

"Let me go. I'll not be second best to the housekeeper." She backed away from him, wiping her lips with the back of her hand. "How could you? I'm not a plaything."

Garrett took a step forward to comfort her but she whirled around and ran from the room, once again slamming the door.

Chapter Four

Callie smiled at Henry. She happily took him up on his offer to ride with him. She needed to get out on the open range. Riding her land always had an uplifting effect, and she needed a pick me up. The sunrise had been spectacular with numerous hues of yellow and pink as it rose high into the bright blue sky. It was going to be another hot one, but that was Texas.

"You okay, Cal girl? You look a might peaked." Henry looked worried.

"I'm fine. Let's go out to the north pasture."

He turned his horse and followed her.

Callie reined in Misty at the fence line and jumped down into the tall Texas grass. The fence had been cut.

Henry dismounted and stood next to Callie, looking at the destruction.

"Something's not right here, Henry. This fence has been cut and it looks like a truck or some kind of equipment parked here." She spotted a brown flag in the ground. It resembled the small flags the water or electric companies used to mark their lines. She picked it up and read the company name on it, S & S Oil, Inc.

"Henry, have you ever heard of this company?"

Henry took the flag from her and puzzled over it. "An oil company approached Garrett a good few months ago. It seems your land sits on a ton of oil. Garrett told them to leave."

"I'm glad he turned them away. I wouldn't want my land marred by oil rigs." Looking around Callie didn't see anything else out of place. "We might as well get the fence fixed."

"I'll do it," Henry offered.

Smiling at his chivalry, Callie shook her head and grabbed the wire, gloves, and tools she needed out of her saddlebag. "You know it's a two person job. It's safer that way."

Henry nodded to her and grabbed his gloves. They carefully ran the barbed wire from one post to the other. Callie secured the wire on the first post, letting Henry do the hard part of stretching, tightening the wire, and attaching it to the other post.

Walking over toward the second post, a razor sharp piece of barbed wire snapped suddenly, slicing her under her chin. It hit her with enough force to drop her to the ground. The throbbing pain was excruciating and when she took her hand away, the amount of blood on it almost made her ill. The cut was deep and it felt long.

Henry came running. "What have I done, Cal girl?" he lamented, sinking to his knees.

"Give me your bandana, I forgot mine," she said, tears poured down her face.

She grabbed the bandana and immediately used it to apply pressure to her wound. "Call for help. I won't be able to ride in. I'm feeling woozy."

Watching Henry on the phone, Callie silently thanked God Garrett had gone against her wishes and allowed the phone company to put up a cell phone tower on their land. It was supposed to look similar to a tree, a very tall fake tree. Now she was grateful.

Henry sat down and gently shifted Callie so her head lay on his lap. "Help is on its way. Seems Garrett ain't far from here and Doc Baker is on his way. I would have called for a truck but I think it would be too jarring of a ride for ya."

Despite the pain, she gave Henry a brief nod of thanks. It hurt too much to talk. Henry ran his hand over her hair, comforting her. Well, the sky was still a cornflower blue and a slight breeze carried the sweetness of the grass on it.

"Henry?" she managed to ground out.

"What is it, Cal girl?"

"The wire. Not your fault. It was the wire. Bring it to the house."

Henry's green eyes widened in shock. "You think something is wrong with the wire?" He kissed her on the forehead. "I'll bring it don't worry baby, you'll be fine."

Callie gave him a slight nod. The pain became unbearable. Finally, she heard the unmistakable sound of a horse galloping her way. She relaxed a bit, hoping Garrett would be able to get her home. It didn't even matter she was furious with him. Last night she tossed and turned all night, reliving the glorious passionate kiss and reliving the shame that he used her.

Tiger had barely stopped before Garrett jumped to the ground. Kneeling down, he took the bandana from Callie. "Looks deep." He returned the cloth to the wound and put Callie's hand back over it.

"Can't keep out of trouble it seems." He gently lifted her off the ground. "Still the same, little tidbit, that was always getting cuts and scrapes."

Callie let her head rest against his shoulder. "I'm not a tidbit."

"I know," he whispered, as he handed her to Henry, got back on Tiger, and leaned down to take her back. Cradling her against him, he took off. He had to hold her with one arm; she was too unsteady to sit a horse. Tiger seemed to sense the urgency and he made his way home without any guidance from Garrett.

"Almost there, Cal, almost there," he reassured her. "Thank God,

Doc Baker is already here. You'll be feeling better in no time honey."

Stamos stood on the porch waiting for them. He reached up, took Callie from Garrett's arms, and carried her into Garret's bedroom. "Shh," he said, as she put up a fuss. "The light is better in this room; Doc Baker wants you in here."

He laid her on the bed and Doc Baker appeared immediately, taking the bandana from her. She passed out.

*****

"So what's the verdict, Doc?" Garrett asked, as the doctor sat at the kitchen table.

"Here have some coffee," Sylvia offered, setting a hot mug before him.

"I had to give her nine stitches. The wound was deep. I gave her a tetanus shot too." He shook his head. "She's going to have a slight scar. It's a shame it happened." He took a swig of his coffee. "She kept mumbling something about the wire."

"She was fixing a cut fence." Garrett got up and looked out the window. He noticed Sylvie rub her breasts against the Doc. Somehow seeing it made him feel dirty. Little wonder Callie couldn't stand her.

Turning back to the Doc, Garrett noticed him smiling at Sylvie. "What kind of care does she need?" he asked, giving Sylvie a hard look. She returned his look with a come hither smile. Shuddering, he wondered why he ever liked her.

"I'll leave a prescription for pain and she'll have to ice her jaw. Her whole face will swell and bruise, so don't worry. Do what you have to do. She needs to stay put this time. No riding, no fixing fences, no stacking bales of hay. I know she's a stubborn woman but you might just have to sit on her. Her ribs are still bruised. It's a wonder she could even ride a horse."

"Wow. She's been acting as though she's fine. I assumed -- Well, that's my fault. I shouldn't assume anything when it comes to that little gal," Garrett said, feeling tender toward his wife.

"Thanks, Doc. I don't know what we'd do without you." Garrett went over, shook the other man's hand, and then turned toward the stairs. He needed to see Callie. He needed to be with her, and he needed to figure out why he suddenly thought of her as his wife.

She looked so small in his big bed. Her skin looked so pale. A lance of pain shot through his heart. She was lucky. It could have been worse. She had probably gone riding because of him. She found solace in the land the same as he did.

Looking toward the doorway he glimpsed Henry standing there, hat in hand. Garrett motioned for him to come in. "What happened out there, Henry?"

"S & S Oil must've been out there again. They cut the fence and left another brown surveying flag." He sighed. "We decided to fix the fence. Honest, Boss we did it right but the wire broke. Callie seemed to think there's something wrong with it. She's right. The wire was filed down in spots, making it weak in places."

Garrett swore. "Where's the wire now?"

"It's in Callie's saddlebag, in the barn."

"Okay, good, thanks, Henry. I'm glad you were there to help her. What about the fence?"

"I sent Stamos out with Karl. I checked the wire first though."

Garrett shook his hand and patted his shoulder. "Good man."

Henry took one last look at Callie, nodded, and walked away.

Garrett sat down heavily onto the antique rocking chair he pulled next to the bed. He really didn't like her color. He fingered his high school ring in his pocket for a moment before pulling it out. He'd been carrying it ever since Callie had given it back to him. He took her dainty hand and slid the ring on her ring finger. Taking his college ring out, he put it back on his ring finger.

He'd been going about things all wrong. He knew she loved him or at least she had. He could actually feel his love for her filling his heart. It made him ache deep inside wishing they had a normal relationship. He'd love to date her, woo her, and ask her to marry him. How had everything spun so out of control? She was dating Stamos and he... Well, he'd played with fire and gotten burned.

He'd have to talk to Sylvie and make her understand her behavior toward him was both unwanted and inappropriate. She'd been down on her luck when he hired her, so he didn't have the heart to turn her out but things were going to change.

He reached over and tucked a piece of Callie's blond hair behind her ear. He caressed her cheek, taking in every detail of her face. She looked so beautiful. Somehow, she didn't even know it. Why hadn't he ever told her? Running his hand over his weary face, he vowed to take better care of her. It frightened him, hopefully he wasn't too late.

*****

Stamos rode into the yard and spotted the flowerpot on the left end of the porch railing. It was their signal. He walked to their spot in the woods, and Sylvie hurried out to meet him.

She launched herself into his arms.

Stamos untangled himself from her hold. "What's so important we had to meet in the day?" he asked gruffly. He could see her wince at his hard words but he didn't care.

"Did you fool with that wire?"

"So, what if I did?" he challenged.

"Well, genius, it's bound to make them closer than ever."

"Callie just got in the way this time. If I can cause enough accidents, men might start leaving, and Garrett would be hard put to run his ranch without help."

Sylvie laughed. "Did you read that in an old western? My God, Stamos, he could just hire more men."

He gave her a dirty look. He didn't appreciate her trying to make him feel the fool. "Listen baby, we can use this to our advantage. You can console Garrett and I will visit Callie. You know just how charming I can be."

He could see by her face he wasn't making her happy. He needed her for his plan to succeed. He gave her his sexiest smile. "You know it's only play. It's you I adore."

Sylvie smiled deeply. "I know Stamos, I'm just getting impatient."

"I know baby, me too. Look at it this way Williams and his gang haven't been able to get to us out here. Once this all plays out we can pay him off and ride away into the sunset." He pulled her into his arms and kissed her. Finally, he set her from him and smiled.

"Okay, Stamos, I'll try harder. The faster we get this done, the faster we can live a free life."

Stamos watched her walk back to the house. He was tired of reassuring her, tired of pretending to adore her. Shaking his head, he went back into the barn.

He looked everywhere but he couldn't find the tampered wire. He figured it must be at the house. He cursed as he wondered who had done it. Everyone knew Callie wanted to ride the fences as soon as she was able. Had someone intentionally tried to target her?

*****

"Looking for something?" Garrett asked. He wanted to find the underlying cause of Callie's accident.

Stamos turned and looked at Garrett in surprise. "I tried to find the wire. I wanted to see if it had been weakened in the same way as Old Henry said."

"Find it?" Garrett sized Stamos up. He looked sincere, but Garrett wasn't so sure anymore. Someone on the ranch had tampered with the barbed wire and he needed to find the culprit.

"I looked but then I figured you had taken it to the house to examine. Bad thing, tampering with that wire. It's dangerous enough without weakening it. Everyone knew Callie was dying to ride the fences as soon as her ribs had healed."

Garrett believed Stamos knew nothing about it. He seemed too incensed. "I don't have it. Henry said he left it in Cal's saddlebag."

"It's on the tack room table. I didn't think to look in her bag."

"Let's get our gloves and take a look." Garrett took his work gloves out of his pocket. He removed the wire from the bag and whistled through his teeth. "Look at that. No wonder it broke."

"Good God, who would do something like that? Anyone of us could have gotten hurt or worse. You don't mess with barbed wire," Stamos said, his tone getting more heated with each word.

"We're going to have to be extra vigilant for now on. I don't know who did this but it might not be the only thing they tampered with. At least Cal will be in bed for a day or two, longer if I have anything to say about it. I'm going to need your help keeping her close to home."

Stamos' eyebrows rose. "I thought you didn't want me near her."

Garrett slapped Stamos on the back. "Normally no, but I need every eye on her. She seems to enjoy your company."

"Just tell me when you need me. I'll look around and see if I see anything out of place. It just sickens me someone wanted to hurt one of us." Stamos shook his head.

"I agree, we'll get the men together tonight and let them know about the possible dangers. Keep an eye out."

Stamos nodded and Garrett could sense he took it all very seriously. He hated to admit it but he'd suspected Stamos of the misdeed. It was good to know he'd been wrong, but if it wasn't Stamos then who did it?

"Stay near the house today. Tell Henry the same. I have a bad feeling."

"Sure thing, Boss."

Garrett nodded at him and walked back to the house. He didn't know what to think but someone had hurt his Cal and for that alone someone had to pay.

The first floor was empty. Garrett climbed the stairs. The loudness and tone of the women's voices concerned him. He stopped at the partially opened bedroom door.

"Sylvie, why don't you just go away for a while?"

"I'm only here to help you."

The fake sweetness of Sylvie's voice grated on him.

"Why don't you go and do well... how about some housework?" Callie said. "Maybe while you're here, you could plump up my pillows?"

Garrett fought a grin.

"You're going to have a big old nasty scar," Sylvie said. "Poor you, no man will have ya now."

"Get out!"

Garrett stepped back as Sylvie ran out. He'd heard enough of the conversation to understand what was going on. It surprised him their truce had lasted this long. Sylvie was bound to be bitter after the talk they had. She hadn't been happy when he told her she was just the help and to keep her hands off him.

Callie turned her head away. He sat in the chair next to her and handed her a tissue. "Honey, don't cry," he said, gently. "Look at me."

Her refusal puzzled him. Her sobs tore at his heavy heart. He climbed into bed with her and pulled her close, hoping to provide some sort of comfort. "It's going to be all right, Cal," he murmured repeatedly, as he stroked her back. She still wouldn't look at him but she snuggled closer, her head on his chest. He could feel her hot tears through his tee shirt and it devastated him.

"Please, Cal, tell me what's wrong." She'd stopped sobbing, but he could still feel her body trembling against his.

"Why won't you let me see a mirror?"

"Oh baby, your face is bruised and swollen; I didn't want to upset you."

"Sylvie said I have a big nasty scar. I feel the pain and I feel the stitches. Please, Garrett, I need to know if I'm hideous or not."

Her impassioned plea went straight to his heart. "Look at me, and I'll tell you the truth."

Her body stiffened against his and she slowly turned her head and looked at him. He wanted to protect her. He wanted to cherish her. "You'll have a scar, but the doctor said it shouldn't be too bad." She started to pull away and he held her close. "It doesn't matter, Cal. You've always been beautiful to me, even when you had pigtails and braces. I still think you're beautiful, Cal, never doubt that."

Callie looked into his eyes. She must have been reassured because she laid her head back on his chest, in a dry spot, and relaxed. Soon enough she fell asleep. Garrett just held her, not wanting to give her up.

Chapter Five

The next day Callie decided enough was enough. She wasn't one to sit around doing nothing. Being stuck in bed made her restless and depressed. It gave her too much time to dwell on her scar. Getting out of bed and going into the bathroom, Callie uncovered the mirror and gasped. She looked ghastly. On second look, the bruising made her look hideous. She leaned closer and examined her cut. Luckily, it was just under her jaw-line. Her eyes narrowed as she remembered Sylvie's comment about a nasty scar. That bitch deserved to fry in hell.

The empty kitchen was a Godsend. Callie wasn't in the mood to see anyone. Pouring a cup of coffee, she thought about Garrett. He'd given her such solace yesterday. She had never found solace in a human being before. It had always been the land that calmed her soul and rejuvenated her spirit. It had always filled her heart. Somehow, Garrett had done all of that and more.

Tapping her cup with her ring finger, she looked out on the bright sunny day. A ding sounded against the cup. Her heart lurched when she looked down and spotted Garrett's ring back on her finger. It frightened her to think about what it meant. It was unmistakable, or was it? She needed to talk to her husband and finally settle things. One day he was fun loving, and the next he pulled away. One day he was her shadow, and the next he ignored her. Her nerves felt frayed.

Turning from the window, she found Sylvie watching her. Sylvie gave her a mock look of horror and then made a show of caressing her flawless face with her hands. Knowing she baited her didn't make it any easier.

"I don't know why Garrett ever hired you."

Sylvie laughed and stuck her chest out. "Girl, if you can't figure that out you're even dumber than I thought."

Callie clenched her hands. "I don't need your constant disrespect. I want you to pack your bags and leave."

Sylvie narrowed her eyes. "You're firing me? I don't think so. Garrett hired me, I only answer to him."

Callie was shocked. One way or the other that bitch had to go, she vowed. "You can't even do your job right. This house is no cleaner than when I got here a few weeks ago."

"Oh, honey, I don't need to do that menial work. I have to save my strength for the evenings. Garrett is a very virile man."

Callie wanted to slap the smile off her face. "I mean it. I don't care what it takes but you're out of here."

"I wouldn't count on it." Sylvie stalked out of the kitchen.

Anger flooded her and she started shaking. She didn't want to believe Sylvie had slept with her husband but she wasn't sure. She wanted to throw up but decided to sit on the porch and get some fresh air. She had a lot to think about.

Sitting in the old rocking chair that Garrett's mother used to sit in gave her some relief from her turmoil. A squirrel raced up the big cottonwood tree chattering at a bird. Everything looked fresh and new, the flowers were just beginning to bloom. It would be time to put in the garden soon. Gardening always soothed her. She'd have to ask one of the men to make the soil ready for her.

Old Henry came by carrying the egg basket. He put it down and sat on the porch swing. "Best air in the whole dang country right here, Cal girl. You don't get this sweet Texas air in no big city, no siree."

Callie reached out and patted him on the arm. "This is as good as it gets," she agreed. "Why are you the one collecting the eggs?"

Henry gave her a sheepish look. "Sylvie is afraid of the chickens so I do it. Ain't no bother."

"Just one more thing she doesn't do."

"Problems in the old hen house?"

If she could have opened her mouth wide, she would have. "Women are not hens, and this is not a hen house."

Henry laughed. "Cal girl, you get your back up over the simplest things."

"Seriously though, Henry, she has to go. I won't live in the same house as her. She implied once again she's sleeping with Garrett." Much to her dismay a lone tear trailed down her face.

Leaning forward, Henry grabbed both of her hands and looked her in the eye. "I don't believe it for one tiny second. Everyone with eyes can see he loves you, honey. We'll just have to find her another place to work. Simple as that. I'm going into town this afternoon for supplies. I'll ask around and see if anyone needs a housekeeper."

Feeling better, she nodded. "That would be the best thing. Garrett's big heart wouldn't allow him to throw her out into the streets."

"I see you're wearing your ring," Henry said, raising his eyebrows.

"He put it on while I slept."

Henry stood up, kissed her hands, and beamed at her. "There you go. That says it all."

"I love you, Henry."

"I know, Cal girl. Same here."

*****

It was almost lunchtime but Callie wasn't hungry. She didn't want to see Sylvie. She had spent most of the morning sitting on the front porch watching the horses frolic in the corral. Surprise filled her when she saw Stamos coming toward her. She hadn't seen much of him lately. "Howdy, cowboy."

"Hey yourself." He bent to kiss her cheek.

She could see his eyes taking in her injuries but he didn't flinch. For that, she was grateful. "Could you do me a favor?"

"You name it."

"Could you go and get me enough apples to feed the horses."

"Sure thing, sugar."

Not long after Stamos went into the house, Nanny came for a visit. She walked up the porch steps and greeted Callie with a soft head butt. Callie laughed. "What in the world are you doing, girl?"

Nanny nickered.

"Oh, you missed me. Well, I missed you too," she replied, stroking her neck. "I don't know what Garrett will say about you being on his porch."

Nanny bobbed her head up and down.

"Oh, I see you've done it before. Well, why didn't you say so?"

The front door opened and Callie grinned at the look on Stamos' face.

"She said Garrett lets her on the porch," Callie told him with a straight face.

Stamos smiled at Callie, took her hand, and led her to the corral. "I know. She told me the same thing last month."

Callie laughed and gladly allowed Stamos to lead her to the other horses. She was startled when he stopped halfway and turned to look at her. "I hear you had it out with Sylvie. I think you're right. She's a menace."

"Glad to know I have you in my corner, cowboy."

"That's a given, Callie. Don't ever forget it. Now let's see those ornery horses of yours."

She had fun feeding the horses and laughing with the man. Her heart had been heavy for so long.

"You'd better go. I see Garrett heading our way."

"No worries." Stamos winked at her. "Garrett gave me his blessing to hang with you."

Callie returned his smile but on the inside, another piece of her heart broke off and shattered. Her throat suddenly hurt and she grew afraid she would cry. Why did he put her ring back on? He'd given her false hope for their future. Now he'd pawned her off on another man. Trembling, she hid her hands in her pockets.

"Hey guys what's up?" Garrett asked, as he stood next to Callie.

Refusing to look at him, she nodded toward the horses. "Looking at the horses," she said, hearing the oddness of her voice. She could feel his warm gaze upon her. Her heart wanted her to be in his arms, her brain wanted her to kick him where it counted the most. Why couldn't she make her face void of all emotions? It was a bad flaw to wear your heart on your sleeve.

"Is something wrong, Cal?" he asked, sounding concerned.

"Just a problem with your housekeeper but we can talk about it later."

"Just tell me."

Using all her inner strength, Callie looked at him. She put her arm through Stamos'. "I don't want to ruin the good time Stamos and I are having by talking about that wench."

Garrett's eyes narrowed. "Well then you two have fun," he bit out, his voice laced with sarcasm.

Watching him storm off didn't make her any happier. She couldn't figure him out and she was just too heart weary to try anymore. Too much downtime was her problem. She couldn't wait to throw herself back into ranching.

"Looks like rain," Stamos commented, looking up at the dark clouds.

Callie shuddered. Storms scared her. "It looks like more than rain. Those clouds look ominous."

The flash of lightening and the roar of thunder woke her from her fitful sleep later that night. Garrett hadn't come home by the time she went to bed. He was avoiding her. He probably didn't want to deal with the Sylvie problem. A crash close to the house made her scream. She put her hands over her ears and closed her eyes but it wasn't working. She didn't even know she was sobbing until she became aware of Garrett's arms around her. He rocked her back and forth and she noticed his state of undress. He only wore jeans, and they weren't even buttoned. She also noticed he wasn't wearing his boxers. Putting her arms around his bare torso seemed so right. She could feel the tightness of his back muscles. "Sorry you had to leave your room for me," she said, once the storm lessened.

"I wasn't in my room."

"I see." How she wanted to slap him. She wasn't going to make a big show of taking her ring off again. She'd grown up a lot these past few weeks. Sometimes you didn't get what you desired no matter how much you wanted it.

Easing out of his embrace, she gave him a sad smile. "Go back to bed. I'll be fine."

The look of tenderness in his eyes became too much. She had

known for a long time now she'd have to move out. Tomorrow would be a good day to do it. "Go," she whispered.

"You sure?"

Not trusting her voice she simply nodded and laid down, turning her back to him. It seemed like forever before he left. Oddly, she was dry eyed. Maybe it was the finality of it. There would be no next time, no hoping, and no dreaming. She was moving on.

*****

The sun shone bright in the window when Callie got out of bed the next morning. She never did get back to sleep after Garrett left. The upheaval in her life left her emotionally drained. What had happened to the woman that had planned to fight for her man? If the man didn't want you, there wasn't a fight. Callie planned to work with the horses today no matter who disagreed. Knowing Garrett would throw a fit if she mentioned moving out before the doctor gave her the all clear, she decided to bide her time. It wasn't worth the fight right now. They had to work together and she didn't want any hard feelings. It would kill her if she couldn't at least still have her best friend.

Some friend, she fumed as she walked into the kitchen. The smell of coffee was welcoming. Callie poured a cup and sat at the table, wondering where that lazy good for nothing Sylvie went. The door to her bedroom was closed. The sun was up now and it made her mad the housekeeper wasn't.

If a wake-up call was what she needed, Callie would be glad to give it to her. She knocked on the door and to her surprise she didn't get a reply. Annoyed she threw open the door, gasping at what she found inside.

Sylvie lay on her mussed bed with her neck at an unnatural angle. Her skin looked pasty white. Her eyes were open. Her black negligee was the only thing in the room that looked untouched. It had been smoothed over her body, not a wrinkle on it, a contrast to the disorder around her. Callie screamed, ran to the bathroom, and got sick. "Oh God, oh God, oh God," she repeated, tears ran down her face. A knock on the bathroom door brought her back to the present and she opened the door.

"Cal, what's wrong?" Garrett looked worried.

"It's Sylvie. I think she's dead," she told him, shaking so badly she could hardly stand.

"Where?"

"Sh she she's in her room."

Garrett ran to Sylvie's room, she reluctantly followed right behind stopping at the door, afraid to go back in.

Garrett stepped into the room. "Looks like she was strangled. I can see the bruises on her neck. How the hell?"

"Garrett?"

"Honey, you don't need to see this. Let me get you to a chair and then I'll call for help," he said softly, as he led her to the family room. "I'll be right back."

A moment later he raced right back into the room and gathered her up tight in his arms.

Callie breathed out a sigh of relief when she spotted the police car coming up the drive. She hoped they would get to the bottom of what happened. She briefly closed her eyes and prayed for the strength she would need to get through the day.

"You stay here, honey. I'll go talk to the police."

Callie simply nodded. Rocking back and forth didn't even comfort her. It must have happened during the storm otherwise she would have heard something. Closing her eyes, she remembered Garrett only wore his jeans when he crawled into her bed. Her heart sank to her stomach. She sensed she was about to break into a million pieces. It just couldn't be. Garrett would never...

"Callie, this is Detective O'Malley. He wants us to remain in separate rooms until back up arrives and they go over the crime scene," Garrett told her.

"Crime scene?" she squeaked. "Oh my God. I'm going to be sick." The bathroom gave her no refuge. She could hear Garrett right outside the door. She had to think. There was no way Garrett was going down for this. Was someone trying to set him up? She'd lie if she had to, after all he'd been with her last night, just not the whole night. Oh God, what a mess.

"Are you all right in there, Miss Daniels?" a female voice inquired.

With trembling hands, Callie opened the door. To her disappointment, Garrett wasn't there. She stood face to face with a sympathetic looking police officer. "Where is Garrett?"

"Ma'am, he's in the other room. I'll sit with you in the family room and keep you company. I heard you discovered the body. That's a tough one."

Callie followed the officer into the family room. The officer was tall and trim. Her police belt didn't even make her look chunky. She wore her light brown hair in a neat ponytail and her brown eyes looked kind. "Yes, it's been a tough one." Callie sat on the couch. She wanted Garrett.

Her legs shook uncontrollably. The air grew very warm bordering on being hot yet she shivered. She felt cold, so cold. She suddenly stood up and looked around. She could feel herself on the edge of hysteria. "I can't sit here. I can't stay in this house," she yelled, in a panic. "Get me out of here. I can't breathe," she said, between gasps of air.

*****

Garrett heard Callie's panic, and against the wishes of the police, he ran into the other room. He grabbed her and held her close. Her distress was almost too much to bear. Her sobbing became louder as he scooped her up, took her upstairs, and put her in his bed. "Call a doctor. Call Doc Baker," he demanded, pulling the covers up over her.

"You really shouldn't be here," Detective O'Malley said.

"Look at her. Do you think I give a damn what you think? I'm not leaving her until the Doc has seen her. She's had the shock of her life." He shook his head, sat on the bed, and gathered Callie to him. She shook so hard her teeth chattered.

Detective O'Malley radioed for the Doctor. "He's on his way. Officer Marks, here will stay with her." He nodded toward the female officer.

Garrett didn't care what was happening around him, his only concern was Callie.

"Mr. O'Neill, I need you to come with us," Detective O'Malley took Garrett by the arm and pulled him from the bed. "I need to take you downtown for questioning."

Shrugging from the Detective's hand, Garrett turned to face him. "I'm not going anywhere until I know she's all right."

"I'm sorry but I need to take you with me."

"Yeah, you already said that," Garrett replied angrily. "Listen O'Malley, I appreciate you have a job to do but I'm not going."

Officer O'Malley took Garrett's wrist and quickly handcuffed him.

"What the hell?" Garrett wanted to beat the man. "There is no downtown. Lasso Springs isn't large enough to have a downtown. This is a joke."

"The dead woman in your house is a joke too?"

Garrett grew quiet realizing just how serious the situation was. "You'll look after her?" he asked Officer Marks.

"I'll go with her to the clinic," she answered.

"Why can't she stay here?"

"This house is a crime scene," Detective O'Malley explained, leading Garrett to the door.

Garrett took one last look at Callie. She still cried but her eyes locked with his. He could see her inner strength shining through. He nodded to her and gave her a reassuring smile. "I'll be back soon, honey." He hoped it was true.

*****

Garrett paced back and forth in the dank holding cell, feeling his anger increase with each step. The smell of urine and vomit permeated his senses. He supposed they expected him to cool his heels in the tiny cell. If anything, it made him hotter.

Did they want him angry? Good God, it was like being in a bad movie. He wondered if they planned the good cop, bad cop thing. If they did, he was going to laugh. He was as concerned about Sylvie's murder as they were. Someone had been in his house. The same house Callie lives in. He wished he had answers. He only hoped his men were looking around the ranch for clues. They wouldn't be able to get near the house, but they might be able to find something in the surrounding area.

Back and forth, back and forth he paced. Now that he had time to think, he was ready to answer their questions calmly. If they expected to use his anger against him, they were in for a surprise.

Chapter Six

Callie's misery lessened when Henry came through the door. She had stopped crying and Doc Baker had managed to keep the police away, at least for the moment.

"Lookin' good, Cal girl. Had me worried that's for sure. Everything is going to the manure pile at home." He gave her a single yellow rose.

Taking the rose, she put it to her nose and breathed in the sweet scent. The petals were silky soft under her fingers. Callie thanked Henry. Yellow roses were his trademark. He was all Texas, all the way. For him there was no other color rose.

"Doc says I can leave this afternoon. What's been going on? What about Garrett? Have you heard anything, has he come home?"

"Whoa, gal, one thing at a time. Garrett is still at the police station. We haven't heard anything. We're in the process of moving base to your homestead. I guess Garrett's house is off limits with Sylvie and all. Stamos, Karl, Corky, and Timms will make the move to your bunkhouse. Old Samuel will stay and look after the Boss' house. We're moving as many horses as your barn will hold." He stopped and took a breath, his green eyes shining with love. "Let's just hope Nanny doesn't visit. I don't know if there's room for her."

"Sounds like everything is in good hands. I must have missed something, who is Timms?"

"Some new saddle tramp the Boss hired last week. You've been down and out so I guess no one told you."

"As long as he earns his pay," Callie said, making Henry smile. That was his saying.

"We're getting your bunkhouse ready and I figured I'd sleep in the house if that's all right with ya."

"Oh Henry, I love you. You've always been my protector."

Henry looked uncomfortable at her praise. "Someone had to look out for a fearless tomboy, all these years," he kidded.

Callie grabbed his hand. "I know," she said, her eyes misted. "You have always been there for me."

"Enough of this frilly talk," he said gruffly. "I need to get you back home where you belong and then we'll work on getting the Boss home too."

*****

Although she had planned to move to her house anyway, it was bittersweet to be there now. Stamos insisted on carrying her. He looked upset and she wondered if he had cared for Sylvie. It was a tragedy and everyone looked somber but the look in Stamos' eyes was different. He put her down when they got to the porch. She wanted to talk to the men.

"Thanks, guys, for all your help today. It's scary to think someone was in the house last night, and it is more tragic than I can say about Sylvie's death. I want things to work a little differently." She held her breath waiting to see if there would be any grumbling, but they showed her respect. "Work in pairs when you're on the range. I will cook all meals and we will all eat at the house. We're a man down until Garrett gets back so I'll tend the animals here with Henry's help. Anything else I can do to make things a bit easier please don't hesitate to let me know."

Waiting until the men dispersed, Callie turned to Henry. "Okay let's go," she said urgently.

Old Henry frowned. "Go where?"

Her eyes opened wide in disbelief. "To go get Garrett, of course."

Henry folded his arms and shook his head. "I have strict orders to keep ya here."

Scowling at him, she wanted to stamp her feet, but that would be juvenile and she was a grown woman now. "Let me guess, Garrett gave you those orders."

"Nope. It was the police. They want to question you and I think you'd do best to co-operate with them. This is serious, Cal girl."

Sighing, her shoulders slumped. She knew he was right. "Okay as soon as we get it done I'm going to Garrett."

Old Henry patted her shoulder. "Well, it looks like ya got your wish, Cal."

Spotting the police car coming her way, Callie panicked. "What if I say something to get Garrett in trouble?" she fretted.

"Tell the truth, that's all you can do. The rest is in God's hands."

Crossing her fingers behind her back, she nodded in agreement. "I just want to get this over with."

Detective O'Malley stared at her from across the kitchen table fifteen minutes later. His eyes narrowed when he observed her bruises and stitched chin.

"What if I told you the murder weapon was Garrett's belt?"

Callie jumped in her chair. "I'd have to tell you I don't believe it."

"Where were you last night?"

"This is ridiculous. Where do you think I was? It was storming and I don't like storms. Ask any of the men. I was screaming and Garrett came in to hold me and calm me."

He looked surprised by her answer. "Garrett didn't say anything about being in your room."

"Oh, for heaven's sake. Garrett would never say anything that would ruin my reputation. He still has high hopes to marry me off to someone."

"How long was he with you?"

"For as long as it stormed, so that would be about all night. I got up the next morning and he was in the barn taking care of the animals. The coffee was already made so I didn't knock on Sylvie's door immediately."

"How did the two of you get along? I see bruises on your face and a cut that most women would kill about. I think you killed her. Rumor has it Garrett was sleeping with her and you didn't like it."

"Leave the Boss alone," Stamos said, walking into the kitchen. "If you ever observed her with the animals, you would know she is kind and caring. Sylvie wasn't worth killing. Garrett was looking for another job for her."

Detective O'Malley smiled. "So, Garrett wanted to get rid of her. Very interesting."

Callie stared him in the eye. "I wanted her gone, not Garrett. She didn't know how to keep house and I wasn't about to do her job. I had enough to do without adding her chores to my list."

She wanted to gouge his eyes out. She needed to stay calm for Garrett's sake, but it wasn't working. "Why don't you ask around town, she had a roving eye and maybe she made the wrong person mad?"

"Such as yourself?"

"What happened to Chief Gordon? I know I've been gone for a while but surely he's still in charge."

Detective O'Malley smiled. "He took a fishing vacation and left me in charge. He'll be gone for about four more weeks."

Callie heard a car approaching and went to the window. She ran out of the house as soon as she spotted Garrett's face. He was just getting out of the car when she jumped into his arms. His arms went right around her holding her close. She pulled back and looked at his face. She wanted to kiss him and yell at him, all at once. He'd said he hadn't come from his room that night. She still wondered if he'd been with Sylvie. He wasn't a murderer that much she knew.

"Happy to see me?" Garrett asked, grinning at her.

She nodded. "We'd better not look too happy. That detective has some strange ideas about us and Sylvie," she whispered.

"Believe me, darlin', I already know. We might as well go in and show him we have nothing to hide."

"Okay," she said, feeling almost giddy inside. She loved him so much and now she knew her love would never go away. If anything, it grew stronger.

Seeing the detective on her front porch made her groan aloud.

"It'll be all right, honey," Garrett said, softly.

"I guess that's all the questions I have for today." Detective O'Malley walked toward them. "As soon as all the evidence is processed I'm sure I'll be back. Don't leave town."

Having had enough of the big, tall, redheaded cop, Callie started to step forward. Garrett's arm snaked around her waist, pulling her to his side. "We'll be here," she said, biting her tongue.

Garrett nodded. "Detective, always a pleasure."

O'Malley looked as though he was going to say something but he didn't. He just nodded to the two of them and got in his car.

Walking back to the house with Garrett at her side, Callie wanted to scream. She wished she could cry at the unfairness of the situation, but she knew Garrett needed her to be strong. "It's been a hell of a day." She tried to sound calm.

Garrett opened the front door, allowing Callie to go in first. He stopped her from going any further into the house and held her close. He didn't say anything; he just seemed to need her closeness.

Callie lifted her face to look at him, His blue eyes looked stormy and his heart beat fast. "Garrett," she whispered.

"Shush." He lowered his head, taking her lips.

The urgency of his kiss surprised Callie. He deepened it, searing her to her toes as he gathered her closer to him. It felt reminiscent of a homecoming to Callie. She'd been waiting for this her whole life but part of her questioned the timing and the reason. Pulling her lips from his she hugged him tight and then let go. It had been such an emotional day and she wanted to know Garrett loved her, but now wasn't the time to ask.

Henry cleared his throat behind them. It drew them apart, yet they only had eyes for each other. Callie searched his eyes but they were filled with so much emotion she wasn't sure if she saw any love in them.

"We'd better come up with a plan for the ranch. Especially a plan to protect our, Cal girl," Old Henry said, not seeming to care he broke up a special moment. Ranching always came first and Callie knew it.

"You're right. Let's fill Garrett in on what we've done so far and see what else we need to do."

Sitting at the kitchen table Henry told Garrett about the move and what each hand was working on. He also told him he was moving into the house with them. Garrett agreed on all points but one. He was going to be the one to protect Callie.

Giving her a long look, he announced they were going to be

joined by the hip at all times."

Callie smiled at him. "Whatever you say, cowboy."

"I'm not kidding. We eat together, we work together, and we sleep together."

Callie knew her mouth hung open. "I'm not too sure about the last part."

"I vote no on that too," Henry chimed in.

Garrett laughed. "I just meant we'd sleep in the same room, I didn't say anything about seducing her."

Henry looked relieved. Callie grew pensive. Things were too confusing right now. She'd much rather have her own room, a place to get away from Garrett to sort out her feelings, but she knew it'd be useless to fight about it.

A few hours later, she rode out to the herd in the pasture closest to the house to check on Maggie Mae. Garrett rode right beside her. He hadn't wanted her to go at all but he gave in. He was taking this joined at the hip thing a bit too far.

Looking over the herd, she tried to locate her favorite bovine, Honey Bun. She was another cow who had come into the world motherless. Callie had hand fed her for almost six months. Try as she might, she couldn't find another cow to let her nurse. Unfortunately, Honey Bun had lost her first calf. It made Callie sad for her friend.

Callie had put both Honey Bun and Maggie Mae in a pen together hoping and praying it would work out. Much to her relief and pleasure, Honey Bun took Maggie Mae on as her own. They were just introduced to the herd a few days ago, and she just had to know her babies were all right.

"You can stay here while I find them," Callie suggested.

"Nope."

Shaking her head, she continued to ride through the herd looking for Honey Bun. As soon as she spotted them, she dismounted and hugged the cow. A 900 pound animal could always be a danger, but Callie knew Honey Bun would never hurt her. She smiled at her white face and black ears. The rest of her was black. Callie loved her.

Callie watched Maggie Mae come to her from behind her adopted mother. She knelt down and hugged her. "You doing okay, little one?" she asked, looking her over. Her weight looked good. "It looks like your mama is taking good care of you."

Callie's heart filled with joy watching the two together. She heard Garrett get down from his horse, but she didn't look at him. As far as she was concerned, she'd seen enough of him today. He even waited right outside the bathroom door for her.

"You did good, Cal," he praised.

"Yes Honey Bun and Maggie Mae will be just fine. Look at how much Maggie has grown."

"You named them?" he asked, sounding surprised.

Turning her head, she gave him an annoyed look. "Of course I did."

Garrett's laughter was deep and long. "They are breeding stock, not pets."

Callie glared at him. "They are mine, and I can name them anything I want."

"Technically they're from my stock, not yours," he stated, returning her glare.

"You know I don't have time for this. I have a ranch to run, a murder to solve, and I have to try to keep you out of jail."

Garrett drew her into an embrace. "I'm sorry, Callie, I was teasing you. I know we have a ranch to run. Keeping me out of jail would be nice but as for solving the murder, stay out of it."

"Why?" she asked, enjoying the feel of his arms around her.

"This is why." He brushed his lips over hers, sending shivers through her body.

Reaching up, Callie put her arms around his neck, drawing his head even closer to her. She opened her mouth to him and he tasted of sweetened coffee. Each time he kissed her, it was better than the kiss before. Arching her body against his, she tried to get closer. He shuddered before he released her. It was good to know she seemed to have the same effect on him.

*****

Garrett looked into her violet eyes, they looked dreamy and happy. Now wasn't the time to make any declarations of love, he didn't know what the future held. She was so lovely and loving. His heart jumped as he watched her with the cow and calf. He smiled as he thought of her naming the cattle. She was one of a kind, and he wanted her to be his.

He watched her get on her horse. For now, he was just going to have to be satisfied with keeping her safe. It still boggled his mind that Sylvie was dead. He wished he could get the look of her cold, white, dead body out of his mind. He kept going over every little thing and still couldn't figure out what the hell had happened.

That night he'd been just about to jump in the shower when he heard Callie screaming. He pulled on his jeans and went to her. He had known about her fear of storms. She had been the same way as a little girl. A storm in Texas was comparable to no other. Big dark clouds in the endless sky and the flashes of lightning looked dangerously close. The rain poured and poured, usually causing a gully washer. He remembered the storm lasting a long time that night. He had brought his weather alert radio with him to Cal's room in case of tornado warnings.

The only new men he had working for him were Stamos and Timms. The rest had worked for him for years. Timms was a baby faced greenhorn that wanted to learn cowboying, so he'd given him a chance. Stamos was no stranger to ranching and he was a good hand. Maybe it had something to do with the cut fence and the weakened wire. Someone had tampered with that new roll of barbed wire. Someone had been on his ranch.

He sighed when the house came into view. The possibilities were endless and he had a bad feeling Detective O'Malley had it in for him. What a nightmare. They wouldn't be able to pay legal costs and keep the ranch. His heart was in his throat just thinking about it.

He dismounted first and grabbed Callie by the waist to help her down. He knew she didn't need or want the help but he needed her closeness. It surprised him she didn't struggle. She just put her arms around him and let him hold her. Her silky softness was not lost on him. Even dusted from head to toe with trail dust she was the sweetest woman he had ever known. She smelled like spring flowers with a hint of musk. He wondered the name of her perfume.

"We'd better get inside. I have to start dinner. I have a lot of hungry men to feed."

"Why did you decide to have us all eat at the house?"

Callie smiled. "Because I wanted to watch each and every man to see who is guilty."

"Playing detective again?"

Frowning she let go of him. "This ain't a joke, cowboy, and you know it. We might be able to find out something if we spend time with the men."

"Yeah, you're probably right. I just seem to push your buttons today."

"It's not you; it's the tense circumstances we're facing. I'm on your side. Now let's get cooking."

Walking side by side they went into the house. They expected to see Henry but to their surprise, Nanny was in the kitchen helping herself to all the apples.

"Oh my, How do you suppose she got in here?" Callie asked.

Garrett laughed. "Nanny does whatever she wants. It does surprise me though. It's a first."

"Dang it. Cal girl, how many times do I have to tell you, no horses in the house?" Henry chastised, grabbing the reins and leading Nanny outside.

Callie almost doubled over, she was laughing so hard. "How

many times?" she barely got the words out between fits of laughter.

"Well, Miss Daniels, how many times?" Garrett asked, enjoying the hilarity of the moment.

As soon as she heard him call her Miss Daniels, the joy left her heart. She wanted to scream her name is Mrs. O'Neill. She turned away from him. He'd only pledged to give her his name, which he forgot, and his protection. He'd told her on their wedding day not to get carried away with the love part. Still it hurt. She knew he didn't kill Sylvie but doubts about their relationship remained.

Once again, she'd dropped her guard. He was only spending time with her to protect her. Now that she acknowledged it, she'd have to deal with it. It wasn't his fault he didn't love her.

"Where's the grub?" Henry asked.

Mustering a smile Callie turned toward him and hugged him. She needed a hug and he seemed to sense it. Old Henry hugged her back. She broke away and looked at him. "Why have we always known you as Old Henry, you couldn't have been old when they first started calling you that."

Henry gave her a sheepish grin. "I have to confess I was a greenhorn once and every time something wasn't done right the other men would just shake their heads and say it must have been Old Henry's doing. The name stuck. Get it? I was new and the called me old."

Kissing him on the cheek, she assured him she got it.

"Now both of you shoo. I have some heavy duty cooking to do."

Both men nodded and went outside but she wasn't fooled. She knew they were sitting just outside the kitchen. Hopefully dinner would be enlightening. She wanted to know more about the new hand, Timms.

Callie greeted each man as he entered the room and sat down. She had expected Garrett to sit at one end and her the other. Didn't happen. Henry was at the other end and Garrett sat down to her left. He just cocked his right eyebrow and gave her a mock look of what-did-I-do-now.

She ignored him. She had to concentrate on the other men. They didn't talk much. They complimented her on the fine dinner of ham, green beans, mashed potatoes, and biscuits. This was getting her nowhere, beside Garrett kept *accidently* touching her foot with his.

"So how was life on the range today?" No one answered. "Karl, what did you do today?" she asked, as brightly as she could.

Karl took forever clearing his throat. He was a bear of a man, huge and very hairy. "I was up in the hills looking for strays, ma'am, just like the Boss told me." He went back to eating.

"Timms, it's nice to have you here. Where are you from?"

This time Garrett kicked her. She gave him a dirty look and turned toward Timms, waiting for his answer.

"A man's got a right to some privacy, Miss Daniels," Garrett said.

Ignoring him, she smiled at Timms who was now beet red. "Ma'am, I'm from a lot of places. Guess I'm just looking for a place to hang my hat and call home for a while."

Nothing suspicious about that, she thought. Garrett had somehow removed his boot and was rubbing his foot up and down her leg. She wanted to kill him. Sometimes he was just a burr under her saddle. She couldn't even think. She had a feeling that's what he intended.

Giving him her I-hate-you-look she expected him to stop. He smiled sweetly at her, making her blood boil.

"How about me?" Garrett asked "Any questions for me?"

"Nope. I've known you from birth so that makes you old enough to be my father."

"I don't think so. I am old enough to be your husband though."

Opening her mouth, she shut it again as his foot found her lap. She'd had enough of him for one day. Smiling at all the men, she grabbed her water glass and fork at the same time. Drinking the water, she jabbed the fork into Garrett's foot causing him to howl. "Something wrong?" she asked, trying not to laugh.

The glare he gave her could have shriveled a cactus. "No, just bit my tongue."

"Well, that does hurt. I try not to do that."

The men all laughed except for Old Henry, he had a puzzled look. There was no fooling him. He wanted them to announce their marriage but Callie refused until she knew Garrett was in it for love. She wanted to be able to walk away without the whole town of Lasso Springs knowing about it.

"I was wondering, Boss, what are the cops doing about Sylvie?" Karl asked.

"They're processing the evidence. It's an awful thing. I liked Sylvie, she had a good sense of humor and she was a help to us all. It also bothers me someone was in my house last night and I didn't know it."

"You didn't hear a thing?" Stamos asked, looking doubtful.

The look of doubt rubbed Callie the wrong way. The men needed to have absolute confidence in Garrett, no matter what. It was akin to the old days, you rode for the brand. "He didn't hear anything because I was screaming and carrying on."

The shocked looks she received made her feel warm. "I didn't mean that. I'm afraid of storms and I get hysterical, always have. Garrett rocked me back and forth, like a baby most of the night."

They still stared. Feeling her face grow hotter, she stood up. "Ask

Henry, he knows how I get." This time she didn't wait for their stupid looks. She marched into the kitchen to start cleaning. Men always thought the worst. They were just like little kids; she knew what they were thinking at first.

Still muttering under her breath, she began to wash the pots and pans. They could clear the table themselves. Feeling the heat of a body behind her, she knew immediately who it was. "I see, my shadow is here," she snipped.

"Don't worry I put my boot back on."

Whirling around, she came face to face with him. "I don't appreciate your humor. I don't appreciate you groping me with your stinky foot, I don't..."

Garrett silenced her with a soul-searing kiss. All thought went flying out of her head as she experienced his sensual lips on hers. He probed with his tongue until she surrendered and opened her mouth. Against her will, she snaked her arms up and wrapped them around his neck. She could feel his fingers undoing her braid, once loose he ran his fingers through her hair. He smelled of spice and leather. Her stomach coiled in anticipation.

"Uh hum," Old Henry cleared his voice.

Garrett seemed content to keep her in the circle of his arms but Callie wasn't. She pushed him away. "I have to get this kitchen cleaned and the biscuits ready for the morning, so you two go away."

She was grateful they knew enough not to laugh. They left the room, leaving her to her rollercoaster feelings. Dang that man.

Chapter Seven

Drying her hair with a towel, Callie entered her bedroom and glowered at Garrett lying on her bed. She stomped to the linen closet. Walking back into her room, she threw the bedding at him.

Seeing her intent, Garrett caught most of the bedding. "What's this for?"

Callie crossed her arms and frowned at him. "So you can sleep on the floor."

Garrett eyed her large tee shirt. It hid her best assets, but he still had a good view of her long legs. He made an obvious act of looking her up and down. He could tell he ruffled her feathers but hell; she was so damn pretty when she was mad. He loved the way her eyes flashed when she was angry. Lately she'd been angry a lot. He gave her a slow lazy grin, watching her trying to control her temper. "But ,cupcake, I thought we'd share this bed." He patted it in invitation.

She sputtered as she tried to tell him to get out. Her anger seemed to have made her tongue-tied. She pointed at him. "Get out. Get out of my bed."

Old Henry came running in. "What in tarnation is goin' on around here?" He looked ready to defend Callie with his last breath.

"Whoa now," Garrett said, raising his hands above his head. "I was just teasing our, little Cal here."

Henry's stance relaxed as he took in the situation. "Yeah, well, I thought the whole joined-at-the-hip idea was as shaky as a bucking bronco."

Garrett got off the bed and waved his hand over the bed. "It's all yours, little Cal."

He could see the little Cal part made her madder. "I'll just get the cot and put it in here."

"Well that should do it. Good night, Cal girl. You holler if you need me."

"Thanks, Henry, sleep tight."

As soon as Henry left, Callie walked over to Garrett. "You are the most insufferable human I know. My name is not, little Cal or, Cupcake. I want to wipe that smile right off your face."

The teasing light in his eyes seemed to have calmed her a fraction. "Don't think you can charm your way out this time, cowboy. You deliberately baited me."

Reaching out to caress her check, he smiled. "You're the most beautiful thing when you're mad."

Callie jerked away. "We'd better get the cot and make it up for you."

*****

Ill-tempered from lack of sleep, Callie tried to smile as she put out big serving plates of scrambled eggs, toast, sausage, and biscuits. Grabbing the coffee pot, she poured each man a cup. They seemed lighthearted this morning with their easy banter. Callie eyed Garrett and he seemed to be suffering from a lack of sleep too. She heard him tossing and turning on that creaky old cot all night. At one point, she almost offered him half the bed, but she couldn't. If he touched her jokingly again, she knew she'd shatter.

Sylvie's funeral was tomorrow, that meant extra chores today, so they could attend. The fear of what happened wasn't far from her thoughts. Deciding to forgo breakfast, she silently went out the door. She needed a breather and she wanted to see Pirate and Misty. She hoped they were settling in.

She relished the quietness of the morning as she walked toward the barn. The birds were singing and the squirrels were chattering, but overall it was quiet. She entered and waited at the door for her eyes to adjust to the dimness. Laughing, she headed toward Pirate's stall. Two heads greeted her instead of one. "Nanny, there isn't enough room for the both of you in there," she chided, as she stroked Nanny's neck. "Tell her, Pirate, that's your stall." Pirate whinnied in agreement.

"Well, let me give you your apples and go greet Misty. I'm sorry Nanny, but you'll have to find another stall to stay in."

She fed them both an apple, chuckling the whole time. She started toward Misty's stall when she was grabbed from behind. An arm imprisoned her waist as the other hand covered her mouth. The hand was covered with a leather glove and it stank. Adrenaline kicked in and Callie began to struggle.

"I've got a knife. Settle down," her assailant ordered in a raspy voice. "Just sign the oil rights over and all of this goes away. Otherwise, I'll be back for you and most likely the Boss will be in prison." Shoving her to the ground, he ran out the back door.

Callie jumped up and followed only to see the man riding away on a black motorcycle. She slumped back against the side of the barn trembling. Somehow this all had to do with the oil. It was a nightmare. She didn't even know who wanted the oil, but Garrett did. She'd have to ask him. It was her land too. Did the attacker think the land rights were independently owned or jointly owned? That would make a big difference. Jointly it was someone who knew about their marriage. Her head started to throb.

"Are you okay?" Garrett asked.

Callie jumped in fright. "No, no," she answered, with tears in her eyes.

Garrett opened his arms and Callie went flying into them, wanting the closeness, needing the security. "Someone was here and he warned me to sign over the oil rights or else you'd go to jail."

Garrett pulled her tighter against him. He didn't say anything.

*****

Soothing words didn't calm her. Garrett had tried more than once to let her go but she held on even tighter. Usually she was fearless, except for thunder storms, but her shaking still hadn't stopped and Garrett wanted to go after the bastard who grabbed her.

Garrett spotted Stamos walking toward him and motioned him to hurry with a jerk of his head.

"What happened, Boss?"

"Looks like someone grabbed Callie and threatened her. Could you take her inside and have Henry see to her. I'll gather the rest of the men and we'll go after him."

Between the two of them, they got Callie to unclasp her hands and let Garrett go. She protested but Stamos swung her up into his arms and carried her to the house. Glad of the other man's help, Garrett began to saddle horses. He figured to use both the horses and the truck to hunt the perpetrator down. No one messed with his woman. He grinned at that thought. Once again, she was foremost in his thoughts.

"She all right?" Garrett asked, as Stamos mounted a chestnut roan.

"She's not too happy. Something about women's rights and she's half owner."

"Being mad is better than being afraid. She'll get over it. We have a lot of ground to cover and he has a damn good head start." They all went over Garrett's plan and headed out.

High hopes of finding the intruder waned as the day wore on. They lost the motorcycle tracks and even though they had all split up, there was no sign of him. Sending a text to all the ranch hands, Garrett headed back to the house. They would meet him there. It didn't sit right with him he couldn't protect the people he was responsible for. He couldn't wait to see Callie. He needed to know she was all right. He called her from his cell at one point but she didn't have much to say. He could hear she was spitting mad though.

Riding toward the barn, he was glad to see Detective

O'Malley, all ready at the site. Maybe he'd believe him this time. There were no illusions. Detective O'Malley had already decided Garrett had killed Sylvie; he just didn't have enough evidence to arrest him yet. Hopefully this latest incident would make the detective look in another direction.

He no sooner rode into the yard, and dismounted than Old Henry took the horse so he could catch a flying Callie. She hurled herself at him so hard he almost went down into the Texas dust.

"I'm so glad you're back," she whispered in his ear, as she wrapped her arms around his neck.

"Cal, I'm all sweaty. Let go, honey."

"I like it when you're sweaty," she assured him.

He almost smiled. "I need to talk to O'Malley."

Callie let go and stepped away, but she didn't take her eyes from him.

He sensed her need and took her by the hand, leading her into the house. Nodding at O'Malley, he sat on the couch with Callie, not letting go of her hand. He had the same need to know she was all right.

"So, Miss Daniels here has told me quite a tale." The detective sounded less than convinced he believed her.

"We had another intruder on the ranch. It makes me sick inside to know he had his filthy hands on Callie," Garrett said.

O'Malley's eyebrows arched. "How did you know the hands were filthy?"

Garrett could feel his eyes all but bug out of his head. "What's that supposed to mean? I wasn't there but any hands that don't belong on Callie would be filthy. Stop your train of thought. I didn't kill Sylvie, and I didn't threaten Callie."

"Getting a little hot under the collar, aren't we?"

Jumping to her feet, Callie stared the detective down. "We aren't anything. I told you what happened. I also told you the man left on a motorcycle. No one here has one."

Grabbing her hand and pulling her back down beside him, Garrett smiled. "Thanks for defending me but I'm positive, the detective doesn't want to jump to any premature conclusions."

Detective O'Malley frowned at them. "Yeah right," he said sarcastically.

Garrett could see they were getting nowhere with O'Malley. "I guess we're done here. Did you even have anyone look for the motorcycle?"

"I'll get on it."

"Yeah, well have a wonderful day, O'Malley." Garrett stood at the front door and opened it waiting for the Detective to leave.

Detective O'Malley scowled at Garrett. He went out the door warning him not to leave town. Garrett slammed the door closed.

"He won't listen to me, Garrett. He thinks I made it up as a type of alibi for you."

"Well, I have a ranch to run and cattle to move. I'll leave Henry here with you." He looked at her sad face and opened his arms to her. She ran into them and he could feel her snuggling as deep as she could. "It'll be okay," he said, kissing the top of her head.

He slowly let her go. He could feel her reluctance but he had things to do. "I'll be back in a few." He smiled at her.

"Okay."

Garrett left the house, making sure Old Henry knew to keep close to Callie. She looked so young, so lost but he couldn't stay, he needed to work off his frustration.

*****

Another cranky day, she bemoaned. She couldn't get the biscuits mouth wateringly flaky. Instead, she was stuck with hockey pucks to serve for breakfast. The scrambled eggs were a bit browned, as was the sausage. At least the coffee tasted good. Garrett hadn't come home for dinner last night. In fact, he didn't get in until after midnight. That was late for a cowboy. She couldn't sleep, waiting and wondering. When he did finally fall into his cot, he tossed and turned again causing the damn thing to make screeching noises all night. To top it off Detective Know-It-All' refused to release Sylvie's body for burial.

She knew her face must have reflected her great mood since not one cowboy complained about the awful breakfast. It almost made her laugh as they tried to chew the biscuits. She began to take pity on them. "I'm sorry about breakfast, guys."

Timms gave her a boyish smile. "Better than my Ma's, Miss Callie."

Finally, she smiled a genuine smile. "I promise to make a wonderful lunch for those of you that'll be around this afternoon."

"You can plan on most, honey. We're going to be in the front pasture, vaccinating the cattle. Doc. Parker will be here too."

"I haven't seen Doc Parker in a long time. Is he still as handsome as a movie star?"

She got her answer in the deep frown Garrett sent her. "Guess so," she laughed. "Can't wait to see him," she said, winking at the men.

"Maybe he'll be too busy for lunch," Garrett suggested, staring at her.

"Oh, I don't know about that, but I'll come out to the pasture later just so I don't miss him."

"Callie, I don't..."

"You heard him boys, get out to the pasture and get the cattle ready," Old Henry interrupted.

Callie smiled at each cowboy as he thanked her for a fine meal. They had nice manners she had to give them that. Her smile vanished when she caught a look at Garret's face. He was cranky too. Riling him wouldn't be to her advantage. "You know, I have a lot of paperwork to get through so I won't be able to make it to the pasture today after all."

Garrett gave her a long hard look. "Good."

Callie watched him walk out the door. His jealousy made her feel warm inside.

"You two young uns need to saddle up and ride into the sunset. The sooner the better," Henry griped.

"So that's what it's called."

"What?"

"Sex."

"Now you wait a minute, young lady. I said no such thing. I meant you need to get your differences out," Henry insisted, his face turning red.

"Oh, you could have fooled me." She laughed as she walked toward the study. She could still hear Old Henry sputtering. She wished it was that easy. She'd adore to ride into the sunset with Garrett, but she needed his love first. He liked her, he was protective of her but sometimes she still viewed herself as the little *sister* following him around. She didn't feel comparable to a full partner in the ranch and she certainly didn't feel like a wife, or girlfriend.

*****

As it turned out Callie didn't even need to flirt with Doc Parker, he did all the flirting himself. Garrett watched as the other man held Callie's chair out for her when they were sitting down to lunch. He seethed when Doc Parker complimented her at every turn and it made him see red when she smiled back at the Doc.

"Did you get the paper work done?" he asked, in a grouchy voice.

Callie looked surprised by his tone of voice. "Yes, well most of it."

"But not all."

"I didn't know there was a due date," she curtly responded.

Garrett looked around the table and realized he was making an ass of himself. He wiped his mouth with his napkin, threw it on his plate, and left the room. He wasn't going to play her game, he thought angrily.

Jumping into his truck, he drove toward town. He wanted to see if Chief Gordon had returned yet. He also wanted to see what progress the police were making. It made everyone irritable and jumpy, well, mostly Callie and him. He needed to get some sleep. It was torture to sleep in the same room as her and not touch her. Every time they grew close, she seemed to pull away from him even further than before. He'd never understand her, but he missed his best friend. They used to be able to talk about anything and now half the time he sensed a wall going up between them.

He stopped at the one stoplight in Lasso Springs. As far as towns went this one was small, a farming and ranching community. Some families had owned their land since before the civil war. The whole town had a gray weather beaten look to it and a few of the stores needed a new coat of paint, but it was home. Garrett looked to his right and was amazed to see Detective O'Malley talking to a man on a motorcycle. He grew excited, it had to be Callie's attacker. They found him.

The light turned green and Garrett made a u-turn and parked next to O'Malley's car. O'Malley looked shocked when he noticed Garrett. The man on the motorcycle wore a helmet with the sun visor down so Garrett couldn't get a look at him. Swearing as the man rode away; Garrett got out of his truck and confronted O'Malley.

"What the hell? That was the guy, wasn't it?"

"Calm down, O'Neill, it wasn't your guy. He's just passing through. He didn't know anything about you or Miss Daniels."

His hands fisted at his sides, he looked at O'Malley in exasperation. "You got his information though, didn't you?"

"Sure, I got his name."

"But since you think I'm guilty you're not taking it seriously. Have I got that right?"

Detective O'Malley looked down the street for a moment, then he looked at Garrett. "That just about sums it up."

"This is a bunch of bull."

"You'd best go home, Mr. O'Neill, before you give me a reason to lock you up," he warned.

Garrett was growing more suspicious by the minute but he knew better than to push O'Malley into a corner. "I'll be at the ranch if you catch the guy." Not waiting for a reply, Garrett jumped into his truck and drove toward home.

He just couldn't wrap his mind around the sordid mess. He tried to remember everything he knew about Sylvie. It wasn't much but maybe Callie could help. He thought back to the night at the Whiskey Barrel when Callie had gone there with Stamos. When Stamos and Sylvie danced, they seemed pretty chummy. In fact, now that he thought about it, they arrived in town about the same time, looking for work. More puzzle pieces that didn't go together.

Chapter Eight

It was time for action. Callie couldn't take being in the house any longer. She'd spent yesterday doing the books and had another sleepless night. Thankfully, she pulled off breakfast without mishap. She planned to take Misty out for a ride, wanting to see what the filly could do. She looked like a runner and Callie needed the wind in her face.

Getting away from Henry proved difficult. He took his responsibilities very seriously. Every time she attempted to walk out of the house, he was there. Finally, she told him to come with her.

Grumbling he saddled his horse Buster. He named all his horses Buster, claiming it was easy to remember.

It drove Callie crazy since she loved to name animals. As a toddler, she always called Henry's horse Bubba. "Quit your grumbling and let's go," Callie called to him.

"You ain't heard grumbling yet, Cal girl," he threw back.

Smiling as they mounted up, she gave him an affectionate look. "Love ya, Henry."

Henry settled down. It always worked with him. Loving Henry was easy.

They rode north. Callie wanted to go back to the spot where the cut fence lay. She needed to find something, some clue. The wind whipped at her face; though warm, it still felt glorious. Breathing in the sweet smell of the Texas grass calmed her. She had such a love for this land. Fear gnawed at her. They could lose it all if they railroaded Garrett. It wasn't something she could put her finger on, but O'Malley smelled fishy.

The earth looked green, the grass, the leaves on the trees and the budding flowers. It was similar to being in her very own piece of art. The sky looked so big. She could see from horizon to horizon. Not a cloud marred the perfection of the huge Texas sky. Just being out on the range gave her strength.

The weight of her gun bothered her. She hadn't carried it in a while. Briefly, she looked down at the holster. It had been a birthday gift from Garrett two years ago. The leather was hand tooled and carved. Callie loved it. Garrett's birthday was coming up. It still stung he had forgotten hers this year, but she planned to help him celebrate his.

Riding up to the fence, both Callie and Henry grew silent. The fence wasn't cut, but there laid a dead calf on the ground. It had been shot and left there to rot. Callie dismounted and started toward the calf. Henry grabbed her arm trying to stop her.

"Henry, I need to know if it's Maggie Mae," she insisted.

"Let me look," he said firmly.

Callie nodded. She stood planted. Tears filled her eyes. Even if it wasn't Maggie someone had murdered her cattle.

Henry turned toward her, "it's not Mags," he shouted.

Breathing out a breath she hadn't realized she held, Callie walked toward Henry and the calf. She noticed the imprint of horseshoes in the dirt, surrounding the calf. She looked into Henry's concerned eyes and nodded to him, letting him know she could do this.

"Henry what is going on around here? Someone on a horse did this." Her heart sank at the implications, it was another threat. She needed to talk to Garrett and find out more about this oil business.

"Let's go back, I don't feel safe here." She swung into her saddle. Patting Misty on the side of her neck, she rode toward home. The feeling of being watched freaked her out. Realizing she had put Henry in danger hit her hard. She needed to think before she acted from now on.

As they rode home, Callie vowed to talk to Garrett. Who were these oil people? They seemed to go to great lengths to get their way. She didn't even make it halfway home before Garrett and Karl rode up.

Callie braced herself when she saw the thunderous expression on Garrett's face. Karl didn't look happy either.

"Where the hell have you been?" Garrett demanded.

It was on the tip of her tongue to tell him off but she didn't. They needed to watch each other's back. "We found a dead calf. Oh, Garrett, it had been shot in the head."

"Damn it." Looking at Karl, Garrett told him and Henry to go and bury it before it invited predators to the ranch. He watched them ride away in silence. He gave her a level look. "I honestly don't know what to do with you."

Callie's face turned white. "I'm sorry, Garrett. I know now it was stupid and I regret it."

"Tell me about the calf."

Garrett listened to the whole story and pulled her from her saddle onto his. He cradled her in front of him. "I'm sorry you had to see that. But you're right it had to be someone on the ranch if they used a horse."

"I hate this. I like all the men, Garrett. Would one of them really betray us?"

Garrett gave her a hug before letting her down. "I suppose we'll have to find out before anything else happens."

"We'd best ride for home." Garrett watched her mount up.

"Who is that?" Callie asked, as they observed a rider on the horizon. The vastness of the Texas sky distorted distance.

"I can't be sure but it looks like Stamos. I wonder what's wrong now." Garrett lifted his face to the sun and sighed.

"Let's not borrow trouble, Garrett. We do need to talk about what's been going on around here. Why haven't you mentioned the oil deal to me?"

"And let them dig up your land? I know you, Cal. The land is what you love most."

She wished she had the guts to tell him she loved him most. He looked so dejected. "If it means your freedom, then yes, I'd let them drill," she said, with conviction.

Garrett gave her a sad smile. "That means a lot, honey. I know how much the land means to you. It's in your blood." He sighed deeply. "I didn't want them on my land either. There's oil under mine, or so they told me, but there is considerably more under yours."

"Do you think this is all about money? My God, someone is willing to ruin our lives for greed?"

"It's Stamos. Let's ride, there might be trouble." He urged his horse to go forward.

Callie's heart dropped. She had a bad feeling. Turning Misty around, she followed Garret.

The beating of her heart increased as she watched the two men talk. From where she sat, it looked like trouble, big trouble. She rode up to them and brought Misty to a halt. Garrett looked defeated and Stamos looked worried. She wished she could just close her eyes and make it all stop. "What's going on?"

Stamos gave her a sympathetic look. "O'Malley is at the house looking to arrest the Boss."

Callie gasped, and she turned toward Garrett. She wanted to take him and run away. However, Garrett prided himself on his integrity so he'd never agree. "The Mexican Border is only days away on horseback," she said, trying to break the tension.

Garrett gave her half a smile. "Yeah, we could ride for the Rio Grande."

"Oh, Garrett, we can't allow you to be arrested. We need to have a plan of action before they take you away. I can't lose you."

"That's why I rode out to meet you. I figured I could escort, Callie back home and you could find a place to lay low for a few days," Stamos explained.

"I appreciate it, Stamos," Garrett said.

"No. I'm not going back with Stamos," she protested. "I have a better plan. Stamos you go back and tell them you didn't see us.

Garrett, we need to talk. We need to plan for the worst and you need to tell me what to do about the ranch. We can go to the western line shack and talk."

Garrett shook his head. "I don't want you involved."

"Oh please. I'm in this up to my eyeballs. We're going to need cash for a lawyer and I need detailed instructions on how to do that without ruining our future," she insisted.

She could see Garrett wavering. "Be smart about it, Garrett. You can turn yourself in tomorrow."

Garrett nodded. "She's right; we have to plan this out." He looked at Stamos intently. "Tell them whatever you feel comfortable with, I don't want you to lie and end up paying for it later."

"I think, Callie would be better off coming home with me," Stamos said, giving Garrett a level look.

"I'm not going home with you, Stamos, but I do appreciate your concern. You've been a good friend to me and I'll have to rely on you if Garrett gets arrested."

Stamos just nodded, turned his horse and rode away.

"I wish you had gone..."

"Garrett, give it a rest, let's go to the north line shack."

"I thought you wanted to go to the western one."

"Right now I don't know who to trust."

"Even Stamos?"

"Even Stamos," she answered ruefully. "Let's get a move on, we have a long night ahead of us."

They rode across the range side by side. Although upset, she knew she couldn't change things now. All she could do was listen, plan, and be there for Garrett. It might be the last night they had together for a long time.

It took a couple hours of riding but they made it to the line shack. It was a wonderful sight to Callie who was getting saddle sore from not riding as much as she used to. The tiny shack nestled against a hill with plenty of trees around it. It would be a great haven in bad weather. It even had a small barn. Usually there would be a makeshift lean-to but Garrett went all out.

"Nice barn." Dismounting, her legs cramped and she had to wait a minute before she took a step.

"I figure if a cowboy needs the line shack, then the horses needs cover too."

Putting her hands against her back, she stretched pushing her chest out. She almost laughed as Garrett tried to pretend he wasn't watching. He was an ornery one she couldn't figure out.

"I'll take care of the horses if you want to see what food is stocked in the cabin."

Callie nodded and then opened the door. It was definitely a shack not a cabin but it would be enough for them. She felt herself blush when she looked at the small bed. She wondered what cowboys did when there was more than one of them stuck out in the bad weather? She also wondered where Garrett planned to sleep. The floor looked anything but comfortable.

She opened a few cupboards and found plenty of canned food, mostly spaghetti. That would have to do. She didn't care, she wanted to know everything Garrett knew. There had to be a way to figure it all out.

Hearing the door open, she turned and watched Garrett take off his hat. He was an impressive man. He seemed to take up the whole shack with his brawny shoulders. She couldn't help but to travel her gaze down to his flat stomach, lean hips, and muscled legs.

Garrett coughed and gave her a strange look. She didn't care. "Tell me everything you know about these oil people," she demanded, folding her arms before her.

Garrett took a step toward the stove and filled it with wood before lighting it. "Hope you know how to use one of these."

"Yes, I do. Let's get to the subject at hand. For all we know O'Malley is on his way here."

Garrett put coffee on the stove, using bottled water. He sat on the bed; it was the only place to sit and patted a place next to him.

Callie went and sat next to him. The shack seemed smaller and smaller.

"Last November the S&S Oil Company sent me letters asking for a meeting. I ignored them. Then I noticed they had left their trademark brown flag on our land as a calling card. Enraged, I called them. They tried to strong arm me into giving them the oil rights. I refused. A couple of heifers were shot, same way that calf you found today. I knew who it was. I called Chief Gordon and he came right away and tried to find enough evidence but there wasn't any. They didn't know of our marriage, only that we had merged the ranches together."

"If we know who it is, why isn't O'Malley going after them?"

"If only it was that simple. O'Malley said he didn't know anything about dead cattle or the Oil Company. He came right out and told me he thought I was trying to shift the blame."

Callie experienced outrage. "There is something about that detective that isn't right."

"I know, honey. I have my suspicions about him too. Don't sell anything to make bail. No matter what. I'm not going to give them the satisfaction."

"But, Garrett." She was cut off by Garrett's lips on hers. The kiss was so sweet and gentle she almost cried. The kiss became more urgent as though he too knew this would be their last night together for a long time.

The little cries and moans she heard were hers and it surprised her. They both had taken their shirts off and Callie grew a bit shy letting Garrett see her without her bra.

He gave her a wicked look. "Surely I'm not the first," he teased.

Callie pulled away, covered herself with her hands and looked at the floor.

"Cal?"

"Would it surprise you if you were the first and only?" she shyly asked.

"Cal, look at me." When she did, he continued. "It's okay."

"I took our vows seriously."

"I know, Cal." He pulled her close, kissing her forehead. "If you don't want to do this just say so."

Callie had never been so warm or excited. It wasn't what she had pictured though. She always pictured herself as a wine and roses kind of gal. This was her one chance. There may not be tomorrow. Seeing the compassion mixed with raw desire in his eyes made her decision for her. Turning she found herself enveloped in his muscled loving arms.

Running her hands up and down his back, she could feel his muscles ripple as he moved. Shifting her so she sat on his lap, Callie put her arms around his neck. She buried her face in his tanned neck and inhaled leather, and spice. She loved his scent. His hands stopped running up and down her back and she pulled away. She realized he had a perfect view of her.

The look of awe on his face puzzled her. She looked down at her breasts and she could see her nipples tightening. She could actually feel it happening. Embarrassed, she moved to cover them with her arms.

"No, don't hide, Cal. My God, you are beautiful. No guy in college ever tried to see these beauties?"

"Garrett, you know I'm not beautiful. I'm just a hick tomboy from the sticks. I didn't even compare to the other girls," she said, with a hint of sadness in her voice.

"Well let me be the first to clue you in honey. You are beautiful. I happen to adore the tomboy in you."

Callie hugged him, feeling his bare chest against hers. Pulling back, she ran her hands over his chest. It was so chiseled, allowing her to see each hard muscle. He had a sprinkling of hair that became darker under his navel, a line that disappeared under his jeans.

Moaning, she relished Garrett's strong hands on her breasts. Callie's mind started spinning out of control. The pleasure she felt was unlike anything she had ever imagined. She turned to putty in his hands as he laid her on the bed. He loomed over her and took one rosy breast into his mouth, making her squirm. She felt a deep coiling in the bottom of her stomach. His hands seemed to be everywhere at once and before she knew it, she lay naked beneath him.

He kissed her soul deep and she arched off the bed in need. She didn't know what she needed but she was sure Garrett could supply it. "Please Garrett," she pleaded.

Garrett fought for control. She made his body sing. Despite her pleading, Garrett didn't think she was ready, just yet. His kissed her breasts and his hand slowly moved downward. Her legs spread for him. She trembled as he touched her. He could feel her readiness as he braced himself above her and entered her body.

She was so tight, so slick. He inched his way, not wanting to hurt her. He came upon her barrier and hesitated. She began moving her hips urging him on so he thrust into her. He heard her small cry of pain and he stilled. Seeing the tears in her eyes nearly broke his heart. "I'm sorry, Cal."

"I'm all right now. The pain was brief."

Her hips rising up seemed to invite him to finish. He thrust into her until she shuddered. She cried out his name and it sent him over the edge. His body quaked with release. She was magnificent.

"Am I too heavy?" he asked, as he collapsed on her.

"No, no I like the feeling of you."

Garrett smiled. He rolled to the side and looked into her eyes. She looked happy and bewildered. Gently he brushed her hair back from her face. He kissed her deeply, feeling shattered to his core. He never imagined it could feel this way.

"Are you okay? Does it still hurt?"

Callie had many smiles but he had never seen this one before. It was so loving and it reflected her satisfaction. "I feel wonderful."

*****

Callie woke with a smile on her face. Her husband had taken her two more times during the night. She could feel the love pouring out of him each time and she rejoiced in it. He wasn't in the shack and she wondered where he went. Slowly, feeling lazy and happy, she got up and dressed. It was a night to remember, her life just starting. They had hardships to face as soon as they rode back, but it was a new beginning for their relationship.

She glowed as she imagined an easy affection between them. She could finally tell everyone they were married. Looking around the shack, she wanted to remember everything about it. She wanted to be able to picture this place and remember the happiness of it.

Putting on a pot of coffee, she wondered where Garrett was. Opening the door, she grew puzzled to see him sitting on a fallen log, looking thunderous. "Garrett?"

The look in his eyes astounded her. He wasn't happy. "Is something wrong?"

She suddenly doubted herself. He was acting so strange.

"I'll be right in."

Callie gave him a long look and flinched at his expression. "Okay."

Sitting back on the bed, she couldn't even begin to understand what had just happened. A sick feeling began to spread throughout her belly. She watched him walk in but he wouldn't look at her. Her heart beat a fast tattoo and she suffered from confusion.

"Garrett..."

"Don't, Cal, just don't. We made a huge mistake last night. I don't know what I thought. I can't have you be my, wife. How stupid could I be? I was enticed by the way you constantly shake your hips at me. I shouldn't have taken you up on your invite. I made a mistake, the biggest one in my life."

Tears formed in her eyes. "Garrett?"

"Let's get going. I have to turn myself in and I want you to start divorce proceedings. I'll do it if you don't. I can't have you hanging around my neck while I'm trying to save it."

Stunned, Callie watched him walk out the door. Numbly she made sure the fire in the stove was out. Looking at the bed, she felt dirty. How could he?

Her heart shattered into pieces and her throat grew dry as she pulled her coat and hat on. It was going to be a long ride home. She should have known better. He never even pretended to love her. She just took everything to heart and he hadn't. It didn't mean anything. He just wanted a woman since he would have to go without in jail. Shivering, she wiped away her tears. He used her and he made her feel dirty about it. If anything she should be mad, but somehow she failed him. She'd been inadequate. She had given him her most cherished gift and he didn't care.

Taking a deep breath, she walked outside, determined to ignore him.

Ignoring him proved near impossible. Watching his rigid back for hours made her want to weep, but she refused to cry. Her mind began whirling. She tried to think of other things but the soreness between her legs as she rode Misty, was a constant reminder of the night before. It bewildered her how he'd treated her this morning. She'd been dreaming of last night forever and now she fervently wished it had never happened.

She finally knew just how pathetic she'd been all her life, waiting for a crumb of approval from him. Well, he gave her what she wanted and now all she had was disgust, coupled with a broken heart. Her heart hurt oh so much. How she was going to bear it she didn't know. It wasn't any consolation knowing he'd be in jail. She didn't wish him ill. Her whole chest tightened, she still loved him. It nearly broke her, knowing she always would.

The sight of her barn and house were welcome. She needed to hide. She needed to lick her wounds in private. O'Malley's car was there. Riding behind Garrett, to her shame, she wanted him to turn and look at her. She needed his reassurance, but painfully she knew it would never be. She rode behind him toward the house, in silence. Garrett dismounted, talked to Old Henry for a minute, and walked with O'Malley to the police car.

The handcuffs on his wrists made her gasp aloud. Dismounting, she waited next to Misty, pathetically waiting until the end for Garrett to turn and look at her, but he didn't. Watching until she could no longer see the car, she waited in vain. She felt so young, and lost standing there. He had always been her rock. Now she stood alone.

Old Henry approached her. She must have looked awful; he winced when he looked at her. Callie couldn't even glance at him, her shame was too much. Handing him the reins, she brushed past him and went inside. Stamos stood there, staring at her, but she ignored him. She needed to be alone. Finally, she reached her bedroom and fell across her bed. Tears released and poured down her face. Using her pillow, she muffled her heart wrenching sobs. He had hurt her heart and her pride many times over the years but he had never broken her before today.

How was she going to survive? The pain she suffered was beyond anything she could have ever imagined. He had used her and tossed her aside. Her life would never be the same. She would never be the same. Her whole being was washed in shame and her love for him had done it to her. Garrett had been right all along, she was too young for him. She was naive and now she was paying the price.

Disappointed in herself, Callie sat up and looked around her room. The wallpaper was peeling. It had once been a princess room her mother and father had decorated for her. Running her hand over the much washed and loved quilt, she tried to make peace with herself. She knew the sick feeling in her stomach and heart wasn't going to go away anytime soon, but she had to put it all aside. She had the weight of the ranch on her shoulders. It was her turn to keep it running and she would. She promised herself she would do her damndest to run it right.

Taking a wet cloth, she pressed it against her swollen eyes. It didn't really matter. All the men would think she'd been crying because of Garret's arrest. It would be easier to allow them to think that. She needed to find out about this character O'Malley. She didn't trust the big Irishman and she knew the perfect place to find out the info she needed, Harriett's Yarn and Tea Shop. It had been a while since she'd been in there but she knew the gossip found there was reliable. Harriett didn't allow malicious gossip, just plain truth. Well, as truthful as gossip could be.

Feeling better for having a plan of action that didn't involve sitting around feeling sorry for herself, Callie left her room and concentrated on getting food on the table. It became business as always and she knew the familiar routine would keep her going. Her hands needed to be kept busy. Tomorrow she would go into town and see what she could ferret out from the women at the tea shop.

*****

Callie woke up to a gray day. A day to match her mood. The men were uncharacteristically quiet as they ate their breakfast, but Callie didn't mind. She had a lot to think about. First Harriett's, and then on to find a lawyer. They should have contacted one as soon as they realized Garrett was the only suspect.

She drove Garrett's truck, a more reliable vehicle than the junker she'd driven the last four years. Funny, the town never seemed to change. She hadn't seen it since going to the Whiskey Barrel with Stamos, but she hadn't paid much attention. Daley's General Store was the biggest building and it was all red brick. Most of the other stores had weathered wooden fronts. The second biggest store was Lasso Spring's Feed Store. It was always a busy place. A sprinkling of smaller shops made up the rest of the town. There were three places to eat, The Whiskey Barrel, Lasso's Pizzeria, and Faye's Café. The familiarity gave Callie comfort.

Parking in front of Harriet's Yarn and Tea Shop, Callie didn't even hesitate. She wanted to find out all she could about Detective O'Malley and she wanted to know what happened to Chief Gordon. Opening the old wooden door, she heard the familiar bell that jingled each time a customer went through it.

The room grew silent as every head turned toward her, but one by one, she received welcoming smiles. Harriett was a tall lean woman of about sixty years of age. She wore her pitch-black hair long. It hung down her back reaching her waist. Everyone knew it was a wig but pretended to admire it. No one wanted to offend the self-proclaimed queen of Lasso Springs. She made a beeline to Callie and clasped her hands. "Oh dear, it is a delight to have you here. Let me look at you. You are the very picture of your mother."

She drew Callie along to the center table where most of the women were gathered. "You sit here, dear. We heard what happened to Garrett. We'll help you run that ranch of yours, don't you worry," she reassured Callie as she scurried behind the counter to get her teapot.

Callie smiled at the town's women. She doubted many of them knew much about the running of a ranch but she was grateful for the support. "I think we'll get by. I've worked that ranch most of my life."

Mable Darling, another sixty year old woman, smiled at her. "I know you can do it, dear. Your parents would be so proud."

Harriett hurried over with the tea. "So, what can we do for you? I know you're not here to buy yarn," she said, with an eager smile.

"Well, I guess I'll just get right to it. What do you know about Detective O'Malley?"

"Oh, that one," Mable said, with a sour look. "He hasn't been here long. I don't like him. He won't let me park in any space unless it's an actual parking space."

"I do know the mayor isn't a big fan. The poor man has had his share of tea, talking about that one," Harriett told her.

"That detective is pompous," Cindy Riley chimed in. She was about Callie's age. "He asked me out and when I refused he started giving me citations for j-walking. I also got one for my little Homer barking. You remember Homer, don't you ,Callie? My precious hardly ever barks."

Callie heard a few grumbles about that. If she remembered correctly, Homer was one of those tiny dogs with big voices. "Where is he from?"

They all looked at each other. No one seemed to have the answer and they all looked very surprised. "Well dang it I guess we don't know, sugar," Harriett said.

"You don't think Garrett is guilty, do you?" Callie asked.

"Of course not," Cindy insisted. "We were just talking about it when you got here. Sad thing when an innocent citizen of Lasso Springs is arrested by that man."

Harriett came over and patted Callie on the shoulder. "I'll make it my personal quest to find out the skinny on the guy. We will not allow him to trifle with one of our own."

Callie smiled. "I appreciate it. Now, does anyone know of a good, but cheap lawyer?"

Mable sat up straight and preened. "My Bobby, is the best lawyer in town and in this case, he'll not charge you a cent. He's been chomping to go after O'Malley. He probably already went to the jail and talked to Garrett. I'll have him call you this evening. We need to stick together."

Callie's eyes misted. "I don't know how to thank you all."

"Oh, sugar, don't you remember when most of us were ready to up and leave and your daddy sold half of his cattle so the rest of us could afford to stay on?" Harriett asked.

"No, I never knew," Callie said.

"Your daddy was the only one of us who didn't get taken by that corrupt Banker Harvey Maves. The rest of us were greedy and we got wiped out," Mable explained.

"Well, thank you. Also if we could get in touch with Chief Gordon?"

"That man has so many fishing holes. We'll try to find out which one he fell into this time," Harriett promised. "You finish that tea and don't be a stranger."

"I promise I won't."

*****

Driving home, Callie had many things to think about. Wondering why she never knew about her father's generosity was on the top of the list. He died when she was so young. Old Henry would be able to tell her more about him. Her thoughts went back to Garrett. The whole truck smelled of leather and hay and of him. It surprised her she hadn't realized it on the trip to town. The once loved scent now brought heartache. Opening the windows, she drove home.

Stamos came out of the house to greet her. His easy smile eased her pain a bit. He opened her door and offered her his hand. His hand seemed so large, work worn, and comforting.

"Everything good in town?"

"Yes."

"Well?"

Callie didn't know what he was fishing for. "The ladies at Harriet's Yarn and Tea Shop were more than kind to me. They made me feel part of the community again," she said, smiling at him.

"Good. What about the Boss? Is he getting out?"

Although she liked Stamos, there was something about his questions that bothered her. They were natural questions but something didn't feel right. "Not today, it seems."

"When?"

Callie drew her hand away from his. Walking away, she shrugged her shoulders. "Don't know."

It didn't feel right not to trust the men that worked for you. It used to be the men who rode for you were the most trusted men but she couldn't bet Garrett's freedom on it, even if he was a mangy dog.

Walking into the house, she spotted Old Henry and greeted him with a much needed hug. "What was Stamos doing in here?"

"Don't rightly know. He seemed to be sticking close by all morning."

"I'm not sure I like it," she said.

"You're the boss, send him out to the north pasture to check fences," Henry suggested.

Callie sighed. Maybe she was making something out of nothing but she didn't trust her instincts anymore. "I'll do that after lunch."

Following Henry into the kitchen she laughed. "Peanut butter and jelly sandwiches?"

Henry looked insulted. "Hey, what's wrong with PB&J?"

Callie squeezed her friend's arm. "Nothing. I can't think of a thing."

After lunch, Callie assigned them each their duties. She glimpsed a flash of irritation from both Stamos and Timms when she assigned them checking the fences in the north pasture. Hang tough, that's what she had to do. She owned the ranch and she was the boss. She didn't have time for hurt feelings.

"Don't worry, Cal girl, it takes a bit of adjustment taking orders from a different person, but you know better than most what needs to be done around here," Henry said.

Callie smiled at him. "Thanks for the vote of confidence, Henry. Make sure you let me know if I get off track, or if I miss anything."

Henry grinned, as he opened the back door. "You can count on that."

Wandering into the family room, Callie experienced the silence keenly. She picked up one of her mother's glass angels and held it to her heart. She was never completely alone, but she seemed alone today. So much had happened in the last week and her emotions were wrung out and weary. It all hurt but the death of her dream for a real marriage hurt the most.

Calling herself every kind of fool, she left the house. She had a barn full of animals that needed tending.

Chapter Nine

Dinner was a bit quiet with the men stealing looks at her but they didn't ask any questions. Callie decided to let the men know what was happening. "I found a good lawyer for Garrett. His name is Bobby Darling; some of you probably know him." A few of the men nodded. "I guess they can hold Garrett for forty-eight hours before they have to either charge him or release him. Bobby seems to think there isn't enough evidence, but he thinks Detective O'Malley will try his damndest to charge Garrett with murder."

"Everyone knows the Boss ain't a killin' man," Karl protested.

All the men agreed. Suddenly they all seemed to be talking at once. Callie smiled at the outpouring of support. No matter how much it hurt she didn't want Garrett in jail either.

"Timms, would you take care of the barn animals tonight?"

"Sure thing, Miss Callie," he responded, with his usual boyish enthusiasm.

Callie smiled her thanks and began to clear the table. All the men, except for Henry filed out the back door. Callie sighed.

"Long day?" Henry asked.

"They all seem long lately." She began to wash the dishes. What she wouldn't have given for a dishwasher. "I'm just worried, I guess. I can't figure out what is going on around here."

"I've been giving it a lot of thought. I'm going to ride over to Garrett's place tomorrow and talk to Old Samuel. He just might know somethin'. He always has his eyes peeled. Could be we just didn't ask the right person."

Hugging him, Callie felt a bit better. "You might be on to something, Henry. I'm grateful for all your help."

Old Henry's face turned bright red. "I'm gonna watch the tellie for a bit, then hit the hay. Don't fret so much, Cal girl. We'll get this figured out."

"Thanks, Henry, good night," she said, heading for the den. It had always been her daddy's den and when he died, her mother wouldn't go in there for the longest time. She did all the paperwork right at the kitchen table up until she got too sick to handle it anymore.

It had to be her imagination but she thought she smelled the cherry tobacco her father used to smoke. She picked up his pipe and caressed it. She didn't remember much about her father but she remembered this smell. She thought about how generous the women at Harriett's had said he was. It gave her a great sense of pride. She ran her hands over the ornate mahogany desk, knowing he had spent a lot of time sitting there. It was all on her shoulders now and she felt up to the challenge.

Her dreams had died but she'd have to make new dreams. No sense mooning over a man who doesn't want you. She drew the line at starting the divorce. He'd have to do it. Her eyes started to well up as she remembered Garrett telling her to get a divorce. Angrily she dashed away her tears. She had a lot of paper work to trudge through and she planned to get it all done tonight.

Earlier she had moved the cot out of her bedroom and put it away in a closet. She even took all his clothes and threw them on a bed in an empty bedroom. Her bedroom still had his irresistible scent so she opened the windows hoping to remove that too.

Later, after hours of paperwork, her eyes were so weary yet still she couldn't find solace in sleep. Her mind refused to stop. She kept reliving her last night with Garrett. It had been pure heaven and he had acted as though she was a precious treasure he'd just found. The next day it seemed as though he realized his treasure was just shiny glass he wanted to throw away.

The hurt and anger ran deep. He'd cut her up pretty bad. Things would never be the same again. She mourned the loss of their friendship and she mourned the loss of her dreams, juvenile dreams. She'd had to grow up fast the last few days. She'd taken a few blows straight to the chin, but she had to get up to fight another day. She just wished it didn't hurt so much.

*****

Forty-eight hours were up. Bobby Darling had called to let her know Garrett was getting out. Callie walked outside trying to think. The silver clouds above and the green grass below gave her a certain consolation. She watched a monarch butterfly waltz through the air. How she wished she could wave her arms and fly. She'd love to see the simple things in life from a butterfly's perspective. The leaves on the trees, the fields of wild flowers, the sprouting garden. Breathing in the fresh country air, she promised herself she wasn't going to blame Garrett for what happened. It wasn't her fault but she should've known better. She never should've taken what he offered that night.

She looked down on her wedding ring and decided to leave it on until after the divorce Part of her wanted him to suffer as she had and maybe he'd remember what he was throwing away every time he looked at it

Wishes, she always had many wishes. Few of them ever came true, except her wish to make love with Garrett. She'd have to be careful of what she wished for.

She went to the old corral where she'd had Honey Bun and Maggie Mae brought. She needed them near her, especially knowing she wouldn't have time to go and check on them anytime soon. She opened the corral gate and smiled as Maggie Mae came toward her

"I should've named you, funny face." She petted Maggie's head. Honey Bun swaggered over to see what was going on. "You're the best mamma, Honey Bun."

A truck roared toward the house and she was reluctant to leave the pair. Nanny watched her at the fence. "If you come in to visit, remember to close the gate."

Nanny whinnied and stayed on the outside looking at her bovine friends. Callie wasn't surprised to see Honey Bun approach Nanny. She was certain they had some kind of communication between them. "You girls be good." She left the corral and closed the gate behind her.

She couldn't avoid Garrett's homecoming any longer. Part of her still wanted to run and jump in his arms. She needed to see for herself he was all right. Straightening her shoulders, she walked as sedately as possible to the front of the house where everyone had gathered and gave Garrett a brief nod. It hurt just to see him. She focused on the ground to hide her pain. She didn't want him to know how much he'd crushed her.

The men all shuffled past her. Garrett had obviously given out orders. Even Old Henry headed toward the barn. Feeling the warmth of his gaze, Callie looked up. "Good to have you back." She stepped around him to head into the house.

"That's it?" he asked.

"That's it," she replied, without even turning around.

Of all the gall, who did he think he was? If he expected a smile and her usual puppy dog look of hero worship, he'd better change his expectations. The more she thought about it the angrier she became. So lost in thought she barely realized she was banging pots and pans all around the kitchen. She stopped and took a deep breath.

"Did you work all your anger out?" Garrett asked.

Callie flashed him a look before continuing to put the beef brisket in the oven. Long, slow, cooking, the thought almost made her laugh, a recipe for both the brisket and her temper. Closing the oven door, she spun around to face him.

He looked good, too good, and her heart ached for him. She didn't want to bring up the divorce but she couldn't live with the constant wondering. "Is Bobby going to take care of the divorce?"

*****

Garrett knew he was a fool. He'd had it all. Just a few short days ago, he'd had it all and foolishly, he'd thrown it away. Callie's eyes no longer shone for him. All he could see in the depths of her violet eyes was anger and hurt. He'd done that to her. The old saying of you don't realize what you have until its gone hit hard. Sighing he took a step toward her, only to be warded off by her hand raised in front of her. "Callie..."

She looked tired and upset. It didn't surprise him when she turned and walked out the door. He felt gut kicked, but he deserved it. He'd become so misguided in his quest to keep her safe. His actions and words did just the opposite. He hurt her and from the looks of it, he hurt her badly. He hadn't talked to Bobby about a divorce. She'd have to be the one to do that, he just couldn't.

"If I were a different man, I'd shoot you," Old Henry said, walking up behind Garrett.

"I know," he responded bleakly. "I'd deserve it too."

"Well, as long as you admit it," Henry grumbled. "You cut up my Cal girl something awful."

"I know. Somehow, I'll make it right."

"You'd better," Henry warned, as he walked out the door.

Garrett walked down the hall to their room. Two days in the same clothes grated on him. Stunned to see his cot gone, he looked for his stuff and finally found it in another bedroom. Hell, what did he expect? He'd played fast and loose with his wife. Damn, that wasn't it at all. He took what he wanted because he loved her. She hated him now and he didn't blame her. He'd been cruel in his treatment of her and he deserved her hate.

His heart dropped to his stomach, there was no fixing it. This wasn't a booboo he could kiss away. Somehow, he'd have to make it up to her, if she let him. The sick feeling in his stomach wouldn't go away. He had caused her misery and for that, he was sorry.

*****

Callie was talking to Pirate, her best friend. In fact, she talked to Pirate and Nanny. Once again, Nanny snuggled up to Pirate during the night. "Well, if it makes the two of you happy who am I to judge? I don't know a thing about love. I know how happy it can make you and I know how devastating it can be when that love turns out to be a lie." Not able to stop the flow of her tears she buried her face in Pirate's neck. It wasn't the first time, and Pirate seemed to understand her need. "I'm such a fool."

Finally, she dried her eyes and gave Pirate a hug of thanks. She had work to do; she didn't have time to cry over that hard-hearted man. She led both Pirate and Nanny out of the barn and let them free in the closest pasture. She went back to the barn and brought Misty out so she could run and graze with her friends. Watching them, she wondered if she would ever feel carefree again. Her sadness became all-encompassing and she couldn't shrug it off.

She had just enough time to weed the garden before she had to start lunch. Pulling her black Stetson lower on her face to keep the sun off, she knelt down in the dirt and began to pull weeds. It looked promising she'd get a good yield this year. Of course, it depended on the weather, but she was optimistic. The feeling of optimism surprised her. She'd get through this.

Somehow, she wasn't surprised to see a pair of brown boots stopping right in front of her. She knew without looking up whose boot's they were and she ignored them. She weeded right around them. Finally, they walked away.

Callie was glad to see the boots disappear. How could he make sweet love to her and then demand a divorce? It boggled her mind. Try as she might she couldn't bring herself to hate him. Loving him had become too ingrained in her. The whole situation killed her. The agony in her heart grew so great she wanted to curl up and die. Nevertheless, the Daniels were made of strong stuff and she'd weather through. She glanced at her watch and stood up. She had sandwiches to make.

The men were full of questions as they sat around the table eating their lunch. Callie found out the police still considered Garrett's house a crime scene. The police didn't have enough evidence to hold him. It seemed up to her and Garrett to ferret out the killer before Garrett ended up paying for it.

Old Henry was uncharacteristically quiet. She wondered if he found out anything from Old Samuel. She had a suspicion he had and she couldn't wait for lunch to end.

Everyone went back to work except for Callie, Garrett, and Old Henry.

"You know something," Callie exclaimed.

"Like I told ya, Old Samuel keeps his eyes peeled and his mouth shut. Got him to open up. Seems Sylvie and Stamos were more than friends. They had some sort of signal thing going on and Stamos would go and meet Sylvie in the woods. Mostly they talked in heated voices. A couple times they kissed."

Callie was amazed. "Old Samuel knew this and didn't say a word?"

"Go figure," Henry replied, with a shrug.

"Did he know anything else?" Garrett eagerly asked.

"Stamos and Sylvie knew each other before they got jobs on the ranch and Old Samuel said they were on the run."

"From the police?" Callie asked.

"Old Samuel didn't know that much. He also said Timms is no greenhorn. He thinks he's faking it."

Callie and Garrett looked at each other. Callie could see the utter confusion on his face. "How'd he learn that?"

"You know how we like to raze the new guys? Well, Old Samuel saddled Timms' horse for him and didn't tighten the cinch. He wanted Timms to fall off as soon as he got on but Timms just went right over, tightened the cinch and mounted the horse like a pro. Old Samuel said not to let his young boy look fool ya."

"What the hell is going on around here? Right under my nose to boot." Garrett shook his head. "We need to keep this information just between the three of us. I don't want the killer to know we know anything."

Callie and Old Henry nodded in agreement.

"I just don't know what to think," Callie confessed.

It was too hard to think about anything with Garrett sitting across from her. To her utter shame her heart yearned to commune with his heart. Even though it hurt, she drank in the sight of him. She hated being weak willed. A sob rose in her throat. She got up and ran from the room. She threw herself across her bed. Her emotions raw, the pain in her heart too fresh, too powerful. Furious at herself for not being able to stem the flow of her tears, she finally gave in and sobbed into her pillow.

*****

Looking in the mirror at her tear swollen eyes a few minutes later, she felt all kinds the fool. It would have been easier if he hadn't taken her virginity. Now she foolishly wanted to feel his hands on her and his lips kissing her all over. Shaking her head, she threw a wet washcloth at her image in the mirror. Who is that woman? Callie turned away in disgust, straightened her shoulders and left her room. No more hiding.

Grateful she had started dinner much earlier, Callie made biscuits, mashed potatoes, and coleslaw. It was uncomfortable at dinner as the men tried not to sneak looks at her tear ravished face. Not one of them said a word, and Callie was relieved.

Old Henry's concerned eyes almost made her break but she put her hands under the table and pinched her leg. Time to show strength, not weakness. They were in crisis mode and her feelings needed to be put on the back burner.

By the time she cleared the table, her emotions were on a more even keel. She was congratulating herself for avoiding Garrett's stare when she sensed his presence behind her. Continuing to wash the dishes as though she didn't have a care in the world didn't make him leave. She heard the sound of a chair being pulled out from the kitchen table.

Hardening her heart toward him became too difficult. However, she could feed off her anger if she needed to. What he'd done to her was cruel. She needed to focus on that. The ranch came first. It always would and she needed to work with Garrett to hold on to it. Bracing herself, she turned around.

The solemn, concerned look in Garret's sky blue eyes almost got to her but she put her hands behind her and pinched her arm this time. She winced as she thought about all the bruises she would have before this was over.

"Honey, we need to talk," Garrett said.

The honey was an arrow to her heart. It was a lie. "I agree we need to figure out our suspect list and make a plan of action. We only have ourselves to solve this."

"That's not what I wanted to speak to you about."

Crossing her arms, she tried to hold in her feelings. "I will not talk about anything else. The ranch comes first, you staying out of jail comes next, and the rest will just have to wait."

"I heard you crying."

"Enough already. I refuse to talk about it so on to the next subject."

Tilting his head, he stared at her. "Okay, we'll do it your way. You're right the ranch comes first. Let's compare notes and see what we come up with. I know it has to do with the oil rights but it seems we have a snake in the chicken coop and we need to find it."

Callie nodded her head and poured them both a cup of coffee. She grabbed a pad of paper and a pen, and then sat down at the table. "Let's start."

"You're really going to be all business?"

"Give me a break. You hurt me, husband of mine, but you know what? I've discovered I can be as hard and callous as you can. So, yes, it is going to be all business."

He gave her a long hard look and nodded. "Number one, S & S Oil seems to be in the very middle of this whole thing. I haven't been able to find out anything about them."

"Did you try the internet?"

"No."

"I'll do that. I think number two should be Timms. Old Samuel is a smart one and if he thinks we can't trust him, we can't." She wrote it down. She started to tap the pad with her pen.

"I think two should be Stamos. Something is off with him."

She wasn't sure about that but she wrote it down as number three. She wanted to laugh at the look on Garret's face. He obviously wasn't used to people not following his commands. Too bad. She smiled.

"Two or three, I guess it doesn't matter," Garrett conceded.

"Nope, doesn't matter." She tapped the pad with her pen. She could tell it irritated him.

"What about Detective O'Malley?"

"Yep, that's a good one considering I don't think he's even a detective." She wrote it down on her list.

Garrett frowned. "What's that supposed to mean?"

"Woman's intuition."

"Oh, come on, there is no such thing," he scoffed.

"You can have your theories, and I'll have mine."

Shaking his head in disbelief, he stood up. "It's my neck on the line, *honey*, not yours so I don't want to hear about intuitions or psychics or whatever else you've got going on in that head of yours."

Callie stood up in front of him and pushed her finger into his chest. "Don't you start with me, *sweetie pie*. I'll eat you for lunch,"

Grabbing her finger, he gave her a slight shove. "That's my, *sweet girl* so soft and loving."

"You know what? You can go to hell," Callie shouted, as she stalked to her room. Jack ass.

She paced around her room but it didn't help. She needed to ride the range. She hoped it would bring her a sense of peace. Quietly she left the house and headed for the barn. She saddled Pirate and rode off.

The afternoon sun burned and she was soon damp with perspiration. That's ranching. It wasn't new to her. In fact, she loved Texas whole heartedly. A little sweat and dust was nothing compared to the sheer beauty of her land. She rode to the Lasso Springs Creek that ran between the two ranches. Texas bluebonnets were out in full bloom and the sight of them made the ride worthwhile. She dismounted and picked one. They were her favorite flower. A sense of calm overcame her as she twirled the stem with her fingers.

She wasn't used to fighting, least of all with Garrett. It seemed so unnatural. It seemed a shame. She looked up at the sound of a horse approaching and spotted Stamos headed her way. He might be number three on their list, but she wasn't frightened. She did wonder what his angle in all this was. though.

"Hey, sunshine. What are you doing alone?" he asked, swinging down from his horse.

"I just needed a peaceful moment. It's not easy being the only female around," she answered, smiling at him. Realizing what she had said, she put her hand over her mouth. "God I'm the only one because Sylvie was murdered. I didn't mean to make light of it. I wasn't even thinking."

Stamos walked over and stood next to her. "Nice peaceful spot. I can see why you come here."

"It's all just getting to be too much. Garrett and I are at each other's throats lately."

"Yeah, I noticed. Just because you're partners doesn't mean you have to spend all your free time together."

Callie turned toward him and cocked her head. "No?"

Stamos laughed. "No. For instance, you still owe me another date. I really had a great time on our last one. I wish you'd give me a chance."

"A chance?"

"I thought you knew how I felt about you. I want to take you into my arms and kiss you. Your lips are so delectable. I wish I had the right to strip you and make sweet, sweet love to you in the green grass."

Callie didn't know what to say. He seemed so sincere. "I have it on good authority you've already done that with Sylvie."

The look of alarm on his face made her realize what a foolish statement she'd made.

"Who said?"

"It was Sylvie. She didn't want me dating you, so she told me you and she liked to do it outside," she lied.

Stamos sighed. "That sounds just like her. Truthfully, we had a fling but nothing more. She might have been beautiful on the outside but on the inside, she was rotten. From the moment I saw you, I knew I had to get to know you better."

"I'm not ready to date right now."

"Garrett?"

"Of course. I've foolishly loved him all my life, but the feelings aren't returned."

Stamos drew her into his muscular arms. "I'm sorry, Callie. I know how painful unrequited love can be."

Callie stayed in his comforting embrace. She didn't want to lead him on but she couldn't deny herself the comfort of his shoulder.

"Damn it, Cal. What they hell do you think you're doing?"

Callie jumped away from Stamos. How could she not have heard him riding up? She spun around ready to give him a scathing retort, but when she perceived the look of panic and concern on his face, she couldn't. "I just needed to find some peace. I'm fine."

Striding to her until they were toe to toe, Garrett looked at her. "Do you know just how worried I've been? Do you?"

Giving him a sad smile, she just nodded. She noticed a few new lines on his face and recognized the toll all of this was taking on him. "Stamos, I need to talk to Garrett. See you later?"

"Sure thing."

Neither Callie nor Garrett moved while they waited for Stamos to ride out of sight. Callie was sorry she caused him to worry. She opened her mouth to apologize and was shocked when Garrett swooped down and kissed her. It was by no means a sweet, tender kiss. It was a kiss of passion, a kiss of possession. She could feel it to the tips of her toes.

She reached up and ran her hands through his brown hair, relishing the thickness of it. She could feel his hands on her back and rear end pulling her closer. The kiss went on and on and Callie cherished every second of it. She already knew how it would end but she didn't care. It was so good; it felt so right to be in his arms. This was her home.

She cried in protest when he broke it off. She watched his face as he stepped away. No look of love, just anger. Sadly, she turned and swung up into her saddle and rode away without looking back.

*****

Garrett watched her retreat in consternation. Throwing his hat on the ground, he swore a blue streak. He related to women easily but with Callie, he became an utter buffoon. He swore he'd never touch her again and first thing he did was seize her and kiss her. What a kiss it was. If she hadn't broken it off he would have taken her right then and there. Feeling disappointed in himself, he vowed once again to leave her alone. There was no way Stamos was going to have her. He didn't trust that yahoo. Something was off and he didn't know what it was. Stamos hadn't done anything, but Garrett was suspicious all the same.

Picking up his hat, he jammed it on his head and jumped into the saddle. He didn't want Callie riding alone. It was too dangerous. He smiled, noticing she wore her gun belt. Good for her. He urged his horse to go faster, needing to catch up with her. He needed to apologize. It was too tiresome to fight with her and then have to walk on eggshells around her.

He finally caught up to her and just rode silently at her side. Her mulish look told him he'd better not say a word. He could respect that. He'd just get her home and apologize later. Her glare was so intense he had to keep his lips from twitching upward. Laughter would bring her wrath down on him, and he had enough trouble.

Seeing her to the barn, he tipped his hat at her and rode away. He knew Old Henry would keep an eye on her. He needed to check the herd. He also wanted to know where each of his men were. Stamos shouldn't have been on that particular part of the ranch, unless he followed Callie. Maybe he was just watching her back, hard to know.

Chapter Ten

Callie was busy washing the dishes when someone knocked on the door. Grabbing a towel to dry her hands, she headed to open it only to be sidestepped by Garrett, who gave her a Neanderthal look. A look that meant, I'm the man I will answer the door. Callie shrugged and waited.

When Garrett opened the door, she could see Officer Marks standing in the dark of night. Garrett stepped aside, inviting the officer inside.

"Officer Marks, I hope there isn't more trouble," Callie said, concerned.

The woman officer smiled. "It depends on what you consider trouble. It seems one of your horses broke into the crime scene and made herself at home, particularly in the deceased's room. Did you know that horse knows how to open drawers and pull apart all the down feather pillows?" She wrinkled her nose. "It-- Well, you'll need to muck that room out."

Garrett's eyes twinkled as he looked at Callie. "What does all this mean?"

"You can have your house back. I know it's serious business but to tell you folks the truth, I've never seen anything so funny in my life."

"Where's the horse now?" Callie asked.

"She wandered away. I put her in a stall and I know I locked it but she's gone." She gave Garrett a sly look. "That wouldn't be the infamous Nanny would it?"

"Yes, it would. Imagine making herself at home, literally."

Callie smiled at him. "She'll show up."

"Detective O'Malley is fit to be tied, but he's such a hard ass. Oops sorry, what I mean..."

"That's okay, Officer Marks, we know what you mean," Callie said.

"You folks have a good night. I'll be glad when Chief Gordon gets back next week."

"Us too," Garrett agreed, walking her to the door. "Thanks for letting us know."

"You two take care, now," she said, as she left.

Callie and Garrett looked at each other and laughed. Callie laughed so hard she half expected her sides to split.

When the laughing stopped, she found herself trapped by Garrett's eyes. He looked at her as though he found her fascinating. It was a bit thrilling yet, the old hurt slammed into her. Callie pulled her gaze away from his. She knew what fascinated him and he wasn't getting any. Her heart longed for him so painfully, but the hurt of his rejection weighed foremost in her thoughts.

She walked to the window and stared sightlessly at the dark of night. "Sounds like we have a big clean up to do tomorrow. Imagine, Nanny ruining things for Detective O'Malley. I knew she was a smart girl."

"She certainly disrupted things. She's always been special and I think we need to bring her a bouquet of carrots when we see her."

Callie smiled a sad smile. She'd never received flowers from a man, except from Old Henry. Now she didn't want to. Turning from the window, she pasted on a smile for Garrett. "I'm going to bed, it's going to be a big day."

"I noticed my things have been moved from your room," he said, not taking his eyes off her face.

She grew uncomfortable as she looked everywhere but at Garrett. "I just can't have you that close to me right now."

"Right now doesn't mean forever. I'll leave my door open so I can hear you if you need me."

Tears pricked at the back of her eyes. "Unfortunately it does mean forever," she replied, her voice shaking. "I'm going to go on with my life. I plan to make a few changes and start over."

"You're not leaving?"

Looking at the ground, Callie tried to measure her words. She wasn't even sure what she had planned, but healing her heart was one of them. "This is my home, my land. It's the only thing I have in my life I can count on. I know someday things will blow over. You'll find a new wife and I'll hopefully find a man to love. Our children will be the best of friends." Callie's throat began to close. She escaped to her bedroom. She couldn't face him. It hurt too much.

The kiss they'd shared earlier was both heaven and hell. His kiss had touched her heart and soul and now she felt sick to the pit of her stomach. She couldn't allow it to happen again. It just ended up opening her wounds. Tears released and poured down her face. It was all too much. She wished she could just stay here at her house but she knew Garrett would have a fit.

She hadn't known this type of loneliness since college. She hadn't fit in with the other students. She was just a plain country hick. Besides, she didn't have the money to go with them if they had invited her. Last Christmas had been bad. She was beside herself when Garrett had told her not to come home. No Christmas, no gifts. She should've realized the score then. Maybe she was just a country hick.

*****

The next day proved hectic, trying to clean the mess Nanny left. Callie and Garrett just stood in the doorway to Sylvie's room with their mouths hanging open. The drawers were all open and most of the items had been taken out and tossed. The bed lay broken, and Callie wondered if the mare had tried to get on it. Feathers were everywhere and it smelled like a stall that needed cleaning, badly.

"I'm going to have Old Henry pack up the old house, you can unpack, and I'll have Timms clean out this room."

"I'd rather have Stamos here than Timms," Callie insisted.

"I don't completely trust Stamos."

Callie looked at him in amazement. "You trust Timms?"

Garrett turned his head and looked into her eyes. "Maybe I don't want Stamos here making a nuisance out of himself."

"He's not a nuisance. I like him."

Garrett smiled at her. "I know and to tell you the truth it makes me jealous to see you together. I'll send Timms over."

Callie's eyes widened as she watched Garrett cross the yard. "Damn that man."

"Hope you weren't talking about me, Cal girl," Old Henry said, putting a box on the table.

Callie gave him an affectionate hug. "You know I wasn't talking about you."

"What did Garrett do now?"

"Nothing and everything. He's got me so turned around. One minute I love him and the next, he rips my heart out. I don't know how much more I can take."

"You hang in there. I know he loves you, girl, he just doesn't know it."

Callie gave him a look of doubt. "I don't think..."

"That's right, don't think, just be the normal sweet woman you are and everything will be all right."

Knowing he meant well, Callie kissed him on the cheek. "Timms is going to be here cleaning out the room."

"Whose idea was that?"

"Garrett's."

"I'll stick close; it'll give you a chance to get to know him. Don't get too close, mind you."

"I'll be careful," she promised.

"Howdy, ma'am, Henry," Timms greeted.

"Good Morning, Timms," Callie greeted with false enthusiasm. "Let me get you a cup of coffee before you start. Here sit at the table, sorry it's covered with stuff but I think we can make room."

Timms removed his hat and sat at the table. "Thank you."

"I have a few more loads to bring in, so I'll be around if you need me, Cal girl."

His words were meant for Timms not her. "Thanks, Henry. Now don't you work too hard. If anything is too heavy, you come get help."

"Wow, I could've sworn my mama died many a year ago," he teased, as he walked to the door only to be hit in the back of the head with the dishtowel Callie was holding. "Good shot," he said, without turning around.

"You really take good care of, Old Henry, ma'am."

"I've known him since I was a little girl. I guess you could say he's family."

"You gots any more family here abouts?" he asked.

"Just Garrett."

"You two related?"

Callie smiled at him, even though his questions started to irritate her. "We're partners in the ranch."

"Legal partners?"

"Well, yes, and we have a few other silent partners," she lied. He was fishing and she didn't like it.

Timms frowned. "Didn't know anything about that."

Callie shrugged and turned away, busying herself with putting the kitchen to rights. "No reason you would know. In fact I don't think anyone knows."

Timms laughed. "Except for Old Henry."

Callie wasn't a good actor and she knew it. She shook her head. "No, I don't think so. It was done before my mother died."

"Well, I best get busy," Timms said.

"Let me know if you need anything, I'll be in other parts of the house putting stuff away."

Callie dried her hands, walked into Garrett's bedroom, and locked the door. Timms' inquisition shocked her. He fished for answers he had no right to know. She made up the fake partners hoping to keep both Garrett and her safe. All Timms had to do was kill Garrett and get her to sign over the property. Was there no end to greed?

It was quite possible Timms' questions were innocent. She'd always trusted the men on the ranch, but now... She'd have to remember to tell Garrett he had silent partners. Somehow, she didn't think she'd have to worry about forgetting her conversation with Timms.

Callie left her room to make lunch for any of the men that happened to come back to the house. She had a special smile for Old Samuel. He was a cantankerous man and he didn't enjoy hugs but she knew he liked her smiles. She didn't know his age but he had to be over seventy. No one would ever dare ask. They'd get their head bitten off and then handed back to them.

Everyone respected him and stayed out of his way. He had worked hard all of his life to keep this ranch afloat and whether he was able to work or not, he always had a place here.

"Was it lonely without us?" Callie asked, serving him a sandwich.

"It was downright peaceful, that's what it was. No one to bother me with questions. It was pert near the vacation I never took."

"Peaceful is nice," Karl commented.

"What would you know about it? You're the one always asking questions," Old Samuel griped.

Callie giggled. It was good to be home. Sadness came over her, this was not her home and it never would be. Broken promises and empty dreams, that's what she had. Try as she might to drive all thoughts of Garrett from her mind, it proved impossible.

She noticed Old Samuel giving Timms the evil eye from time to time. They were a cast of characters. She loved them. Well most of them. Timms might just deserve the evil eye. She'd have to ask Garrett what he thought.

The door opened and Garrett and Stamos walked in. Callie stood to make more sandwiches when she found herself in Garrett's arms. He gave her a big hug and kissed her cheek. Too bad, she knew what it was all about. It was a way of telling Stamos to stay away. Callie stiffened and waited for Garrett to let her go. His intense perusal made her feel strange.

"Sit, I'll make more sandwiches, the coffee is ready though. Help yourself."

"Do you need any help?" Stamos asked.

Callie just shook her head and went back to her sandwich making. He played with fire. Why would he put his job in jeopardy? It made no sense to her, but she could see the anger in Garrett's eyes when she turned around. He looked mad at her and she experienced a jolt of annoyance.

She handed Stamos his plate and walked toward Garrett. Dumping his sandwich in his lap, she put the empty plate on the table with a clatter and stepped out of the kitchen.

The hard scraping of the chair legs gave her pause but she continued to her room. She just about made it but Garrett was fast on his feet. He grabbed her and put her over his shoulder. "I think we need to talk."

Callie pounded on his back, she tried twisting, and kicking, but Garrett was determined. He carried her to his study and slammed the door and locked it. Callie grew frightened. In all her years, he had never manhandled her this way. "Garrett, please," she begged, her voice trembling.

He put her down on the sofa and pinned her arms. "I think you need to apologize," he told her, his voice hard and low.

"Sorry."

"Are you?"

"Yes. I'm sorry. It was juvenile and I regret it so get your big hurting hands off me."

"Hurting you, am I? Honey, you don't know what hurting is. You are a, spoiled little girl."

Tears formed in her eyes. "Garrett, please."

"Please what? Please kiss me? Please make love to me? Is that what you want? It must be with you shaking your tail at Stamos every chance you get."

"Garrett, no, no."

His kiss was hard and it hurt. She tried to turn her head away but he took her jaw between his fingers and squeezed her until she stopped struggling. Callie was shocked. Garrett pulled her top off and then her bra.

She stopped fighting. She lay there, tears pouring down her face. She sobbed and he suddenly looked at her. She could see the disgust in his face as he edged away from her.

"Put your clothes back on," he told her, his voice harsh.

Her hands trembled as she tried to latch her bra. Garrett swore and came behind her to help her. He pulled her shirt over her head. She had to hold the top edges together to cover herself. She refused to look at him. He'd abused her.

"Cal..."

"No, don't talk to me," she said, her voice shaking. Her whole body shook. "I know I've been a burden to you all these years. You don't have to worry about me anymore. I got the message loud and clear. It's not the first time you've left me bruised without a care. I'll call Bobby and... and..." She couldn't go on. Callie turned and ran from the room. Oh, mama, what were you thinking by having me marry him?

*****

Callie felt sore the next morning. Her arms hurt as she rose from her bed. Looking in the mirror the amount of bruising horrified her. Blue finger sized marks darkened along her jaw. Tears of shame filled her eyes and she wiped them away. She needed to be strong. She was strong, she amended. She couldn't show any weakness, especially to the men. She wanted their respect, not their pity.

Taking a deep breath, she walked tall into the kitchen. She smiled when she saw Old Samuel and Old Henry busy making breakfast. "Thanks, guys," she said softly, touched by their kindness.

Old Henry looked her up and down. "Want me to kill him for ya?"

It touched her, because Henry was serious. "No, I'm fine. Thanks for the offer, though."

Henry nodded and turned back to the stove.

Pouring a cup of coffee, Callie stole a piece of bacon and left the house. She didn't want the other men to have the chance to study her throughout breakfast. What she wanted most in the world was to talk to Pirate. She needed to hug his neck and tell him her problems.

Pirate greeted her with a gentle head-butt. He stood still as Callie cried against his neck. He nodded his head from time to time as though he was sympathizing with her. Feeling a bit better, Callie led her friend out to the corral. "I'll ride you later," she said, turning back toward the barn.

On her way to grab Misty, she encountered Stamos. His expression of anger and concern became her undoing. He opened his arms and she ran right to him, needing the comfort he offered. "That bastard," she heard him whisper.

He lifted her and sat down on a hay bale. She sat facing him, her legs on each side of him. She laid her head on his shoulder, feeling his strength, his comfort. It felt so non-sexual and Callie was extremely grateful.

"He left bruises. Are you all right?"

Callie nodded against his shoulder, afraid to speak, afraid she would cry.

"Did he...?"

"No, no."

She sensed the tension drain from his body. She didn't care what Garrett said, Stamos had always been there for her.

"I guess today wouldn't be a good time to ask you for that date."

Callie smiled slightly. "No, not today."

"Not any day. Stamos, get to the house and eat. Callie, I would like to speak with you if it's all right with you." Garrett frowned at the two of them.

"Callie?" Stamos asked.

"I'll be fine."

Stamos seemed reluctant but he left.

Garrett took a step toward her. She began to tremble, but she held her ground. She looked him in the eyes. "You'll not put your hands on me again."

Garrett nodded but walked toward her until they were toe to toe.

She could see him wince as he examined her face. "Cal..."

"There's nothing left to say," she told him sadly.

"I'm so sorry. I don't know what came over me. I'm jealous and, damn it Callie, I love you."

Callie could feel the tears on her cheeks when she looked at him. He had finally said the words she had always dreamed of and it was too late. "I wish I could take you at your word, Garrett. But I can't."

Garrett reached up as though he was going to touch her and she jumped back in fear. "Don't touch me."

Garrett nodded. "I'd take it back if I could. I am sorry and I do love you. We have a ranch to run."

"I know. I'm going to get Misty and put her in the corral. I'll be back up to the house after that."

*****

Callie grabbed a cup of coffee and slowly walked the plank. That was what the long hall leading to the study seemed to be today. Part of her wanted to shrivel up and part of her wanted to fight. Her fighting spirit won out. She pulled back her shoulders and walked to the office.

Her steps must have been silent as well as slow. When she reached the open door, Garrett didn't even look her way. He looked defeated and lost. The unhappiness she observed on his face made her heart turn over. He hadn't shaved and his eyes had a look of hopelessness to them.

"Hey partner." She sat down in front of his desk, not able to take her eyes from him.

Giving her a ghost of a smile, Garrett returned her stare. "I feel like I've bungled everything, especially where you're concerned."

Callie could feel the ice around her heart thaw and it frightened her. She refused to be hurt by him again. "Let's just talk about the ranch."

Garrett got out of his chair and rounded his desk. He winced. "You're face. I left bruises on your face too."

Callie looked away; she couldn't stand to see the look of despair in his eyes. "I thought I'd spend some time on the internet and see if I could come up with anything about S & S Oil."

Garrett didn't take his eyes off her. "I did that last night. I couldn't sleep, not after what I did to you."

Callie took a deep breath. He was making it hard to stay angry. "What did you find out?"

"There is no S & S Oil. I called around this morning and I couldn't find one person that's ever heard of them."

"They called, didn't they?"

"You know that's the rub. I can't remember what company called me originally but I don't think it was S & S."

Puzzled, she mulled it over. "What about the man that came to talk to you? Where was he from?"

"That Yankee yahoo? He gave me his business card. Must be in here somewhere."

"I'll look for it, you go work the ranch," Callie suggested, hoping he would leave. She started softening toward him and she couldn't allow it.

"Cal, I am sorry. I know you don't believe it but I do love you."

Callie could see his heart in his eyes and she wanted to weep. She couldn't trust him not to hurt her, physically and emotionally. "Garrett..."

Garrett gave her a long look and left. Callie held her breath until she heard the front door slam. Funny how he thought a few flowery words would make everything fine. It was going to take time. Her wound was deep and she just couldn't forget what he'd done to her. He'd taken her virginity and made her feel dirty and ashamed, and then he manhandled her. No, she didn't believe him, or his love.

His scent surrounded her when she sat at his desk. Musk and spice mixed with the smell of leather. Every time she came home from college, she would swap an old shirt of his for a new one with his scent on it. She'd put that shirt under her pillow. Now it made her feel foolish, but she had to admit she loved the smell of him.

This had all started with oil, and she had a feeling it would end with oil. Who knew how much time they had before Detective O'Malley arrived again with new accusations.

*****

Garrett walked into the study. He'd been a bear all morning and his men were getting ready to mutiny. He didn't want to take his foul mood out on them, but he did. Callie was on the phone, so he went back into the kitchen, grabbed a couple of the sandwiches Old Samuel had made, and two cups of coffee. Heading back to the study, he promised he would be all business. He wouldn't do anything to make her afraid of him again.

He had somehow thought, hoped that she would forgive him. She hadn't taken his declaration of love seriously. The bruises on her fair skin made his heart ache. He'd never treated another being the way he'd treated Callie and it shamed him. He was a monster, the same as his father. His father had always made his mother cry and he'd done the same to his wife.

He'd lost her for sure and he only had himself to blame. She was sunshine, happiness and innocence and he'd taken it all away. He was a fool.

Callie frowned as he walked into the room. She took the sandwich and coffee he offered. "Thanks."

"We both need to eat."

She nodded and she took a big bite of the ham sandwich.

"Been busy?" Garrett asked.

"Yes. I found the business card and follow-up letter from the Briggs Oil Company. They are legit. In fact, I just talked to Joe Briggs. According to his geologists, there is a fair amount of oil on our land. He made me an offer on the phone but I told him I had to talk to my other partners."

Garrett was confused. "Other partners?"

Callie got up from behind the desk and closed the study door. She looked good in her tight jeans and pink tee shirt. Her glistening blond hair, pulled back into a ponytail, made her look younger than her twenty-one years. She didn't wear make-up, but she didn't need it. Her skin was peaches and cream. Peaches and cream marred by blue bruises. He wanted to apologize again but he knew she wouldn't be receptive.

"The partners I told you about."

"You didn't tell me anything, what's going on?"

"I guess I forgot to tell you. I can't believe I forgot," she said, her dismay clear in her voice.

"You've had a lot on your mind," Garrett said. She seemed to be missing her usual confidence and he knew that it was his fault. He bore the guilt deep in his soul. He tried catching her gaze but she looked everywhere except at him and when she did look at him she seemed to focus on his ear, not his eyes.

"Yesterday when we were moving in, Timms cleaned out Sylvie's room. He asked me a few questions that made me nervous."

"What types of questions?" Garrett asked, trying to hold in his anger.

"He asked about my family and if we were related or just business partners. I don't know why, maybe it was a weird look in his eyes but it made me afraid for you. It dawned on me if he could get rid of you, I'd be fair game." Callie stopped and looked at Garrett. Her eyes full of concern. "I told him we had silent partners. He said he hadn't known about it. I told him there was no reason he would know. Then he asked if Old Henry knew. Garrett, that shook me. His questions were not idle curiosity."

"Did you tell him Henry knew?"

"I told him no one knew. I hope I did the right thing."

"You did a great thing. There is so much that doesn't seem right. I know it'll be hard but I need you to trust me."

Callie gave him a long, measured look. "Of course I trust you," she responded quietly. "Oh, I also asked Joe Briggs about S & S Oil and he laughed. He wondered if it was the pair that tried to make a deal with our land. They said they had the rights and were trying to sell them."

"You've got to be kidding me? Did he say who they were?"

"He said he'd get back to me, he'd have to go through his records but he did say it was a man and a woman. The woman was a sexy dark eyed blond, that much he remembered. The man, well, Joe confessed he was too busy looking down the woman's dress to notice too much."

"So it seems we have silent partners after all," he mused.

"I'm trying so hard to be strong but I..."

Garrett stood up and went behind the desk. He looked at Callie and offered her his hand. She took it, hesitated for a moment before stepping into his arms. He enfolded her, kissing the top of her head. "I'm sorry, Cal. You're my best friend, my comfort, my strength, and I've lost it all."

Callie tipped her head back and looked into his eyes. He could see all of her loneliness and misery in her violet eyes. "We have to have each other's back. This is serious trouble and I refuse to lose you." She laid her head over his heart. "Hold me, Garrett. I need to feel your reassurance. I need to feel your strength."

Garrett felt humbled by her words. He didn't deserve them, he didn't deserve her or her trust, but she gave it to him. He rocked her back and forth. Somehow, he'd prove to her he did love her. It would take some time but he was determined.

*****

Sleep was impossible for Callie. It was as though she had an angel on one shoulder and the devil on the other. One telling her to lead with her heart and the other calling her a fool for even having feelings for Garrett. Maybe she was too tenderhearted and in need of toughening up. Quietly, she slipped out of her bed and headed for the back door. She needed some fresh air and the men wouldn't be able to see her from the back.

Staring at the huge moon hanging in the sky, she could feel a warm breeze wash through her hair and ruffle her nightgown. It felt deliciously rebellious to stand outside barefoot, with her nightgown as her only covering. The trees behind the house swayed, their leaves making music. It sounded like rain and it brought Callie a sense of serenity, something she keenly needed.

Hearing a sound behind her, she didn't even bother to turn around. She knew who it was; she could feel him, smell him. Closing her eyes, she wished he wouldn't touch her. He was sorry about hurting her. He'd apologized. He even declared his love, but she knew once a man hurts you that way, he'd do it again. It was too much to process.

Feeling the heat of him surround her when he stood close to her back made her shiver. He stood as close as he could get without touching her. A fluttering happened in her stomach and somehow she recognized it as desire. Neither talked.

Suddenly the sound of a motorcycle roared through the night. It came out of the tree line behind the house and the driver headed straight toward them. Callie was stunned. Garrett grabbed her around the waist and tossed her to the floor. He fell on top of her, knocking the breath from her. Were those gun shots? Hearing the sound of the motorcycle becoming fainter, she pushed at Garrett.

He jumped up, reminding her of a cat with his fast reflexes. Garrett scooped her up and brought her into the house. He quickly set her down and locked the door. "Run. Lock the front."

Callie flew to the front door and turned the lock as she heard the motorcycle out front. "Garrett."

"I hear him, get down." He loaded his rifle. "Get to the hall, close all the doors and lay on the floor."

"I..."

"Callie, just do it. Grab the phone on your way and call the police. Hurry up, Stay down, don't give him a target."

Biting her lip, she nodded at Garrett. Somehow, she had turned scatter brained in this crisis. Shots rang out and shattered the window Callie had just been in front of. She crawled to the inside hall, closed the doors, and grabbed a phone. She was on the line with the dispatcher, when more shots echoed in the night.

Tears ran down her face and she dropped the phone. Was Garrett all right? Crawling into her bedroom, she reached up and grabbed her gun. She made her way to the edge of the hall and peeked around the corner. She wanted to cry out. Garrett was fine. All the front windows were shattered, but Garrett was fine.

Once again, they could hear the motorcycle leaving, followed by the sounds of boots running up the porch steps. Garrett unlocked the door, letting the men in. Old Henry rushed to her side, took her gun away, and held her. "I thought Garrett was dead," she repeated over and over.

Garrett stationed every man at a window with instructions to keep down. Then he made his way to Callie. He took her from Henry's arms and put her on his lap. Her arms snaked around his neck and she buried her head in his chest. "We might have been killed," she whispered.

"I know, Callie, I know."

Callie trembled but she was glad Garrett didn't try to paint a rosy picture with untrue words. He didn't say everything was going to be all right, and she was grateful.

Leaning back, Callie touched his face, his chest, his arms. She needed to know he wasn't hurt. "Thank God."

Garrett smoothed her hair back from her face. He gave her a slow kiss on her lips. He stopped when he heard Callie moan, looking straight into her eyes.

Callie knew her love for him shone in her eyes and for once, she didn't care. She wanted to tell him but she couldn't work up the courage. The sound of sirens made her choice final. Reluctantly she let go of Garrett and stood up on shaky legs. He seemed to lend her strength by standing next to her clasping her hand, entwining his finger with hers.

Stamos opened the door and let Officer Marks and Chief Gordon in. Callie watched them approach and looked behind them for Detective O'Malley. It didn't bother her any he wasn't there. She couldn't stand him.

Garrett greeted the Police and shook their hands. He offered them a seat while he led Callie to the family room couch. Sitting next to her, he reached for her hand. "He could have killed us. I believe that is what he tried to do."

Chief Gordon looked at Garrett. His bushy black brows furrowed together. Taking his hat off, his midnight hair came into view. He was about fifty years old and built like an ox, big and strong. "You sure the person on the motorcycle was a he?"

"It was the same motorcycle the person who threatened Callie rode. The same one I witnessed Detective O'Malley standing beside, talking to the driver. It was a man."

Chief Gordon looked at Officer Marks in confusion. "Did you know about this?"

She looked puzzled. "I knew about the threat but I never knew that Detective... I mean O'Malley talked to the guy."

Callie looked from one to the other. "What's going on?"

"Yeah, where is O'Malley?"

Callie watched Gordon and Marks exchange looks. Marks' face grew red, and Chief Gordon's looked angry. "There is no Detective O'Malley."

"What?" both Garrett and Callie exclaimed.

"I never requested someone to take over while I was gone. The Missus had my number and she'd have called if anything were wrong.

O'Malley had her fooled too. Boy is she hopping mad. Now it seems O'Malley left right before I returned, disappeared actually. I called around and there is no Detective O'Malley fitting his description in the whole state of Texas."

"What the hell?"

"I wonder the same thing, Garrett. I hear he put you in jail. I'm sorry as can be about the whole thing."

"What about the investigation into Sylvie's death?" Callie asked angrily.

Chief Gordon stood up and started to pace. "I was going to come out here first thing in the morning. All evidence has disappeared and from what I could tell her name isn't even Sylvie." Stopping before the fireplace, he turned and looked at Garrett. "What name did you put on her paycheck?"

His face grew red. "I paid her cash."

"Not uncommon on the ranches around here, I guess," Chief Gordon commented. "I have some of my guys sweeping the perimeter, checking for clues. Tell your men to go back to the bunkhouse; we'll take it from here."

Callie looked around the room at the concerned and angry faces. Her thoughts churned. She shook as she listened to Garrett explain everything that had happened while the chief was away O'Malley wasn't O'Malley and Sylvie... Who the heck knew who she was? She wondered if they sold the oil rights, would they be safe again? It would break her heart to see those big oilrigs marring her land, but if it would keep Garrett safe, it'd be worth it.

"Callie?" Garrett asked gently.

"I'm sorry. I was just wool gathering I suppose. I can't wrap my brain around everything that has happened."

Chief Gordon smiled at her. "That's natural in these types of situations. The trouble is our police force is so small I can't offer round the clock protection. I could call in the Texas Rangers."

"No. I don't want any more strangers on my land," Garrett insisted.

"Chief, I just had a thought. What if S&S Oil was Sylvie? Maybe she was one or both of the S'." Seeing the looks of doubt on Chief Gordon and Garrett's faces, Callie sighed. "Never mind. I'm just so tired."

"We'll take this up in the A.M. I know I don't have to tell you folks to be careful, but do it just the same. I doubt anything else will happen tonight."

Callie smiled at the chief. He was right; they could go over this in the morning. "Thank you for your quick response." Callie stood up and shook his hand.

Garrett stood up too and walked Chief Gordon and Officer Marks to the door. He locked the door after them and gave her a weak smile.

"What?"

"It seems ridiculous to lock the door with all the windows shot out."

Callie returned his smile and took his hand. "Let's go to bed, cowboy. It's been a bad day all around."

Callie could read the questions in Garrett's eyes. She could also read his hopefulness. Life was too short to be so mad. "Your room or mine?"

Garrett took her into his arms and held her. "I don't want you to make any hasty decisions."

She knew he was warning her his feelings hadn't changed. "It's not hasty, Garrett. I need to feel alive and you're the only person that can do that for me."

*****

Garrett tipped her head back and looked into her violet eyes. They glowed with passion. He also observed the scar on her jaw line and the bruises he had left on her. He didn't deserve her, but she was right. They had almost died out there. He knew she didn't love him but he needed her. Hopefully someday she'd see the love he had for her.

Taking her hand, he led her toward his room. "Mine of course."

"Mine is neater," Callie teased.

"Mine is bigger," Garrett shot back playfully.

"Is it"?

"Is it what?"

"Is yours bigger?"

Seeing her mischievous smile, he was shocked. "We're not talking about beds, are we?"

Callie laughed and shook her head. "No, cowboy, we are not."

Garrett picked her up and threw her on the bed. "I'll let you decide."

"I have nothing to compare it to."

Feeling as though he was going to bust out of his jeans he leaned over and kissed her. "You'd better keep it that way."

"What way? The way it is now or did you mean you don't want me to make a comparison?"

"Just my luck to get the, world's funniest woman in my bed."

Callie pushed out her lower lip, giving her a pouty look. "I was hoping for world's sexiest."

Garrett groaned as he slid naked in the bed beside her. "By the time I get you undressed, I will definitely be thinking that."

Gentleness and tenderness were in order for tonight. He still couldn't believe he had treated her so rough before. She didn't deserve it, no woman did. He removed her tee shirt and bra and winced when he saw the bruises on her. "Oh God, Callie, I am so sorry. More sorry than I could ever say."

"I'm not going to say it's all right, because it isn't. I need you tonight, Garrett."

Garrett kissed each and every bruise. By the time he had her jeans and panties off, she was begging him for release. Kissing her, he entered her, slowly, carefully, and was wholly surprised when she thrust back taking him deeper. She tried to set a faster pace and Garrett gladly obliged. Her cry of passion undid him. He wished he could have told her he loved her but he just held her afterward, feeling blessed she was even in his bed.

Chapter Eleven

Waking up slowly, stretching her arms above her head, Callie's heart soared. The fact that Garrett wasn't still in bed with her didn't dim her joy one bit. She was a woman who had been thoroughly loved. His tender touch and words drove her over the edge repeatedly last night. It was little wonder she had slept later than usual.

Her clothes were scattered throughout the room. She put them on quickly. Opening the door, she peeked out. It was clear. She ran to her room. She didn't want anyone to know what took place in Garrett's room last night. It was a delightful secret she held in her heart. Showering and changing, Callie walked into the kitchen.

The sound of hammering was prevalent as was the smell of sawdust. The windows were being fixed and the bullet holes repaired. After pouring a cup of coffee, she wandered out to the front porch. Timms and Karl nodded to her in greeting. She could see Stamos working at the barn. Old Samuel worked fixing the walls. She was able to locate everyone except for the one she wanted most.

"Looking for someone?" Old Henry asked her.

Nodding toward the corral Callie asked, "What are Tiger and Nanny doing in the corral? I didn't think Tiger liked her around."

"She must have sweet talked him," Henry said with a grin. "Speaking of sweet talkin'..."

Callie's face grew red. "You just stop that line of thinking right now," she said, trying to sound indignant.

Old Henry just smiled at her. "I think love is in the air."

"Henry."

"I was just sayin'."

"Well, quit."

"I'm just funning you, Cal girl," Henry said, affectionately.

Callie walked down the porch steps and hugged Henry. "I love you too."

"Oh shucks, Cal girl, give a man a break. I can't have you huggin' me in front of the men."

Callie grinned and let him go. "Where is the Boss anyway?"

"Out back."

"I'll see you for lunch," she called, heading out back.

Stopping at the corner of the house, Callie had an unbelievable view of Garrett's shirtless body. He was pulling out the back stairs or what was left of them. His arm muscles bulged as he pulled. His back muscles tightened and she could remember the feel of him under her hands. He glistened with sweat and his abs made her insides coil. Her hands shook. How would he treat her this morning? She didn't think she could survive another rejection by him. Last time almost killed her.

Garrett turned toward her. "What's up? Are you okay?" he asked, never taking his eyes off her. He looked like he wanted to bolt.

"Yes...yes I'm fine, just fine," she rambled.

"Good," Garrett replied.

"You?"

"Cal..."

Callie turned around giving him her back. "Garrett, if you're going to tell me last night didn't mean anything, I just can't hear it."

Callie waited. It seemed to take forever for him to answer. Still she couldn't turn around.

"Cal... Hell, I'm no good at this," Garrett said gruffly.

Callie's heart lodged in her throat. She couldn't even answer him. He wounded her yet again. When was she ever going to learn not to be the fool? "I understand."

Where was she to go? The whole house was full and Stamos was in the barn. Taking a ride on her horse was out of the question. Pulling her shoulders back, she took a deep breath. She gathered her gardening gloves and tools. The garden needed her TLC even if Garrett didn't.

*****

It was hot out in the Texas sun. She was just about done weeding when a big shadow blocked her sunshine. Looking up she was surprised to see Garrett, hat in hand looking at her.

"Did you need something?" she asked, the chill in her voice evident.

"You left before I could tell you that you look beautiful today."

"Thanks for the message."

"Callie, is something wrong?"

"Yes. I'm the one who is wrong." She stood up and brushed the dirt from her jeans. "I have lunch to make, tell the guys half hour?"

Garrett looked bewildered, bordering on angry. "If that's what you want."

She nodded and left Garrett standing alone in the garden. She would never understand him. Everyone had been right; she was wearing her heart out on him. It seemed useless, but it wasn't his fault. She could've said no last night. Now she officially believed herself a whore. She bypassed the kitchen and grabbed a pair of scissors from her room.

Looking in the mirror, she couldn't stand to see the pitiful sadness in her eyes. Quickly she cut one part of her long blond hair then the next. By the time she was done, it was short and uneven. Tears sprang into her eyes when she saw all the hair on the floor. It was what they did to whores in the 18th century, wasn't it? Now her crowning glory was gone, no one would give her a second glance and that's what she wanted.

There was no bemoaning it now. Without sweeping up her hair, she went into the kitchen and made lunch, soup and sandwiches. She heard a couple gasps but she ignored them. Feeling everyone's eyes on her made her uncomfortable. Holding her head high, she fed them. The sympathy she glimpsed in Old Henry's eyes became her undoing. Running out of the house, she headed for the barn.

Climbing up to the hayloft, she burrowed herself into a corner and cried.

*****

Garrett knew something was afoot; all the men were staring at him. The looks weren't exactly friendly. "Okay, out with it."

Old Henry glared at him. Throwing down his napkin, he stalked out of the kitchen. Garrett was shocked. "Someone had better tell me what the hell is going on around here. Where is Callie?"

Old Samuel frowned at him. "Go into the bathroom and look on the floor. That should answer a few questions. As for that little gal, she's in the hayloft."

His chair scraped loudly as Garrett pushed back from the table. When he saw the hair on the bathroom floor, he felt sick. It was Callie's beautiful blond hair. Hair that had draped over both of them just last night. He picked up a lock of it and held it to his cheek, then put it in his pocket. He had to find her.

He didn't know what to say to her. He knew she'd been a bit touchy this morning, but she was a female. Wasn't that how they acted occasionally? He felt clueless. Cutting her hair was a very drastic act. He didn't know what to think. Maybe it was a cry for help.

Climbing the ladder to the hayloft had him sweating. He didn't want to say anything that would send her over the edge. He'd have to hide all knives, razor blades, and pills when he went back to the house. He'd heard of cutters, maybe she was one of them.

"Cal?" he softly called.

The only answer he got was sniffling. It pinpointed her location and he made his way around the bales of hay to find her. She looked pitiful with her chopped off hair and red swollen eyes. He wondered what was wrong with her.

Sitting down on the bale next to her, he put his arms around her, hoping to lend her some comfort. She stiffened against him. "No matter what, it's just a bump in the road of life," he said. He remembered hearing that somewhere.

"We can get you help now you have made your cry for it. Geeze, Cal you could have just told me you wanted to talk to a shrink. You didn't have to cut off your hair to get my attention."

*****

Callie wasn't sure she heard him correctly. A bump in the road? A shrink? Was he crazy? Then it occurred to her he thought she was the crazy one. A fool, yes, crazy, no. Shaking his arms off, she stood up and put her hands on her hips. "You know for a well-educated man you are stupid. You have no idea what you're talking about."

"Honey, I know you're a cutter."

Callie stared at him, shaking her head. "A cutter? Oh, please. A cutter cuts their flesh, not their hair."

"Really? Well, I guess you got me there. I don't know much about female flighty ways."

"You know what? Open mouth and insert foot."

He looked so confused she wanted to slap him. "You put your foot in your mouth. I don't have flighty ways, you, big oaf. It's obvious you don't even know me. I know every little detail about you. I know you hate raisins and always pick them out of your cereal. I know you wear boxers. I know you like to sing in the shower and you never blow-dry your hair. I know how much you loved your mother, and how much you hated your father. I know your first horse was a bay named Ranger. I even know how you got that slight scar on your knee. Your favorite color is green, the color of the sweet Texas grass. You love ranching above all else. Now I know you are clueless,"

"Close your mouth, you'll attract flies." She scrambled by him and went down the ladder. Now she was just plain mad. Mad at him, mad at herself. How could she have built all her hopes and dreams around him? Maybe she did need a shrink because it was a crazy thing to do. She'd wasted so much time, loving him. She was strong and she'd just push through the pain.

*****

Garrett had stayed out of her way for the rest of the day and she was grateful. Sitting back in the desk chair, she looked out of the new windows. Darkness surrounded the house but she could see Karl standing guard on the front porch. Garrett probably told him to spy on her to make sure she wasn't hurting herself. It amazed her Garrett hadn't taken all the pencils and then there was the letter opener, he'd overlooked that.

Shaking her head, she closed her eyes. Earlier she'd had a headache and found all the aspirin, cold medicine; everything had been removed from the bathroom cabinet. She'd be damned if she would ask Garrett for an aspirin. He was a controlling, irritating, cold man. It was all true and he was clueless.

Her stomach growled. She'd made dinner and retreated to the study to do the accounting. It had been stupid to cut her hair, but it was too late now. It had seemed right at the time.

Someone knocked on the door but she ignored it. It didn't surprise her it opened anyway. Old Henry stuck his head in, obviously concerned about her. "I have a surprise for you in the barn, Cal girl."

"Does it involve Garrett?"

"Nope."

Callie jumped up and followed Old Henry out of the house. She smiled as she entered the barn. Old Samuel stood with his scissors and plastic bib. He cut all the men's hair and he was quite good. "Thanks guys."

Old Samuel kissed her cheek, which he never did before, and led her to an old barber's chair he'd found long ago. "Don't you worry, missy. I'll make you look like a movie star."

Old Henry winked at her and left.

"If you could just make it look presentable, I'd be happy," Callie told him.

"I'm really talented you know," Old Samuel told her. He cut away.

He seemed to be cutting a bit fast. It reminded her of a movie she had once seen, that man could cut bushes too. "I appreciate you taking time to do this, Samuel. I wasn't sure what I was going to do."

"Let me get a mirror." He reached toward the hay bale he had his barbering stuff on, "here we go, take a look."

Her hands shook when she took the mirror. Maybe looking wasn't a good idea but she'd do it for Old Samuel. Raising it so she could see her reflection, she was stunned. She looked pretty. Her hair curled all around her face looked wonderful. "Oh, Samuel, you performed a miracle. I actually look pretty."

"You've always been pretty. You just needed my talent to bring it out."

"You are indeed talented."

Callie got up and hugged Old Samuel before he could protest. "Thank you."

"You are welcome."

She felt dismissed when he turned from her and gathered his equipment. She bit back a smile before she returned to the house and raced to her bathroom. She turned her head left, then right and laughed in delight. The laughter was gone when she saw the bane of her existence, Garrett O'Neill, standing in her room.

"Closed doors are closed for a reason."

Garrett just stood and stared at her. "You look beautiful, Callie."

Walking across the room, Callie stood next to the open door. "Thank you, now if you'll excuse me, I have some names to think up. Names I haven't called you yet."

"Honey..."

"Don't you dare, honey me. Now if you want to retain our business relationship you will leave this room now." Her heart beat quickly. "I said now."

Shaking his head, Garrett gave her a long searching look. He looked disappointed at what he glimpsed in her eyes. "Okay, Cal, have it your way. Good night," he whispered.

Callie closed the door and leaned her back against it. It had been hard to remain cold to him, but it was for the best. Now she had to push through the pain. Why was everything so hard?

*****

Garrett could hear the men talking as he walked down the hall toward the kitchen. He'd had a sleepless night worrying about Callie and the ranch. He wanted to make things right between them but now wasn't the time. A killer was loose and a whole slew of strange things were going on. He got to thinking and he decided Callie's observation about Sylvie being part of S & S Oil had merit. He felt stupid for not knowing her last name.

The silence was deafening when he reached the kitchen. It looked close to a freeze frame, no one moved, except Callie.

She stood up and got him a cup of coffee. "Here you go, cowboy," she said, barely looking at him.

Garrett nodded his thanks. He couldn't take his eyes off her. The bruises on her face had faded and her hair looked so becoming. He'd miss the way it wrapped around his naked body, but if it made her happy...

Corky, one of the younger ranch hands, beamed at them. "Well, since y'all are done being mad, what's the plan for the day. I want to be done in time to go to town. I have a hot date."

The other men snickered. Corky was not the most handsome man around and he usually mumbled when talking to the opposite sex.

"Takin' your Ma to the movies, are you?" Karl teased.

"Say what you will, but I got me a pretty little gal waiting for me," Corky bragged.

"I didn't know you had a younger sister," Karl shot back.

Corky grinned. "Tell them, Timms, tell them about those girls we met last week."

Timms grinned shyly. "Well, I hate to ruin your funnin' but we do have dates."

"Good for you," Callie said.

"Thanks, ma'am," Corky replied, giving Karl the stink eye.

Garrett relaxed and smiled, listening to the other men's banter. "I want the herd brought in closer to the house. Callie and I are going to have tea at Harriett's Yarn and Tea Shop."

"Callie, is it knitting time?" Old Henry asked.

Callie's eyes narrowed. Knitting time meant a baby. "It most certainly is not. But a nice cup of tea is always nice."

"Sorry, I was just kidding you," Old Henry apologized.

Callie grinned. "I know you were. Keep an eye on the place while we're gone, all right?"

"You can count on me."

After a hasty breakfast, Garrett was ready to leave. He found Callie waiting for him on the front porch. He yearned to take her in his arms and kiss her. The disappointment of their relationship hit him hard. He tried to catch her look when she turned toward him but she averted her face. "Ready?" he asked.

"Sure. Now tell me why we are going to the yarn place?" she asked.

"Who knows more about the going ons of Lasso Springs then the women who have tea there? I bet they know more about O'Malley than they think they do. He wasn't too bad looking and that fact wouldn't have escaped their eyes."

Climbing into the truck Callie looked at him. "You're right,"

"First Harriett's, then a picnic," he said.

"Did I mention a picnic?" she asked.

"Well now that you mention it, I like the idea," Garrett teased.

Callie gave him a swat on his arm and looked out the window for the remainder of the ride.

*****

Callie smiled at all the ladies at Harriett's Yarn and Tea Shop. They were warm, inviting, people and they gave Callie a sense of belonging. Their eyes widened at the site of Garrett walking in behind her and she could imagine their minds whirling and making assumptions.

She knew she was right by the sweet little smiles they gave the couple. It was an 'aren't they cute together' smile. Tempted to roll her eyes, she smiled instead.

Harriett came rushing over, her wig starting to slant slightly on her head in her haste. "Well well," she said giving them a brilliant smile, "just look at the two of you. Well, sit, sit. I'll bring you some tea."

"Thank you, Miss Harriett," Garrett responded giving her a big old grin.

Callie wasn't sure she liked the direction this visit seemed to be taking. "Good morning, Mable, Cindy." She settled into the wooden chair Garrett had pulled out for her.

"Comfortable, my love?" he asked, much to her irritation.

The happy sighs from the other woman made her want to slug Garrett. If she didn't play along, they would think horrible things about her. "Yes, my little boo bear," she replied, her voice heavily sugared.

Cindy grabbed Callie's hand, "I just love your hair."

Harriett had fixed her long pitch black hair and was placing the tea in front of the couple. "It is cute, but as you can see I've never had mine cut, except for an occasional trim."

Callie could see Mable's eyes narrowing as though she was going to say something she shouldn't. "Thanks Cindy, it's different for me. I'm the same as, Harriett, I love long hair." She turned to Garrett, "what's your opinion, boo bear?"

Garrett coughed as if his tea went down the wrong way. "I um, I like, Miss Harriet's hair. Long hair is my favorite but each woman has her own style." He made a show of looking at each woman. "Everyone here has a unique style that flatters them."

The smiles and preening of the other's was a bit much. Callie kicked Garrett under the table.

"Honey, you don't have to tap me with your foot, all you have to do is ask." He leaned over and kissed her.

He was going to die; she would make sure of it. She couldn't push him away in front of the others. Finally, she bit his lip, lightly.

"Ouch, Callie, how many times do I have to tell you not to get so aggressive in public?"

Feeling her face grow warmer and warmer, she knew it must be bright red. "You are so right, my little submissive slave."

The whole room grew silent and the woman looked puzzled. "He likes me to bite him and, all I can say is, he likes to be hog-tied."

Garrett laughed. "What a kidder she is. I just love her wit."

"You two are such a cute couple," Mable praised.

"Thank you, Miss Mable. You know I wouldn't be here if it hadn't been for your son, Bobby. He is one fine lawyer," Garrett said, turning toward the younger woman. "Miss Cindy, how's that precious dog of yours? I haven't seen Homer in a long time."

Cindy look flustered to have Garrett's attention. "He's just fine, just fine."

"I'm just going to cut to the chase here, ladies. What do you know about O'Malley? Garrett asked. "I was shocked to find out he wasn't a detective at all."

"You're not kidding," Harriett said, outraged. "To think I thought him a fine young man. I knew he wasn't from Texas, his accent wasn't quite right. I'm going to go out on a limb but I think he's from the Northern Midwest. He sounded a bit like my cousin Joey." She turned to Mable, "You remember Joey, don't you?"

"Oh course I do. Where does he live?"

"He's from Chicago," Harriett answered.

"There you have it, Harriett has an uncanny ear for accents," Cindy explained. "O'Malley is from Chicago."

"Anything else?" Garrett asked.

"He had a friend named Derek Rider. He owns a motorcycle, is thirty years old and single. He had the look of a handsome devil. Gave me goose bumps," Cindy said.

"Goose bumps?" Mable scoffed. "He was ugly as sin. His hair was black with a purple streak in it and he had one of those bull rings through his snout."

"If you had looked beyond those few things Derek was handsome," Cindy insisted.

"Is he still in town?" Garrett asked.

"Unfortunately, no," Cindy replied, with a sighed.

"Now Derek was from a little town right outside of Chicago," Harriett supplied. "I asked him."

"Do you remember the town?" Callie asked eagerly.

"Well of course, He's from Tyrone."

Callie and Garrett looked at each other. It was their first real clue.

*****

Garrett held Callie's hand until they were out of sight of The Yarn and Tea Shop.

"You know something? You're a real, ass. Who do you think you are kissing me in front of the whole town?" Callie asked crossly, pulling her hand away.

Garrett was just about to open the truck door for her but pinned her against it instead. Leaning in he kissed her, savoring her soft luscious lips. He heard her moan and he pulled back, watching her. Her eyes glowed with pleasure. "Now that was a kiss in front of the whole town."

Callie pushed him away. "Just drive me home. I've had enough of you for one day."

Garrett laughed. "But I thought I was your boo bear? What happened?"

"Why? Why do you always bring out the worst in me?"

Garrett gave her a long lazy grin. "Sweetheart, I also bring out the best in you."

He laughed and she sputtered. Opening the door, she scrambled in, refusing to look at him. At least she wasn't ignoring him. Somehow, he was going to break through to her. He didn't know how'd he accomplish such a thing but he was determined.

"Do we know anyone else from Chicago?" Callie asked.

"You don't really believe Harriett can tell where someone is from, by a slight twang, do you?"

"Yes I do. So do we know anyone from Chicago?" she asked again, getting more annoyed by the minute.

"No one I can think of." He frowned.

"We might but you don't like for me to question any of the men."

Sighing, Garrett nodded. "Okay, I'll give you that. You were right, and I was wrong."

"Could you repeat that? Especially the part where you were wrong?"

Garrett pulled over to the side of the dirt road. He reached over and pulled Callie toward him. Kissing her in the crook of her neck, he whispered, "I was wrong, so very, very, very, wrong." He punctuated each very with another kiss and he could feel Callie shiver. "We could have some fun in the truck you know."

Pushing him away, Callie scowled at him. "I'm not that type of girl. I am not your personal good time whore."

Garrett's eyes grew wide. "Callie, you are not a whore and I never, I repeat never, thought that of you. Good God, you're my, wife! I love you."

Looking doubtful, Callie crossed her arms in front of her. "You always have the love light in your eyes when you want me. Funny thing the light fades and the heartbreak returns when you are done. I have fought so hard for your love but it isn't real. You always regret it, and I can't bear it any more. I need to get home now if you don't mind."

Starting the truck, Garrett drove them home.

*****

Garrett was worried; he hadn't seen much of Callie over the past few days. It was blatantly obvious she was avoiding him. He'd declared his love for her, what more did she want? He would never understand her. He'd made mistakes. He hurt her the first time they made love at the line shack but he had good reason. The last time they'd been together had been amazing. He told her that, didn't he? He knew deep down she loved him but for some reason she was fighting that love with the ferocity of a cowboy hog-tying a bull.

He tried to put himself into her path but she was a sneaky gal, he gave her that. Somehow, she seemed to sense his intentions and always went the opposite way. If she wanted to be a prickly cactus, then so be it, but he had to protect her. She wasn't making it easy.

The misery in her eyes when he did see her, made him flinch. He didn't like her sudden paleness and lack of appetite, it worried him. He had thought they were on the right path. The more he tried to hold Callie the more she shied away. He'd think of something. No way in hell, he was going to lose her.

"Looks like trouble," Stamos warned. They rode toward the fence.

Garrett was immediately jarred out of his musing. He spotted the dead cow and calf. "Not again," he bit off, swinging down out of saddle.

They stood beside each other and surveyed the damage. "Think it's the same people as before?" Stamos asked the disgust obvious in his voice.

Garrett took off his Stetson and slapped it against his thigh in anger. "This can't go on. Maybe I should just sell the oil rights. I can't take the chance of someone trying to hurt Cal again."

"I thought we had men riding the fence last night." Stamos frowned at the carnage.

Garrett walked over to the dead animals. "At least it's not Honey Bun and Maggie Mae."

"I'll cut them from the herd and bring them closer to the house. Callie sure does love those animals," Stamos said. "Want me to bury them, Boss?"

Garrett shook his head. "No, I think we'll let Timms and Corky have the honor since they were supposed to prevent this from happening." He climbed back into the saddle. He wished he knew what to do.

*****

Callie hadn't been feeling well all day. In fact, she'd been queasy for about a week now but today seemed different. She was starting to cramp and it wasn't at the right time of the month. Calling out for Old Henry, she asked him to take her to the Lasso Springs Clinic. Something was wrong.

Biting her tongue to keep the screams in, Callie was whisked away to an examination room. An IV drip was started and that was the last thing Callie remembered until the doctor came into the room to tell her she'd miscarried. Silent tears poured down her face when she realized what she'd lost. She didn't even have time to love her child, or to experience the joy of finding out she was going to have Garrett's baby.

She'd been in the hospital most of the day and still there was no sign of Garrett. She had expected him to come running to her side but he wasn't there. It was her own fault. The ache in her heart was almost too much for her to bear. Turning to her side, she put her hands over her abdomen and wept in grief.

*****

Garrett was out of his mind with fear. He hadn't taken his cell phone with him and now he drove recklessly to the clinic. He knew she needed him. She needed his comfort as much as he needed hers. A baby. His heart ached for their loss.

Reaching the clinic, he barely stopped at the front desk to inquire about her room number before he sprinted down the hall. He had an undeniable urge to hold her. Stopping right outside her door, he took a deep breath. Walking into the room broke his heart all over again. Callie looked so very pale. Her eyes were red and puffy, her misery evident. In just two strides, he was by her side whispering her name, but she didn't acknowledge him.

Garrett reached out to take her into his arms but she resisted. She turned her back on him and his heart shattered. She was grieving but he grieved too. Reaching out to stroke her back, he was devastated when she stiffened and pulled away. Still he stayed, hoping she would turn to him, but she didn't.

Visitor's hours were over. Garrett stood up and gazed at her lifeless form. "Callie, I love you," he said, but there was no response. Heavy hearted he walked away.

Chapter Twelve

Coldness had its price. Callie had never been so unhappy. It had been Old Henry, not Garrett who picked her up from the hospital. It hurt deeply but she knew she had sent him away. Her heart wasn't encased in stone. It couldn't be, it hurt too much. She wished it were, she needed some peace in her life. It was torture to watch Garrett ignore her all week.

Seeing it caused a rift between Garrett and the men, Callie got a new job. She now worked part time as an accountant for a local real estate company. Her boss, Stewart Kline was a sweetheart of a boss and Callie enjoyed working for him.

Her lack of presence at the ranch seemed to calm the hands and it eased her heart a bit not having to see Garrett at every turn. She loved him but she didn't know how to bridge the horrible gap between them. He was up and gone before she rose and he didn't come home until her bedroom light was off.

It saddened her to know she was the reason he wasn't comfortable in his own home anymore. The ache of losing her baby was ever present. Saddling Misty, Callie took off for her favorite place along the Lasso Springs Creek.

The warm wind on her face soothed her. The sun shined and the whole world looked bright and green. The leaves on the massive oak trees danced with the breeze and it left her with a grin on her face.

Dismounting, she noticed the serenity. The flowers were all in bloom and the grass had such a sweet scent. The gurgling of the water was a balm to her broken heart. Somehow being here renewed her. It made her feel hopeful.

"Misty, you will never be a gentle, Southern Belle," she said watching her horse drink from the creek. It was a large creek; personally, she thought it should be called a river.

Sitting at its edge, she took her shoes off and put her feet into the water. It was heaven sitting there with her toes warmed by the flowing stream, enjoying the singing of the birds as they flittered about. Closing her eyes, she breathed in the clean Texas air. She took her hat off and let the breeze blow through her short curls. This land was in her blood.

Opening her eyes, she could see a rider on the horizon. At first, she cursed for not bringing her gun, but soon enough she recognized the rider. It was Garrett. Watching his approach, her stomach filled with butterflies and her heart turned over.

Was he going to be angry with her yet again? Maybe it was just ranch business or maybe he just stumbled across her. She had no reason to believe he would seek her out. The closer he came, the more nervous she got. She missed him, but he had made it clear he wanted nothing to do with her.

He looked so handsome on Tiger, sitting so straight and proud. His Stetson sat lowered over his eyes and she couldn't see what he was feeling. No smile greeted her and her heart dropped to her feet. Jumping on Misty and riding away seemed like a good idea, but she had to face him.

"Garrett."

He swung down out of his saddle, but didn't reply immediately. He took Tiger to the creek instead, allowing him to drink. His back looked tense and it made her all the more afraid.

"Garrett?"

Garrett turned around and looked at her. She could see storm clouds in his eyes. A lump grew in her throat making it hard for her to swallow. Tears misted her eyes, this was it. She had foolishly thrown it all away. Her head hung in defeat as she turned away.

"Callie," Garrett called to her.

Turning around she watched his strong arms opening to her. She ran to him and flung herself into his arms. He tightened his embrace and pulled her close. It was too much for her and she started to cry.

"It's okay, Cal, cry it out. We both lost something that day and we haven't grieved. I know I need you. I can't do this anymore, it's tearing me apart."

Callie laid her head over his heart and listened to its forceful beat. "I need you too. I always have and I always will. I don't want to be apart from you ever again."

Garrett let go of her and kissed her on the forehead. He walked to his horse, grabbed a blanket, and spread it out among the flowers on the creek's bank. He grabbed Callie's hand and tugged her down next to him.

"Garrett, I can't, I -- we can't," she mumbled feeling her face grow red.

"Honey, all I want to do is lay down with you and hold you close. I need to feel you next to me."

"Oh, Garrett, can you ever forgive me?"

"Shhh." He pulled her into his arms. He stroked her back, giving her comfort.

*****

A wet nose woke Garrett sometime later. Opening his eyes, he was surprised to see a Billy goat staring at him. "You smell awful, girl."

"Thanks," Callie mumbled, without opening her eyes.

"You could use a toothbrush," he told the goat, knowing Callie would think he was talking about her.

"You're mean," Callie accused. When she opened her eyes, she began to laugh.

"Hey Billy." she chuckled. "How'd you get here?"

A loud whinny answered her question. Nanny stood not five feet away.

"Her name is Billy?" Garrett asked.

"Yep. It's short for Willimina. She's Nanny's best friend."

Garrett laughed, only on his ranch could this happen. "Who does Billy belong to?"

"She belongs to the Grange family. Nanny goes there a lot."

"I knew she wandered over there but I didn't know why."

Billy had run over to Nanny and the two friends seemed to be nuzzling their noses together. It was both amusing and sweet.

"They are giving me ideas," Garrett teased. He kissed Callie's neck. Her soft sigh was all the response he needed. She still wanted him and it made his heart swell.

Callie smiled up at him. "We'd better get back."

Garrett kissed her on the lips. "Tastes so good," he murmured.

"Ummm. It does."

"Callie, I love you."

"Of course you do, cowboy. I love you too, always have," she said, her love shining in her eyes.

Garrett pulled her into his arms and held her. "Maybe we should announce that we're married."

Callie pulled away. She looked at him and smiled. "I'd like that but I think we should wait until we know who killed Sylvie. Announcing our marriage might put us in more danger."

"Wise woman." He got up from the blanket and pulled her up beside him. "I don't want to lose what we have."

Touching his face with her small hands, she looked into his eyes. "We won't."

"About your job."

"My job is here working the ranch. I'll give my notice."

*****

Mable paced back and forth on their front porch. Callie and Garrett dismounted, gave the reins to Old Henry, and hurried to the house.

"Mable, what's the matter?" Callie asked, taking the older

woman's hand.

"Oh dear, I came as soon as I heard. It seems there's been a sighting of O'Malley."

Surprised, Callie led Mable to a chair. "Where?"

"I'm so flustered. I drove straight out here as soon as my Bobby told me," she explained.

Garrett knelt down next to her and took her hand. "You take your time, darlin'."

Mable took an old piece of paper out of her purse and began to fan her face with it. Old Henry handed her a glass of water and she gave him a great big smile. Callie wanted to laugh as Old Henry blushed and moved away.

"My Bobby was in Dallas. He is an important man and he goes to all the important places. He walked into a restaurant and saw O'Malley having dinner."

"Did Bobby mention if he knew who O'Malley was eating with?" Garrett asked.

"Well, that's the most puzzling part. He was eating with that nice Mr. Briggs. You know the oil guy that was pestering everyone a couple months ago."

Callie's gaze shot to Garrett's. She could tell they were thinking the same thing; Briggs was one person that wasn't on their suspect list.

"Did Bobby talk to him?" Callie asked.

Mable held her hand out for Garrett to take again. "No. He didn't want O'Malley to know he'd been seen. Oh I hope they didn't see him."

Garrett stood and helped Mable up. He took her into his reassuring arms and hugged her. "Your Bobby is a mighty smart man. I'm sure he wasn't spotted. I can't thank you enough for coming all the way out here to tell us this. You are a good neighbor."

Mable pulled back and preened. "I try."

Garrett smiled at her. "You went beyond and I appreciate it. Now Henry will drive your car home, and I'll have one of the men come get him in a bit. How does that sound?"

Callie wouldn't have believed it if she hadn't seen it. He walked her to the car all the while talking to her. He was a charmer. Old Henry was still blushing as he got into the driver's side of the old Cadillac.

Garrett walked back to the porch and put his arm around Callie's shoulder. "Wave, darlin'," he teased. Callie jabbed him with her elbow.

Taking her into his arms, he gave her a long lingering kiss. She couldn't help her response to him. She didn't have to control her emotions around him and it was freeing.

"How long are you going to make Henry sweat it out before you send someone after him?" Callie asked.

"At least an hour." They both laughed.

"Let's go into the study and figure this out," Garrett suggested.

Callie didn't want to end the embrace, but there would be others. "Let's go, cowboy."

Garrett took her hand and intertwined his fingers intimately with hers. He seemed to touch her every chance he got. She shivered at his touch, but she had to admit it made her feel good, very good.

He tried to get her on his lap but she squirmed away.

"This is serious," she admonished.

"So is this," he said, giving her a roguish grin.

"Briggs said two people went to his office claiming to have the oil rights. He said the woman had blond hair. Obviously he was lying. He must be behind everything that has happened," Callie said heatedly.

"I agree. He also has some inside help. I've suspected Stamos for a long time."

Callie gasped. "Really? Stamos? I don't think of him as a suspect anymore."

"He was having a fling with Sylvie, and he came out of nowhere."

"What about Timms or Corky?" she asked.

"Timms maybe, but I know Corky's Pa and he asked me to take him on and teach him the ropes. I guess he and his Pa were butting heads too much. Now Corky isn't supposed to know I know who he is."

"Then logically its Timms," Callie reasoned.

"We have no proof. We need to keep our eyes open. Incidentally, I hired a new housekeeper. She starts tomorrow."

Callie frowned. "Where did you find her and how large are her breasts?"

"Do I really deserve that?" Garrett asked.

"Yes. Answer the question, who is she?"

"Chief Gordon recommended her. She's his niece or something. She's going through a divorce and is having a tough time of it," Garrett explained. "Don't look that way, Cal. It's you I want, not any other woman."

Callie nodded. Old hurts just didn't go away overnight. Giving him a weak smile she told him she had dinner to make and left the room. Her heart suffered as though it was in a vise. She couldn't help it. They needed the help she knew that, she just wanted an older, ugly woman. She knew she was being totally ridiculous but her heart still hurt.

*****

The side of her bed sagged and she stirred from her sleep. She rolled over and gaped at a naked Garrett. "What are you doing?"

Garrett gave her one of his sexy grins and she wanted to hit him.

"I'm sleeping with my wife, of course," he replied, his eyes twinkling in the moonlight.

"Oh."

"Well?" he asked.

Callie could see a certain vulnerability in his expression. She wanted a new start and here it was. "Of course, you big ofe just don't try anything."

Garrett got into bed and immediately drew Callie into his muscular arms. He fitted her to his side with her head on his shoulder. "Not until the doctor gives the okay."

Callie smiled. This was her dream. "This feels nice."

Garrett playfully yanked a strand of her blond hair. "Just nice?"

Callie nipped his shoulder. "All right, very nice," she conceded.

"Good. It feels so right, don't you think?"

"Garrett?"

"Yes, love?"

"Go to sleep."

Garrett laughed and hugged her tighter. Loosening his hold on her, he did what she requested, he fell asleep.

*****

Callie stretched her arms over her head as she sat up in bed. Garrett was gone, but that didn't surprise her. The smell of bacon and cinnamon rolls did surprise her though. She jumped out of bed, dressed, and made her way to the kitchen.

Just as she suspected, the new housekeeper was a buxom, platinum blond. "Good morning," Callie greeted.

"Good morning. You must be, Callie. I'm Janey. It's nice to meet you. Is it true you can do anything a man can do on this ranch?"

Callie smiled. "Mostly."

"Sit down and I'll get you your breakfast. You'll have to let me know your likes and dislikes, and I'll need to know the routine around here. Garrett is certainly a man of few words." She placed a plate and coffee in front of Callie.

Callie wanted to dislike her. In fact, she'd prepared to hate her, but she seemed nice enough. "Sure, I'd be glad to show you the ropes. I'm glad you're here it saves me from having to be in the house so much. I love to ride the ranch and work the cattle."

Callie turned when the door opened. Her eyes caught Garrett's and he cocked one eyebrow at her. "Good morning," she said.

Garrett was in front of her in two strides. He leaned down and kissed her. It was a gentle, sweet kiss. "Good morning to you too," he said huskily.

Callie looked deep into his eyes and she knew Janey wouldn't be a threat. It seemed she had this cowboy hog tied. "I'm going to hang back and show Janey the schedule and stuff today."

Garrett still stared at her. "Did you hear me?"

"Of course, darlin'. You'll be at the house all day."

"Another cup of coffee?" Janey asked Garrett.

Finally, he broke eye contact with Callie and nodded. "Make it to go. I have a ton of work to do. Don't be surprised if I don't make it back for lunch."

"I'll just make you something to take with you," Janey offered.

"Thanks," Garrett said, barely looking at her. He seemed to only have eyes for Callie.

Her heart soared at his attention. This new start was going to be a good thing. She could tell. She felt herself blush under his intense perusal and she giggled. She watched in delight while Garrett laughed.

Putting his Stetson on, Garrett started to walk out the door. He turned back and gave Callie another kiss. She watched him leave as she put her fingers to her lips.

"You've got a fine man there," Janey commented with a smile.

Filled with joy she wouldn't have been able to stop smiling if she wanted to. "Yes I do."

"So, you're, Chief Gordon's niece?" she asked, as she helped to clear the table.

"Well, not really but I've always called him uncle. He was close friends with my dad. Sure am glad he found me a job. Money ran out of my college fund and I wasn't sure what I was going to do."

Callie glanced at her. "What about your parents?"

Janey sadly shook her head. "Dead."

Callie pitied the other woman. She'd never had a girl for a friend before, but she hoped she and Janey would be. "You can stay here as long as you need. No worries."

Janey sent her a grateful smile. "That's kind, thank you."

"Well, I have animals to tend. Lunch is at noon so I'll be back before that." Callie bounded out the door. It was a luxurious sense of freedom, knowing the housework would be done. Boy it was hot, similar to standing in front of a hairdryer set on its highest heat. Jamming her hat on her head, she headed for the barn. She needed to check on Pirate. They had to call the vet a few days ago because Pirate had started limping, and Callie had been concerned.

"Hey Pirate, what's up?" she asked patting his neck. "How's the leg?"

"Better than yours is going to be."

Callie turned and was shocked to see O'Malley standing close to her. Swallowing hard, she stood up straight. She didn't want to show any fear. "What do you want?"

O'Malley grabbed her arm and jerked her toward him. She was too close for comfort and his hold on her hurt. "You know what I want. I want the oil."

Callie gave him look of disgust. "That damn oil has caused enough trouble. I already sold the rights to an outfit in Houston, so sorry, you're too late."

The look of fury on his face terrified her. Then he suddenly smiled. "Honey, you are the worst actress ever. I can see it in your eyes, you're lying."

Callie felt the blood leave her face.

"Don't even try to tell me about other partners. I know that was another one of your lies. You have twenty-four hours to sign the oil rights over to Briggs or your houses are going to start burning and more animals will be killed, starting with this horse you seem so fond of."

Callie tried to wrestle her arm away, but he pulled her until she was against him. "Mm, nice and soft in all the right places. I'm going to have some fun with you before I kill you."

Callie vomited on O'Malley.

"You, bitch," he yelled, slapping her face. "Twenty-four hours, got it?"

Callie nodded and sank to the ground. She watched O'Malley walk away. Good Lord, he just implicated Timms. He was the only one she'd told about multiple partners. She needed Garrett.

Janey came running into the barn and instantly put her arms around Callie. "Are you okay? I saw that man my uncle has been after just leave here. Did he hurt you?"

Callie gave Janey a weak smile. "We'd better call your uncle."

*****

Garrett saw the police car as soon as he drove up. His stomach clenched as he ran to the house, praying Callie was all right. Bounding into the kitchen, he met her gaze and held it. He let out his held breath and raced to her side. "What happened?"

The men started to pile in for lunch. They all stood and stared at Chief Gordon.

"Janey, sweetheart, if you could feed these boys and then bring us some coffee, it would be much appreciated," Chief Gordon said.

"Sure thing."

As soon as the study door closed, Garrett drew Callie into his arms. "Are you okay?"

Callie snuggled closer to him. "I'm fine."

Garrett let her go and looked at her. A faint bruise was forming on the left side of her face. Putting his hand under her chin, he turned her face so he could get a better look. "What the hell? Who did this? What is going on?"

"Callie, Garrett, sit," Chief Gordon ordered. "We have a lot to sort through and we'd better get started."

Still fuming, Garrett pulled Callie down next to him on the leather couch. "Will someone tell me what is going on?"

Callie turned her head and looked at her husband's angry face. "O'Malley cornered me in the barn."

"He hit you?"

Callie nodded. Garrett clenched his fist. He wanted to go looking for O'Malley, but he knew he'd have to hear Chief Gordon out.

"This is what we know. O'Malley works for Briggs Oil. This isn't his first go round with getting people to sign over their rights. Seems he's been burning people out of their houses to get his way."

"Good God. Callie, are you sure you're all right?" Garrett asked anxiously.

Callie took one of his fists and unclenched it so she could hold his hand. "I'm fine."

"It seems O'Malley implicated Timms out in the barn," Chief Gordon began.

Garrett jumped to his feet. "Let's go get him."

"Simmer down, boy. We have numerous players in this, and we don't want to make any missteps."

Garrett sighed. It went against his nature to sit and chat.

"Besides Timms we have Stamos..."

"I knew it," Garrett interrupted.

"What the hell, Garrett? Let me finish a sentence at least."

"Sorry."

"Stamos is a Fed. He's working undercover as is my niece."

Callie shook her head. "Really? Wow, he had me fooled. I mean, really fooled."

"The problem is I don't know why Stamos is here and I need to talk to him before I blow some Fed operation."

"Stamos won't be back until later. I sent him into town to get supplies," Garrett explained. "We thought he might be a suspect. It's a bit disconcerting to find out he isn't who we thought.

Janey entered the room with a tray of coffee. "What did I miss?"

"Make sure no one is listening at the door," Chief Gordon instructed her, then waved her toward him when she was done. "It seems Timms and O'Malley are working together for Briggs Oil."

"I knew he smelled fishy," Janey replied.

"What we need is proof. Callie, was given twenty-four hours to sign over her oil rights or the house will burn," Chief Gordon explained.

"Why can't we just bring Briggs in? Good God, he's killed my cattle, cut my fences, and now threats?" Garrett got up and began to pace. "I will not take a chance of, Callie getting hurt. I'll just sign the rights over."

Callie jumped up and stood in front of him. She took both of his hands in hers. "No, Garrett. It's our land. Our hard work and sweat built it along with that of our ancestors. I refuse to sign."

"How else am I to keep you safe?" he asked bleakly.

Janey stood up and smiled. "That's why I'm here. For now on, I'm Callie's shadow at least until we can find out Stamos' involvement in all this."

Garrett glanced at Janey, then at Callie. "I don't want to sign but..."

Callie put a finger across his lips. "We won't have to. We have to have faith in the police."

"I do have some good news. We captured the motorcycle rider who threatened, Callie and shot up your house, Garrett," Chief Gordon said. His stomach rumbled loudly.

"I'll go get you a sandwich," Janey volunteered, walking out the door.

"What did he have to say?" Callie asked eagerly.

"Nothing, but we have the gun. Right now he's in the local jail."

"Here's your sandwich." Janey handed a plate to the chief.

"Thanks, honey. I'm going to take it to go. I think you have everything under control here. Keep me posted. I'll try to find out more about Timms, O'Malley, Briggs, and Mr. Motorcycle."

"He didn't give you his name?" Callie asked.

"Nope, and his fingerprints don't seem to be on file either. Don't worry; Janey here is the best agent the FBI ever had."

Garrett looked at Janey in surprise. "Wow, FBI."

"It's a serious case with lots of victims," Janey explained.

"Let me walk you out, Uncle," Janey offered.

As soon as they were alone, Garrett drew Callie into his arms. "I can't believe that bastard put his hands on you."

Callie turned her face upward and stood on her toes to kiss him. Garrett cradled her head in his hands and deepened the kiss. Callie made the sweetest little moaning noises and Garrett thought he'd go crazy if he didn't have her, but he couldn't. Not for about six weeks.

Stepping back, he admired his wife. "You are one hell of a woman."

Callie blushed at his praise. "We need to have each other's back."

Garrett reached out and grabbed her rear end. "I have yours," he said playfully.

*****

Callie was still blushing when she left the study. Garrett had such a playful, frisky side to him. It brought a smile to her face remembering his praise and his rear end grabbing. Feeling hopeful about their future, she was determined to protect it.

She paced the length of the family room. How she wished she were the undercover agent and not the victim. Thinking about O'Malley and his threats made her livid. She was glad she had vomited on him. Twenty-four hours he'd said, but what if he tried something else before then? Garrett was out on the range unprotected. It was going to be a long day and she wished she could take some type of action. She wanted to shoot Timms and question Stamos but that wasn't going to happen.

"You'll wear a hole in that carpet, Cal girl," Old Henry commented.

Callie gave him a slight smile until she saw his rifle. "What's that for?"

"Protection. I was entrusted with your life and I take that responsibility very seriously."

Callie walked over to the older man and kissed his whiskered cheek. "You've done very well so far."

"Only because you have nine lives," he responded gruffly.

"How much do you know?" Callie asked.

"Enough. I was briefed and told not to talk about it. You never know who might be sneaking around listening."

Callie sighed. "It's like being in a spy thriller. I'll have more compassion for the victims in the next one I read."

"Glad I am to see you and Garrett sparkin'."

Callie laughed. "Sparkin'?"

Old Henry frowned. "You know courtin' and the like."

Callie patted him on the arm. "I know what you meant I just hadn't heard that word since forever," she teased.

"You're distracting me, Cal girl. I'm on guard duty so let me be."

"I guess I'll go help Janey with dinner."

"Now she seems like a nice little gal," Henry commented.

"What about Mable? Aren't you sparkin'?"

"You respect your elders, young lady."

His face might have looked stern but his eyes were dancing.

"Okay I'll let you be," she said.

Walking into the kitchen, she could hear him mumbling, "Sparkin'." It made her smile. Old Henry needed a woman. He never dated as far as she could remember.

Taking one look at Janey, Callie laughed. "Am I the only one not carrying a gun?"

Janey smiled at her. "Actually, your gun and gun belt are on the table, I suggest you put them on."

Callie's heart grew heavy again. The danger was all too real. Garrett should be home with her. She was worried about him. The uneasy feeling she had just wouldn't go away.

*****

The heartfelt greeting he received from Cal when he arrived home pleased Garrett. She kissed him so passionately he had to set her away from him before he embarrassed himself. She was a damn beautiful woman. She looked so cute in her cutoff jeans and pink tee shirt, looking so feminine he wanted to sweep her up into his arms and take her to bed. Too bad, they had to wait.

Callie exchanged warm glances with him throughout the meal. Her smiles made promises for the night to come. Garrett was so lost in Callie he was surprised that Stamos stayed behind wanting to talk to them. When Garrett invited Janey into the study, Stamos objected until Garrett assured him he wouldn't be sorry.

"What's going on?" Stamos asked.

"You tell us," Garrett challenged.

"I'm an undercover agent with the FBI." They all nodded. "What the hell is going on?"

Janey laughed. "I'm Agent Reddy with the FBI. I knew you were undercover but not which agency you were with."

"You made me that easily?" he asked, looking a bit put out.

"No. Chief Gordon found out somehow and planned to talk to you tonight. O'Malley was here and threatened Callie."

Stamos looked at Callie. "You okay?"

"My, wife is fine," Garrett said in warning.

"I know you're married."

Callie looked stunned. "You do?"

He ignored her comment. "Let's get down to business. Timms is the inside man. His contact is O'Malley, who works for Briggs, who works for the syndicate I've been looking to bust. I landed here by accident. The heat was on and Sylvie almost blew my cover so I had to get her away from Dallas. Unfortunately, Sylvie paid for my choice with her life."

"But you were lovers," Callie accused.

"Not exactly, it was part of the cover. She didn't know at first but she grew suspicious. Her father was the mob and she stole from him. Sylvie was a conniving one." He looked at Garrett. "She planned to get you to marry her by pretending to be pregnant with your child but, Garrett, old boy, you wouldn't sleep with her."

Garrett felt hot under the collar. "You were going to let her set me up?"

"She can't have children. I figured if she was busy with you I could start to investigate who was cutting your fences. I would've told you before she demanded you marry her. Then I did a bit of digging and found out the two of you were already married."

Callie shook her head. "Who killed her?"

"I don't know yet but I intend to find out. It has to be tied in with Briggs and the mob."

Garrett could see Callie begin to tremble. "Cal, come here."

She got up from her chair, and was immediately drawn down onto Garrett's lap. He could still feel her shaking as he stroked her back. Finally, she relaxed against him. "What now?"

Janey stood up, walked to the window, and drew the curtains. "We sit tight. We have agents all over this property so don't shoot first and ask questions later. In fact, I'd better tell Old Henry that one. If they try anything tonight, we're covered."

Janey left the study and Stamos gave the couple a sheepish look. "I'm sorry about the deception."

"You had good reason," Garrett told him.

Stamos nodded and left.

"How did life get to be so complicated?" Callie asked. She kissed Garrett's cheek.

Tucking her head under his chin, he hugged her tight. "I don't know, baby, I don't know."

*****

Waking up in Garrett's arms was the ultimate pleasure. It surprised her they were in his bed, she must have fallen asleep in the study. Garrett's sky blue eyes watched her. Smiling she kissed his chin. "Did you sleep?"

"No, I did something better, I watched you sleep."

Callie's eyes misted. "You romantic fool, you're making me cry."

"I love you, Callie O'Neill. Always have, always will."

Callie looked into his eyes. "I love you, Garrett O'Neill. Always have, always will."

It was Garrett's turn to look a bit misty. His smile was big and bright as he leaned down and kissed her. "Music to my ears."

"I go to the doctor next week; maybe we could be making music sooner than we thought."

"We'll let the doctor decide. I don't want to risk hurting you."

Callie snuggled closer, loving the smell of him. If it weren't for all the crazy oil stuff, she'd think this moment was perfect. "We'd better get up and see what's going on," she said, with a sigh.

"Everything's fine. Someone would have been in here if it wasn't,'

"Still..."

Garrett gave her one last lingering kiss and shot out of bed. "We could take a shower together," he suggested, with a sexy grin.

"Those slow easy grins have no power over me," she lied.

Garrett laughed heartily as he walked into the bathroom.

Men! She had to admit this particular one was fine. More than fine. He filled her heart and soul with joy. She grinned and got out of bed.

Getting dressed, she wished for the first time to have a cute little sundress to wear. She wanted to look as feminine as she felt. It was Garrett's doing she supposed but she was never going to outgrow being a tomboy.

By all the excitement in the kitchen, something must have happened. It seemed as though everyone was talking at once. She was glad when Jancy grabbed her hand and led her into the study.

"We got Timms."

Callie's eyes widened.

"He killed another calf before we could stop him and he had S & S Oil flags in his pocket. A red herring. While we were trying to find out who S & S Oil was, Briggs paid to have your ranch in chaos."

"Timms was arrested?"

"Yes, one of our agents got him. Luckily, no one was hurt."

Callie stood there taking it all in. "It's over?"

"No. Timms isn't talking and O'Malley and Briggs are still out there. Plus there is the mob angle Stamos is working on but we're close."

Feeling both relieved and frustrated, Callie walked back to the kitchen. Sitting at the table, she looked at Corky "What's the sad sack for, Cork?"

"Timms and me were supposed to have another double date with those girls I told you about. I could kill Timms for all he's done but I swear to God, Miss Callie he was the best dang wingman I ever had. No more girls for me."

"Oh Corky, any woman would consider herself lucky to have you. Call your date and set something up for just the two of you." Seeing his eager face she went on, "in a week or two after all the trouble is over but you should call her and cancel for tonight."

Corky's smile filled the room. He puffed up his chest. "Thank you, Miss Callie. That's what I'm gonna do."

"Do what?" Garrett asked, slipping his arm around her waist. He kissed her cheek and let go.

"Miss Callie, was giving advice on how to rope me a filly," Corky told him eagerly.

Garrett grinned. "Oh she was, was she? If you need advice on how to rope and tie them, I'm here for you. I roped and tied the most stubborn of fillies but it was worth it."

Callie punched him playfully. "Honestly, women do not like to be compared to horses."

Garrett kissed her again. "I know."

Chapter Thirteen

Callie stood at the window, wishing to be outside. Janey was a fun friend but still she longed for the wide open spaces. Her mind would not turn off and it gave her a headache. The tightness in her neck and shoulders had become uncomfortable. They still had two more hours left before the deadline O'Malley had set.

Even knowing the ranch was crawling with police, Callie couldn't shake the awful feeling of dread.

"Get away from the window!" Janey yelled. "What are you thinking? I go to the restroom for one minute and you make yourself a target."

Callie gave the Texas sky one last look before moving away. "Sorry," she said disheartened.

"I know it's hard but it is what it is. My job is to protect you and that is what I plan to do."

Feeling contrite Callie walked over to the big stone fireplace. The mantle was jammed with photos. Most of them were pictures of her and Garrett over the years; from her birth until her high school graduation. She remembered her mother snapping the pictures and Callie would run the developed photo over to Garrett. Garrett always acted as excited as she did when she handed it to him. The ones his mother had framed were on the ornate side. Garrett's were in black wooden frames, still on display.

He had put up with her all his life. He was never given a choice; she had just torpedoed her way into his life and ended up married to him. He said he loved her and she believed him, but it confused her to know he never had a choice. Would he have made a different one?

The ticking of the antique grandfather clock made her crazy. One more hour and her twenty-four hours would be up. "I can't take it anymore, Janey."

"I know, waiting is the hardest part," she sympathized.

"What do you think will happen?" Callie asked.

"I'd like to believe they would back off, especially since we have Timms but you never know."

"You enjoy your work." Callie studied the other woman.

"I do. I like to think I make a difference."

Callie nodded and stared at the clock. "Do you think twenty-four hours means exactly twenty-four hours?"

"No, so stop staring at the clock. I can see how anxious it's making you."

The sound of a truck approaching had both women jumping to their feet. Janey peeked out the front. "Good God, its O'Malley."

Callie began to feel woozy. "What do we do?"

"Act naturally. He obviously doesn't know Timms' been arrested. Sign the damn paper and I'll arrest him."

Feeling doubtful, Callie nodded. Shaking, she answered the door. "What do you want?"

O'Malley's superior grin had her itching to slap his face. "I'm here for a signature." He pushed his way into the house.

"Come in," she said sarcastically. Her heart lodged in her throat and she wanted to call out for Janey, but she knew she couldn't. Too much was riding on her remaining calm.

"Give me the papers. I guess I have no choice in the matter."

Callie signed them, feeling her heart in her throat. "There all done. Now leave."

O'Malley smiled and shook his head. "I need your partner's signature before I leave."

"Look at the signature. It says O'Neill. Garrett and I are married and we have each other's power of attorney. You only need one signature."

O'Malley looked puzzled, then relieved. "Nice doing business with you." He put the document in his pocket.

Callie shuddered looking at his slimy smile. "You're, scum."

Laughing at her, he started for the door. "Rich scum," he said.

"Hold it right there, O'Malley," Janey commanded, her gun drawn and pointed at him.

If she hadn't been so frightened, Callie would have enjoyed the look of surprise on his face.

Janey quickly handcuffed O'Malley and shoved him out the door. Radioing for back up, she turned to Callie. "You'll have to make dinner yourself I'm afraid," she said with a chuckle.

The tension drained out of Callie's body. "That's okay."

They both smiled in triumph when they heard on Janey's radio Briggs was also in custody. Callie wanted to hug Janey but she still had her gun drawn.

It was akin to watching a movie. A car came barreling up the driveway and two agents got out and took O'Malley away. Janey apologized as she left, not wanting to miss the interrogation. An agent still stood outside the house. Callie closed the door and fell back against it, drained. There were still so many unanswered questions, but right now she just needed Garrett.

*****

Garrett rode for home the instant Callie called. The rest of the men still guarded the cattle. He couldn't wait to have her in his arms. She said she was fine but he could hear the tremor in her voice. It had been a long nerve racking day and he needed to see for himself she was all right.

Jumping off his horse, he handed Tiger off to Old Henry who'd been armed, waiting in the barn. "We got them," Garrett yelled over his shoulder as he ran to the house.

Callie came running out of the door and straight into his arms. The feel of her safe and whole was a relief. He could feel her shaking and he realized she was crying. Picking her up into his arms, he carried her inside and strode straight to their bedroom. He sat on the bed and rocked her back and forth, murmuring that everything was all right.

Finally, she was still. Pulling away from him, she studied his face, trying to smile at him.

Her tear ravished face looked tight and drawn. "You were very brave today," he praised.

She gave him a real smile this time. "I was so nervous but I did it," she said proudly.

"That's, my girl."

"Am I?" she asked shyly.

"Are you what?"

"Am I, your girl?"

Garrett pulled her into a big bear hug, then he pulled away covering her face with kisses. "You better believe it. You are most certainly, my girl."

Still holding her, he wondered why she had asked. Stress and strain was all he could come up with. They loved each other. Maybe women just needed reassurance often. He wished he could make love to her. That would erase all doubts.

"Hopefully we'll have a quiet night," he murmured.

Callie nodded. "Somehow I managed to make beef stew and cornbread for dinner. The men should be in soon."

Garrett reluctantly let her go. "You're right. Let's go to the kitchen and see what's up."

Garrett entwined his fingers with hers and led her out of the bedroom, their bedroom. It was going to be a lively dinner, that was for sure.

*****

The hot bathwater eased her. It was heavenly and Callie enjoyed it. A Reba McIntyre's song played on the radio and she found herself singing along. It occurred to her she hadn't sung in a very long time. She used her favorite bath set with a Japanese cherry blossom scent. The smell exuded romance and despite the awful day, she found herself smiling.

She couldn't wait to snuggle up with Garrett tonight. It was a fine thing to have him in her bed. They planned to announce their marriage tomorrow. Doubts still crept up on her. She couldn't shake the fact Garrett never had a choice in marrying her. Her mind kept going back to the day she found Sylvie in his arms. It would have been so nice to have dated for a while, and then gotten married. Maybe she was inviting trouble with such thoughts but she couldn't help it.

Garrett made her feel pretty but that didn't mean she was. She knew the plain face she saw in the mirror every day. He deserved better. He deserved a choice. One more night she decided. She wanted one more night in his wondrous arms before she gave the situation any more merit.

Walking into his bedroom, she was surprised to see champagne and roses. There were even strawberries dipped in chocolate. Smiling through her sudden tears, she walked over to Garrett who stood by the window watching her. "It's beautiful," she whispered.

Handing her a fluted glass of champagne he smiled. "Not as beautiful as you."

"You've always been my champion. You're quite a charmer too."

His warm gaze made her feel on top of the world, the hell with her doubts.

"It's a gift, being charming," he teased, as he took the glass from her and fed her a strawberry, licking the juices rolling down her chin.

It tickled and she laughed and squirmed. "I'm sorry," she said. "I know this is supposed to be romantic and I shouldn't be laughing."

"I love your laugh and it is romantic."

She got lost in his eyes. "Yes it is."

Garrett carried her to the bed and put her under the covers. He undressed and slid in beside her. Taking her into his arms, he kissed her. "I feel so blessed neither of us got hurt today."

Callie kissed him back. "Me too," she said, feeling warmer and warmer.

"Good night, Cal," he said.

"Good night," she whispered, wishing they could make love.

*****

Callie was thrilled when Garrett announced their marriage at breakfast. There was a lot of backslapping and hugs. The men all seemed to be happy for them. It seemed they knew about her miscarriage and they were a bit concerned Garrett might be taking advantage of her.

"I almost went after you with my shotgun," Old Samuel told Garrett, still eyeing him with suspicion.

"I admit we should have told you but Cal's mother didn't want anyone to know right away and well..."

"I want to know why Old Henry doesn't look surprised," Karl said.

Old Henry threw his shoulders back. "Because her ma and I were seeing each other before she died."

That took Callie by surprise but it didn't matter. She loved Old Henry. "We still have to be vigilant. We still don't know who killed Sylvie and I don't know if the oil ends with Briggs. I don't want anyone else hurt."

"Callie is right," Garrett said. He looked at Corky. "Sorry you lost your wingman but the fact is we're a man short and I'm not bringing any stranger to this ranch."

"I guess that means no new housekeeper," she said glumly.

Garrett put his arms around her and kissed her cheek. "Sorry, babe. I know how much you like ranching but for now I need you close to the house."

The sympathetic look he gave her warmed her heart. "I understand. It'll all be over soon."

"That's, my girl."

Callie smiled at him. "So you keep telling me," she teased.

The men all filed outside and as soon as the door closed, Garrett took Callie into his arms and kissed her neck, making her shiver in delight. "You, rascal."

He rained more kisses over her neck as he laughed. "You like me that way."

"Your ego is growing like Pinocchio's nose. You'd better go while your head still fits through the door."

"You be careful," Garrett said, letting her go.

"You too, cowboy."

Callie watched him ride out on Tiger. She laughed when she spied Nanny helping herself to the vegetable garden. Walking outside she called to the horse. "Let me guess, carrots right?"

Nanny nodded her head at Callie and then continued to pull them up from the ground.

"Nanny, there is a fence around this garden for a reason. What would your friends think if they knew you were greedy with their treats?" Callie scolded.

Callie heard a whinny and looked behind her. To her surprise, Pirate and Misty were out of their stalls waiting by the fence. Nanny grabbed on to a couple of carrot tops, walked over, and threw them over the fence to her friends.

"We'll, I'll be damned. What am I going to do with you, Nanny?"

Callie watched as Nanny grabbed a few more carrots, walked out the gate, and led the other two horses back into their stalls. Callie followed amazed. Nanny led Misty to her stall and locked it behind her then she and Pirate went into another stall, which Nanny closed and locked. Callie could have sworn they were trying to look innocent.

"You made my day, Nanny. Thank you." She turned to walk to the house, hearing a whinny in response.

*****

The next few weeks went by slowly for Callie. Being housebound was not to her liking. She hadn't been on a horse and she was going crazy. Garrett had been affectionate but she still couldn't get the fact that he never had a choice, out of her head. He could feel her holding back, she just knew it. Often she would find him gazing at her with a troubled look. Telling herself she was wrong and crazy didn't help. It was foremost in her thoughts and she couldn't shake it.

None of the prisoners were talking. Chief Gordon seemed to think they hadn't caught the "king pin". Hyper vigilant became the new buzzword at the ranch. Callie became so tired of it all.

Then there was the guilt. The guilt of accepting Garrett's love and comfort while she held back. She had her doctor's appointment earlier that morning and he told her everything was fine. Now she had to decide what to say to Garrett. He'd be home soon and he'd want to know the results of her visit.

The bird made such a racket outside Callie had to go and see what was happening. She was hit by the thick, hot, Texas, air the moment she stepped outside. Summer had arrived full force. She smiled when she spotted Honey Bun and Maggie Mae in their fenced pasture. Giving them a closer look, she realized something wasn't right. Maggie seemed to be limping.

Running Callie jumped the fence and breathlessly reached the calf. What she saw sickened her. Two huge dollar signs were carved into her side and her leg had a chunk taken off it. Callie tried to hug Maggie but she was having none of it. Quickly looking Honey Bun over, Callie called the vet with her cell phone, and then she called Garrett.

Old Samuel came running as he heard Maggie Mae bellowing. "Oh my God! Who could be so cruel?"

Maggie wouldn't let him near her either. Callie's heart was in a vise as she watched her beloved friend in pain. Callie's determination to calm Maggie paid off; she finally let Callie near her. She murmured reassuring words to Maggie and she seemed to understand.

Garrett and Tiger came charging into the yard. He hopped off the horse and ran to Callie. "Damn it!"

Callie grabbed his arms and looked right into his eyes. "Maggie needs us calm. I finally was able to get close to her, so be gentle."

Callie wanted to be in his arms but now wasn't the time. "The vet will be here soon," she told him.

He nodded as he stared at Maggie. "Whoever did this was too close to the house. It could have been you."

The color drained from her face. "Not now please. I'm already on overload, and I can't take anymore."

"I'm sorry. Looks like Doc Parker is here."

Callie had to shade her eyes with her hand. The sun was so bright and she hadn't thought to put her hat on. Just knowing Doc Parker had arrived gave her a small measure of encouragement.

It took some doing but Maggie allowed Doc Parker to come near her. He had a gentle way about him. He worked on her with Garrett's help for a long while. It wasn't until he was out of the pasture Doc started to curse. Seeing Callie next to him his face grew red in embarrassment. "Sorry about my language," Doc said.

"Nothing I haven't already said since I found her in pain," Callie commented.

"I'll be back out tomorrow. She'll be fine, scarred, but fine. I've never seen the like." The vet shook his head.

Garrett shook Doc Parker's hand and walked him to his truck. "Thanks again."

Most of the men had ridden in for the evening and they were shocked anyone could be so cruel to an animal. Callie was glad she had put a huge brisket in the oven earlier to slow cook. Her appetite had fled but she was sure the hard working men were hungry.

Autopilot kicked in and Callie got the meal on the table. It was a quiet dinner. No one seemed to know what to say. Callie could feel their eyes on her and she gave them a weak smile. "I need to check on Maggie Mae." She sped out the door.

Knowing Garrett was right behind her didn't slow her down. He'd catch up. She needed to see her baby. Running into the barn, her heart broke, seeing how sad both Maggie Mae and Honey Bun looked. It felt all too personal to Callie, these were her animals, her friends, and she believed this was done because of her. She knew it was because of her and that damn oil.

She couldn't live in fear anymore. She didn't know whom to contact about selling the oil even if she wanted to. The big strong arms that took her and held her became her redemption. She turned and buried her face against his chest. The comfort she drew from Garrett was immense. It was life changing, he was giving her the will to go on and fight another day.

Garrett leaned down and covered her mouth with his, putting his tongue in her mouth. His kiss felt so intense, so intimate.

Callie could feel his urgency in his kiss. He pulled her closer as she moaned.

Grabbing her hand, he led her across the yard and into the house. He pulled her into the bedroom and closed the door. Leaning against it, he stared at her.

She felt his gaze as she took off her tee shirt and bra. She walked over to him putting her arms around his neck. She pulled his head down for a passionate kiss. Reaching down she unbuttoned his shirt. She wanted to feel his warm skin against hers...

"Did the doctor say it was okay? I don't want to hurt you."

Callie took a step back and nodded her head. "We're good to go, cowboy," she teased, smiling at him.

Scooping her up, he laid her on the bed and quickly stripped them both. Leaning down he kissed her stomach and laughed as she nearly jumped off the bed. He touched her thigh, inching his big hand upward to the heat of her.

"Please, Garrett I need you now," she begged.

Garrett thrust into her and she thrust back. They were so in tune with each other it took only seconds for them to fly. Callie cried out his name. Gently, he eased away from her and gathered her into his arms.

"You are, one sexy woman," he growled. "You plumb wore me out."

Callie's body sung and his praise made her warm all over. Being in his arms was a feeling she would never forget. The feeling they were made for each other enveloped her and she snuggled closer to him. Her head lay on his chest, over his heart and she could hear each beat. It beat for her, a special tattoo just for them.

Her love for him knew no bounds. It seemed larger than life and she didn't quite know what to do with her feelings. She wished she could just enjoy the passion and love they had found, but she couldn't shake the feeling of guilt she carried. Garrett never had a choice. He'd been saddled with her his whole life, and it wasn't fair.

Knowing she was foolish didn't help. Every time he declared his love, she felt more and more guilty. Reaching between them, she reached down to stroke him. The need for him was greater than her guilt. At least for tonight.

*****

The next morning Callie poured a cup of coffee and stood at the front window. She loved this land, this house, most of all she loved Garrett. The thought made her want to cry as she observed the birds flying in the sky so carefree. A lone tear slid down her face while she watched two black birds with bright yellow beaks building a nest together. They planned a family, she supposed.

Why couldn't she just allow herself to be happy? Garrett seemed so happy with her. Her doubts were crushing her. Calling herself all kinds of fool, she put her coffee down and walked outside. She gave Old Samuel a brief smile when she entered the barn. "How is Maggie Mae?"

"Skittish," Old Samuel responded.

Walking further into the barn, Callie smiled at her two bovine friends. She stayed outside of the big pen until she could gage the safety of going inside. Both animals came over to her. The breath she hadn't been aware she'd been holding expelled in relief. "Hey, babies."

Callie opened the gate and stepped in. Honey Bun gave her a gentle head butt and Callie hugged her in response. Maggie held back a bit but Callie went to her and gently talked as she reached out and touched her head. Finally, Maggie Mae took a step toward her and Callie was able to hug her too.

Callie's heart hurt as she observed the knife cuts. They would scar and always be there, the two dollar signs. Maggie had a bandage on her leg that looked fresh; the vet must have been here earlier. "You look better today, girl." She patted her side.

It wasn't right. Who could be so vicious to carve into an animal? It was obvious the threat was all too real. She wished there wasn't oil on her land. There had to be a way to sell the oil to a reputable company so the danger was no longer theirs.

She looked up and found Stamos staring at her. Giving him a quick smile, she eased out of the pen. "What's up?"

"Just watching you with the cattle. You make a very pretty picture."

"Compliments will get you everywhere," she said, not knowing how to take his words.

"Maybe I should leave you be now I know you're a married lady."

"Yes, I am."

"I'd better go," he said, giving her one last long look.

*****

Garrett couldn't put his finger on it but something wasn't right. After last night, he had expected to be greeted with a hug and kiss at least. Instead, all he got was a distracted smile, the same smile she gave everyone at the lunch table. He went from flying high to feeling comparable to a swatted fly.

He watched her throughout the entire meal and not once did she look at him. Confused and hurt he intended to get to the bottom of it after lunch. It seemed the men were taking a very long time to eat and he grew more and more irritated by the minute. Waiting for them to file out was torture.

Callie stood at the sink washing dishes. She was obviously ignoring him and he couldn't fathom why.

"Cal?"

"What?" she asked, with her back to him.

Garrett had had enough. He crossed the room and stood behind her, his body touching hers. "What's wrong? Don't even bother to deny it, I know you too well."

Callie turned and looked at him. He could see misery in her eyes and his heart sunk. "What's wrong? You didn't even look at me once during lunch."

Callie shook her head. "I'm just tired. I spent the morning with Maggie Mae and I guess it sucked my happiness away. I'm sorry."

Garrett studied her face. He wasn't sure she told him everything. Leaning down, he kissed her soft sweet lips. He lingered, kissing her soundly and was rewarded with one of her little moans.

"That's better." He held her against him. Finally pulling away, he lifted her chin with his finger. "You all right?"

Callie smiled a real smile. "Yes. Go rope something and let me be."

"Yes, ma'am." He kissed the tip of her nose. Walking out of the house, he turned and gave her one last look. "Love you."

Callie smiled and nodded. "Me too."

*****

She watched him ride off, admiring how well he rode. He was a handsome man, for sure. He was everything she had ever wanted Hell, he was who she wanted and her conscious wouldn't let her have the happiness she'd been reaching for all these years.

She deemed herself foolish, plain, and simple. She winced when she glanced into the hall mirror. Her hair looked boyish. It gave her a pixie appearance and that wasn't what she was going for. The scar everyone said wasn't noticeable practically jumped out of the mirror at her. That barbed wire had really done a job on her. The doctor had recommended plastic surgery, but there was no money for that. Hell, Garrett had gone out and bought her a few new pairs of jeans the other day. Her old ones were letting her bright colored panties show through.

The front door slammed. She whirled around surprised to see Stamos. "I thought you were out herding cattle."

"My horse threw me and my shoulder is pretty scraped up. Garrett sent me back to you." He gave her a searching glance. "It's okay isn't it?"

"Of course it is. Come on into the kitchen and I'll play doctor."

Stamos hesitated. "You do know what you're doing, don't you?"

"Do the rest of the men seem fine? I doctor them up all the time," she said, enjoying his discomfort. "Don't be, a sissy. Sit in the chair and let me take a look at you. It probably just needs to be cleaned and bandaged."

"Okay." He sat in the kitchen chair. "If stitches are involved, I'd like a real doctor."

Callie couldn't contain her amusement. "Let's just see what we're dealing with first." She laughed at the face he made. "Come on, cowboy off with your shirt."

Stamos reached out and grabbed her hand as she reached for his buttons. "I have to warn you it isn't a pretty sight. I have two bullet wounds and a knife wound."

Callie just nodded and as soon as he released her, she unbuttoned his shirt. He had warned her but she still breathed in sharply. He had a bullet wound near each shoulder and his abdomen seemed cut in half by a long scar. "Law enforcement has been dangerous for you."

"I got the bullet wounds due to a drug bust that went bad and the knifing happened while I was undercover in a prison." He grimaced as she took a cloth and began to wash his abrasions.

"You didn't mention the horse dragged you," she said with a chuckle, trying to lighten the mood.

"As a matter of fact..."

Callie laughed, as his face grew red. "My foot got stuck. If it hadn't been for Garrett that mangy horse would have dragged me all the way back to the barn."

"So how long have you been a cop?"

He winced from the antiseptic as he answered her. "Right out of college. It was all I wanted to do."

"It's taken a toll on your body," she observed.

"That and my marriage. My wife just divorced me."

"I'm sorry."

"I knew going in what the lifestyle would be like. She didn't sign up for an absent husband," he explained.

"You still love her."

"Always will, it seems." His regret clear in his voice.

"I don't know what to make of you. I know you're undercover and all but I have a tough time trusting you."

Giving her a lopsided grin, he stood up and put his shirt back on. "Good, then I'm doing my job. Thank you."

Callie walked him to the door. "You're entirely welcome. Try to stay put in the saddle this time."

Stamos' laugh echoed as he walked away.

Callie mulled over the whole conversation. Nothing seemed real, nothing seemed simple. Who was Stamos? She didn't even know who she was anymore. She itched to ride Pirate but she couldn't., She had to find something else to do. Garrett wouldn't want her leaving the house. There was always the accounting. Maybe she could help figure out how to make the ranch more profitable. She dug right in.

It was the usual expenses associated with the ranch. Garrett had kept everything very organized and easy to read. All the bills had been paid except for the few from this month. She'd send out the checks tomorrow.

What started out as simple bookkeeping ended up with Callie seeing red. Feeling her jaw hanging open she closed her mouth, making her lips purse. Her pain dwarfed the anger. Looking at the receipts left her with no other explanation. Garrett had bought two pieces of jewelry while she was away at college. Both pieces were pricey. Unfortunately, there wasn't a description, just the price.

She threw her coffee cup against the far wall. She remembered spending both Christmas and her birthday alone and homesick. She hadn't gotten any jewelry. Hell, she'd gotten a second job to afford books. Briefly, she thought of Sylvie, but discounted it. There hadn't been any jewelry in her possessions.

No, there was someone else. Hadn't she heard the ribbing about Garrett's revolving bedroom door? Foolishly, she thought it to be a big joke. Problem solved. She had wanted to distance herself from him and now... She'd been wondering what he would have done if he'd had a choice. Now she knew that he wouldn't have chosen her.

She should've recognized he was too handsome, too charming to be interested in her. The fact he'd never bought her a wedding ring said it all. Angry and disillusioned, she decided to get away from the ranch. A ride in the truck might cool her down. Why would he toy with her heart?

She hadn't seen one hint of another woman, beside Sylvie. Why would he buy expensive jewelry when the ranch was struggling? Who was this woman that he lavished with jewels?

Grabbing the keys, she flew out the door. Starting the truck, she turned it around and raced down the dirt road, leaving a wide berth of dust behind her.

*****

Garrett was in a foul mood as he tracked mud into the house. A couple steers were caught in a bog and it took forever to free them. It had been hard sweaty work and all he wanted was Callie, sweet tea, and dinner. All in that order. Callie and a shower would be a good combo. Thinking about her made him feel better.

He frowned when he noticed dinner wasn't ready. The kitchen looked spotless. A pot of coffee was made, but that was all. Figuring he'd worn her out last night, he headed for the bedroom. His puzzlement intensified when he found it empty. "Cal?" he yelled.

Worried when he didn't get a response, Garrett started looking in each room. It alarmed him when he spotted coffee splattered on the wall and the cup broken on the floor beneath. Something had happened. He looked out the front window and noticed his truck was gone. A lump grew in his throat as he picked up the phone and called Callie's cell. Getting no answer, he slammed down the phone. What the hell?

Running his fingers in his hair, he wondered what to do. Picking up the phone again, he called Chief Gordon. Something wasn't right and he was determined to find out where she was.

Old Henry drove up to the house in one of the ranch trucks. Garrett saw him hurrying toward the house and ran to meet him on the front porch.

"What in tarnation did you do to Callie?" Old Henry demanded.

"Where is she?"

"After driving like race car driver, she almost slammed into The Whiskey Barrel's front door."

"She what? Why didn't you call me?" Garrett demanded.

"Because Cal girl threatened me with castration if I called you. She's drinking."

"Cal rarely drinks," Garrett said. It didn't make sense.

"She's swearing a blue streak about you. Better get down there."

"Thanks." Garrett jumped into the truck Old Henry had just gotten out of and gunned the engine. He was off to find out what was wrong with his little wife.

It was dark inside The Whiskey Barrel when he arrived a few minutes later and it took Garrett a minute for his eyes to adjust. He didn't see Callie at the bar and looked around the room. All he could see was a small line of men, near the dance floor. They all held a shot of whiskey.

Impatient, Garrett headed for the bar. "Hey, Billy," he said to the oversized bartender, "have you seen Callie?"

"Try the dance floor. Last I heard was she was dancing with any man who bought her a shot."

Shocked, Garrett stomped to the dance floor. Sure enough, Callie was doing the Texas two-step with a cowboy from another ranch. The music stopped and the next man in line approached Callie. She smiled, took the shot, downed it, and began to dance with her new partner.

Heatedly he strode across the dance floor. He could feel the eyes of every man in line on him. He hoped he could get her out of the bar without someone trying to play hero. He could see Callie staring at him. She seemed to be sending him daggers with her eyes. Garrett didn't care; he was getting her out of there.

Surprise was on his side. Her dancing partner didn't even see him coming. Tapping him on the shoulder, Garrett wasted no time as the couple came to a stop. He lifted Callie and put her over his shoulder. When she tried to struggle, he swatted her on her rear end.

The other men began to voice their displeasure. Garrett swung around and faced them. "I'm sorry to ruin your fun but I need to get my wife home where she belongs."

Each man stood back and kept quiet. They knew enough to leave a married woman alone.

Garrett heard a couple of whistles as he charged outside. He reached for his sunglasses to fight off the blazing Texas sun. Callie had stopped struggling and Garrett figured she knew she was wrong.

Setting her down on her feet, Garrett unlocked the passenger side door to the truck. Callie took off like a shot, running across the gravel parking lot as if the devil was after her. Luckily, for Garrett he was faster than the devil. Catching her, he hefted her onto his shoulder again and this time he put her in the truck. She looked hot under the collar and Garrett wondered what she had to be mad about.

"What the hell do you think you're doing?" Callie demanded. "Is my face still red from all the humiliation?"

Garrett looked at her. "I'm not the one who was dancing with strange men."

"Maybe just maybe I have to dance with strange men since my, so called husband is obviously having an affair." She was spitting mad. "What? No denials?"

"There is nothing to comment on."

"Oh, really?"

"Listen, Cal, it's obvious you've had more than enough to drink. I don't think you know what you're saying."

"For your information, I've hardly had anything to drink. Just some little itty bitty glasses of booze."

"You, my dear are shit faced," he said, between laughs.

When they drove up to the house, she jumped out yelling, "I'll see you in the study."

She almost stumbled going up the steps but she caught herself and walked sedately with her shoulders back and her head held high.

Garrett walked into the study and closed the door. Standing behind the desk, he leaned down so his big hands spread wide. He looked into her eyes and shook his head. "Dare to explain yourself?"

"Humph. You don't treat me with respect."

"You'll get it when you earn it. Now tell what is wrong."

"I don't feel well and the room is spinning." Jumping up she ran for the bathroom.

Garrett heard her vomiting. What had gotten into her? He thought everything was okay between them. Actually he thought they were better than okay. He decided to make some coffee, for him not for her. The sooner she slept the better.

Garrett turned from the sink when he heard the screen door slam. "I found her."

Old Henry looked worried. "What was she doing down there? My Cal girl is not a drinker."

Shrugging his shoulders, Garrett shook his head. "I don't know. She seems to think I'm steppin' out on her."

Old Henry's gray eyebrows drew together. "Where'd she get a hair-brained idea like that?"

"That's what I want to find out. Unfortunately, I'll probably have to wait until morning. You might as well grab the aspirin and some water to put by the bed. I have a feeling she's going to need it."

*****

"Oh God, who's making so much noise? My head is pounding. What happened?"

"So, our little alkie has come around," Garrett said.

Callie sat up and put her head in her hands. "Go away."

"Sorry no can do. I have to take care of my, wife."

"Then go find a new one, this one isn't in the mood for you," she said sharply, then groaned at the pain.

Garrett chuckled softly and sat on the bed, leaning against the headboard. Gently he pulled her into his arms and held her. "It's all right Cal. You'll live but you're going to have a miserable day."

"What happened?"

"Now that is not a good sign, honey. You drank an awful lot yesterday."

Callie winced. "Don't remind me. Did I make a jackass out of myself?"

"Not so much." His tone of voice implied the opposite.

Callie groaned and fell asleep.

Garrett watched his sleeping wife for a moment before deciding to check the books. He wanted to be around the house in case Cal needed him. He didn't know what was going on inside that pretty head of hers. Sitting behind the desk, he ran his fingers through his hair. Cheating? Really? When was he supposed to have had the time to see another woman?

Turning on the computer, he opened their accounting program. It looked as though everything was up to date. He even found a list of things that could help their bottom line. He smiled proudly. Callie was a good rancher. Leaning back he looked at the high ceiling and wondered what made her think he was cheating. He wasn't getting any answers here.

He stood up and spotted two receipts on the desk. One was for the jewelry he had gotten Callie for Christmas, the other as a birthday gift. How come he never saw her wear any of it, he wondered.

*****

Callie cooked breakfast the next morning. She'd gotten up with the sun, grateful for feeling better than the previous day. It had been a miserable day, one she vowed never to repeat. It disturbed her she was probably the talk of the town. Talk about being a complete fool. She wasn't sure what happened when Garrett took her home. Hopefully the men weren't around to observe her behavior. She'd know shortly when they filed in to eat. She planned to just brave it out and pretend it never happened.

She sighed as she heard the door open, She closed her eyes and prayed for strength. Pasting a smile on her face, Callie grabbed the coffee pot and greeted everyone. Each cowboy was polite and acted as though nothing was wrong with the exception of Garrett. His eyes were on her the entire time. It made her nervous.

Expelling a deep breath, she couldn't believe her luck. Everyone had left including Garrett. Maybe her actions weren't as bad as she imagined. Her peace didn't last long. Garrett came stalking into the house, stood in the middle of the kitchen and stared at her. His eyes seemed to bore holes through her and she began to sweat.

"Feeling better?" he asked.

"Yes," she replied, wondering where this was going to lead.

"So you don't want to go down to The Whiskey Barrel for lunch?"

"No thanks." She turned her back on him and pretended to wipe down the already clean counters.

"Cal, look at me," he said softly.

"I can't. I'm too embarrassed," she said, her voice shaking.

"All right I'll say what I have to, even if it is to your back. You made some accusations that night and I need to know why. Why in the world would you accuse me of cheating on you?"

Callie shrugged her shoulders. She wasn't ready for a fight.

"I need an answer, and I'm not leaving until you tell me," he warned.

"It's common knowledge your bedroom door is considered to be a revolving one," she said defensively.

"What are you talking about?"

She twisted around and glared at him. Her angry eyes met his amused ones. "I know about the other woman."

Garrett's eyebrow shot up in surprise. "When exactly do I have the time for another woman?"

"When I was in college. Don't forget I saw you with Sylvie in your arms."

"There hasn't been any other woman, Cal. It's always been you." Garrett reached for her only to have her back away from him.

"I don't believe you." She turned and fled the kitchen.

*****

Garrett was amazed. He thought it was the whiskey talking but obviously, she believed he had a woman on the side. It was almost comical. He told her often, he loved her. He needed to take care of this now before it blew up even bigger.

He found Callie in her old bedroom, looking out the window. He could tell by her heaving shoulders she was crying, maybe sobbing was a better word. Immediately, he walked up behind her and wrapped her in his arms. After a token resistance, she calmed, turned, and buried her face into his chest.

Garrett stroked her short blond curls. Her sobs made his body vibrate and he wished she would listen to reason. Rocking her back and forth in his arms, he waited for the storm to blow over. Finally, her body calmed and she started hiccupping. Garrett let go of her and took her hand. He led her to the twin bed and hastened her to sit next to him.

"Now tell me what this is all about."

"You didn't want me here for Christmas."

Garrett sighed. "I was trying to put some distance between us."

"I knew it," Callie responded.

"I believed I was too old for you. I wanted you to have choices, and I didn't want either of us to have to suffer the heartache of a breakup if things got heated. It was my job to protect you, not to take advantage of you."

"You changed your mind," she said quietly.

"Because I love you."

Callie shook her head. "No it's not true and I have proof," she said sadly.

"What proof would that be?"

Tears began to pour down her face again and her bottom lip quivered. "You didn't even send me anything for Christmas or my birthday but you bought jewelry for someone else. Who is she?"

Garrett smiled. This he could fix. "Those pieces of jewelry were for you."

Callie jumped off the bed. "Think again, cowboy. I never received any jewelry from you."

"I don't know what happened."

Giving him a look of disgust, she left the room. Damn she was always walking away from him and he did not like it one little bit.

Chapter Fourteen

It was his fault. He should've called her on both occasions instead of depending on the jeweler to send the gifts. Tom Sisco, the owner, still had the items at his store. He said a woman had called and told him Garrett would pick them up instead. Tom said he'd called a few times but was told Garrett would get around to it eventually. It must have been Sylvie.

Garrett shook his head. He had the pieces plus an extra one. All he had to do now was convince Callie to stay in the same room with him long enough for him to explain. He didn't blame her. They'd both been contrary since she'd graduated college.

They were meant to be together, now all he had to do was to prove it to his wife. Where she was, he couldn't even begin to guess. His attention was diverted as he spotted Stamos riding in with a stranger. Puzzled, Garrett walked out to the yard to meet them. To his surprise, the stranger was in handcuffs.

"What's going on?" he asked.

Stamos swung down from his horse and shook Garrett's hand. "I got him."

"Who is he?"

"This fine example is no other than Siggy Williams," Stamos replied.

"No way. The crime boss you've been after?"

Stamos laughed. "He kind of stands out with his suit and all. I found him cutting the fence and he was carrying a rifle."

"Get me down off this animal," Siggy demanded.

"You don't call the shots anymore. Cattle killing is serious business." He turned to Garrett. "I had to let him kill a calf so we'd have concrete proof, sorry."

"If it keeps him off my ranch it was worth it."

"I'm hoping with Williams in custody the others will talk. We might get to the bottom of Sylvie's murder."

"She was my daughter, you ass," Siggy bellowed. "I had nothing to do with her death."

"She felt so safe she begged me to hide her," Stamos sneered.

"I never should've trusted you. I treated you like a son and look where it got me."

Garrett looked Siggy in the eye. "Looks to me you're where you belong."

"This is your fault too. Why wouldn't you just sell the damn oil rights? Sylvie's death is on you. Don't think I will forget about that."

Garrett was relieved to see Chief Gordon's police car coming toward the house. He watched the two lawmen put Siggy into the back of the car. Watching them drive away gave him a sense of relief. Some of his burdens were gone. Now he needed to find Callie. There were still a lot of unanswered questions but he knew Stamos would come through.

He sensed her presence behind him. He loved her perfume, Japanese cherry blossom. He was going to have to get her more. He turned and looked into her pain filled eyes. "Stamos caught the crime boss."

"Good," she said, looking into his eyes. "The jeweler called. I don't even know where to begin with my apology. I was jealous. I'm sorry."

Garrett looked at her and smiled. "Come inside, darlin' I have a few gifts for you."

*****

Callie grabbed the hand he offered. It felt good to have her small hand in his bigger, stronger one. She could feel the calluses on his palm and knew she had similar marks on her own. Garrett led her into the family room and had her sit on the couch. She watched him leave the room with the promise of a quick return.

Hopefully, all the troubles about the oil were gone along with the constant danger. Her heart felt heavy. She wondered if Garrett could forgive her accusations. She had kept her love from him and it wasn't right. There had been many times over the last weeks when he looked puzzled and hurt. Hopefully she would be able to rectify their marriage.

Garrett came back into the room with three packages. Callie didn't feel worthy of his gifts. She smiled at him but she knew the smile came off as false.

"It's all right, Cal. I want us to get back on track. I want us to be a family. Now here's your Christmas present." He handed her a square jeweler's box with a red bow on it.

Callie looked at the velvet covered box and then at Garrett. He looked so eager for her to open it. Lifting the top, she gasped. It was a gold filigree heart pendent. "It's beautiful," she whispered.

Garrett winked at her. "Now here's your birthday present," he said, handing her another box.

She accepted the box. It was heavier and bigger than the last one. She looked at him and he gestured for her to open it. Her eyes grew wide when she saw what was inside. Laughing she took out the sterling silver belt buckle that had the Texas lone star engraved on it.

"This is perfect," she said in delight. She had always admired the one Garrett wore, though his was much bigger.

"I have one more for you," Garrett said huskily. He got down on one knee. "We got married four years ago because it was the only thing to do to keep your land safe. I want you to have a choice. Callie O'Neill, will you marry me?"

Callie stared at his face in surprise. The look of love he gave her was almost too much for her already full heart. She looked down and saw a diamond cut gold wedding band. It was lovely. Nodding her head, Garrett removed the ring from the box. He slipped his high school ring off her finger and replaced it with his wedding band.

"You didn't have a choice back then either," Callie said.

"Believe me, I chose you then and choose you now. In fact, I was relieved you were mine before you went away. I didn't want anyone else to steal you from me."

"Then why did you push me away?"

"I wanted you too much and I believed it would be taking advantage of you if I pushed the marriage. I foolishly decided I was too old for you. I think I was grasping at excuses. I wanted you to know your mind."

Callie looked from her ring to his earnest face. The love shining in his eyes humbled her. Had they been shining all the time and she just refused to see it? "I thought I was going to die when you rode away from the line shack. You broke my heart by rejecting me, but I can see now you were going through your own hell."

Leaning forward she touched his lips with hers. Opening her mouth to him, she deepened the kiss. The air seemed charged as they drew closer. "I love you, Garrett," she breathed into his mouth.

He pulled her down on the soft rug, his hard body beneath her. She stared into his eyes. She'd never felt so cherished. His large hands cupped her face and drew it down to his for yet another kiss. It was a searing kiss of desire, a kiss of possession. Her heart soared and she laughed to herself. She could belong to no other, it would be impossible.

"Tears?" he asked, wiping them away with his thumb.

Callie was so overcome with emotion she couldn't even answer him. She kissed his cheek, then the other one. Next, she kissed the tip of his nose, and each eyelid, then she kissed his loving lips again. The feel of his strong biceps wrapped around her made her want him, with her whole being. "Garrett, please."

Garrett smiled into her eyes. "Please what?" he teased. "Please let me up, please kiss my neck, please not here, or is it please make love to me?"

Callie laughed and kissed his neck instead. She wanted to hear him begging, she could already feel evidence of his arousal.

"Um hum." Someone cleared their throat.

"Tell me no one is there," Garrett warned. They couldn't see whoever it was from in front of the couch.

"Sorry."

Groaning Callie got off Garrett and stood up. Stamos stood in the doorway, hat in hand looking very embarrassed. He shifted his weight from one foot to the other. "I have some news and I have some explanations for you both."

She looked at Garrett, he didn't seem to be embarrassed in the least. "Well, let's all sit and talk," she said, giving Garrett a glower.

Garrett plopped down on the couch taking Callie with him. "What's up?"

"Well, for one thing, it looks like the danger is over. I have to tell you arresting Siggy Williams is as good as it gets in my world. I couldn't believe it when the boss himself came onto your land. I guess you want the whole story." He settled in a chair opposite the couch. "I'm Robert Walker, a special agent with the FBI. I worked out of the Dallas office until they needed someone to go undercover. Stamos was born then. Siggy had me doing nickel and dime stuff but I caught wind of his oil scam. Apparently, that was where he got most of his money. He was the gambling king in Dallas, but with everyone's income drying up so did his money. Strong arming wasn't working. People just didn't have the cash.

Sylvie and I became friends, a bit more than friends. It seemed to be a good idea at the time but she didn't deserve what she got. She stole a bundle of cash from her father and Siggy wasn't one to forgive or forget. He ordered me to kill her. I took off with her and headed for the smaller towns. I remembered Siggy talking about Lasso Springs and I thought what the heck we might as well gather information while we were on the run. That decision cost Sylvie her life."

"It's not your fault," Callie said sympathetically.

Stamos gave her a ghost of a smile. "I wanted you to sign the oil over to us so no harm would come to you. Just by owning the oil rights made you targets. Sylvie and I were S&S Oil. I did cut your fence the first time but not after that. I didn't kill any of your cattle, and I did not tamper with that barbed wire that nearly took your head off."

"Just the one time?" Garrett asked, sounding doubtful.

"Swear to God. It was Timms. Apparently, he worked for Siggy but he didn't know me and I only suspected him. I couldn't catch him at anything. I can't figure out how he managed to leave the S&S Oil flags at each of his sites of destruction."

"I probably know the answer to that," Callie said, as the two men turned and stared at her. "Sylvie was fooling around with both you and Timms. Seems Old Samuel notices everything."

Stamos nodded. "Makes sense. Sorry about putting her on you, Garrett. I figured if she was busy trying to entice you she'd stay out of trouble."

"What about O'Malley?" Garrett asked.

"Siggy arranged for a 'Detective O'Malley' to cover for Chief Gordon while he went on vacation. Jake O'Toole a player out of Chicago, who owed Siggy, made all the arrangements. They planned to strong arm the rights from you if they had to."

Callie shook her head. "So complicated? Don't they know the simple plans work best? Too many people were their downfall."

"Timms is the murderer. I feel like a damn fool for not catching on to that. I seemed to have missed a lot."

"Stamos, I mean Robert," Callie began.

"Call me Stamos if you want. I've come to think of it as my name."

"What about the guy on the motorcycle?" she asked.

"One of Siggy's goons. He's in jail too."

"So, we are safe? The ranch is safe?" Garrett asked.

"Yes, and thanks to Callie's lie about silent partners you two are alive." Stamos stood up, shook Garrett's hand, and kissed Callie on the cheek. "I'm going to miss it here. I'd forgotten just how much I enjoy ranch life."

"If you ever want a change of careers, we're here," Garrett offered.

"You two take care of each other," Stamos said, as he walked out of the house.

They stood up and went to the window. Callie wrapped her arms around Garret's waist and leaned her head against his muscular chest watching Stamos' car drive away. She was relieved and battle weary. "It's over," she said, hugging him tight.

"No, sweetheart, it's just beginning."

*****

Callie silently laughed as Garrett glowed at all the men around the table. They planned to be alone but there seemed to be question after question with too many commentaries on top. The men were excited and she didn't think they'd be out of there anytime soon.

She couldn't help but admire her wedding band and she had a constant urge to touch her necklace. Happiness almost made her heart explode. She admired Garrett's handsome face. Her heartbeat echoed in her ears and she was almost afraid it was all a dream. Swallowing hard she comprehended the depth of his love. It was a scary thing, a fragile thing but it was worth it.

Garrett stood up and walked outside.

Curious, Callie left the men and stood on the porch waiting for him.

Leading Tiger and Pirate out of the barn, he approached her. "Go with me?"

Callie smiled and nodded. "I thought we'd never be alone."

She settled in the saddle.

"Well, I have an idea about that," Garrett said, grinning at her.

"Where are we going?"

"You'll see. I have to talk to Old Henry and let him know we're going. Be right back."

Callie sat patiently astride Pirate. "Wonder where we're going, old boy. Garrett didn't tell you, did he?"

"No, he did not," Garrett responded. He laughed out loud. "Come on woman just follow me."

"Okay just this once I'll let you boss me around, but mister, do not take this as a sign of how things will be," she teased.

"No problem. Let's make tracks I want to get there before dark."

Ten minutes later Callie knew their destination. It was the line shack where they had first made love. She wanted to be with Garrett but that place ended with bad memories. Her stomach clenched and she sat stiffly in the saddle. Part of her considered turning Pirate around and heading for home. All of her self doubts came pouring back and she wasn't sure if she could do it.

Following Garrett reminded her of his rejection. Garrett slowed Tiger until they were riding side by side but she just couldn't shake the feeling of dread. Garrett didn't seem to notice, he just smiled at her, often. By the time the line shack was in view, Callie was a nervous wreck and at the end of her tether.

Garrett swung down from his horse and looked at Callie. "Need some help down?" he asked when she stayed in her saddle.

Hesitating before she nodded her head, she gave him a quick smile. Help wasn't needed, but she needed Garrett's comforting arms around her. She put her hands on his shoulders and her heart started thumping in her chest. He lifted her down and her body slid against his. It was a sexy feeling and her heightened emotions began to crackle. She desired this man, her husband. She trembled hanging on to him.

"Cal?"

Taking a giant step back, she looked into his worried eyes. She loved him. "It's just this place," she explained. "It holds bad memories for me. You broke my heart the last time we were here."

Garrett pulled her into his arms and rubbed her back. "That's why I chose this place. I want to erase all the bad memories and make new ones."

Feeling herself relax, she hugged him back. "I don't know if you are the craziest man I know or the most romantic."

He laughed and picked her up. "Well, Mrs. O'Neill, you can decide later," he teased, carrying her into the tiny shack.

It looked just the same. Of course, it'd been restocked and cleaned since the last time. Callie blushed, the proof of her virginity had been on the sheets.

"Don't worry. I restocked. I know I acted the biggest fool to treat you so shabbily. You gave me your proof of love and commitment, and I acted like a first class jerk."

Her heart started to heal. "Polecat, is a better word for you."

"Oh really?" He laughed deeply.

"Really." She began to unbutton her blouse.

"Oh please allow me." Garrett reached for her. He unbuttoned her blouse slowly, sensually until he had her panting with anticipation.

"You're taking too long," she complained, breathlessly.

"Nice and slow, it can be good that way." He laid her on the bed, covering her with his body.

Opening her mouth to him, she was rewarded with a passionate kiss. Groaning she pressed herself against him. The feel of his hard toned body excited her. Reaching between them, she made quick work of the snaps on his western shirt. Her hands tingled as they touched his bare chest and slid down to his chiseled abs. Heavenly came to mind. Her body began singing when he unhooked her bra. For a moment she wished she'd put on sexy under garments. He'd only remove them, though.

Her exploration halted while he slid her bra down her arms. Her nipples tightened and tingled. The feel of his tongue on her hard nipple made her want to come off the bed. She arched toward him, offering herself to him. Her stomach coiled with need when he took one of her nipples into his mouth.

Garrett fumbled with the button on her jeans. Finally, he got it undone. Feeling his hand inside of her pants made her squirm. Her breathing sounded labored. He lowered her pants and removed them. The look in his eyes made her feel incredibly sexy.

Callie ran her fingers through his thick hair as he continued to pay homage to her breasts. She could feel her release coming and cried out his name as she convulsed repeatedly. Before she even stopped, Garrett shucked his pants and became one with her. The feeling of love was almost too much. Holding on tight, she went over the moon with him again.

She could tell by his cry of passion she had made him happy. Each time it seemed to get better and better. Her whole body ignited. A feeling of wonder sizzled through her. "I love you, Garrett."

"You're going to be the death of me yet. I love you too." He sprinkled kisses on her face. "My heart is yours, Callie; it's always belonged to you."

"Don't go getting all mushy with me, cowboy. You're going to make me cry."

"That's fine. I know how to make you sing again."

*****

Singing birds brought the wondrous sounds of the morning. Callie gazed at Garrett while he slept. He was such a sexy, handsome man, and he was all hers. A fierce feeling of possession overtook her. It'd been a hard bumpy road, but it all worked out in the end. His eyes opened and he gave her a long, lazy smile, causing her heart to soar.

"There is nothing better than, Callie in the morning," he teased, kissing her, making her feel the fire.

Callie moaned into his mouth when he stroked her. Suddenly they stilled. The sound they were now hearing wasn't their passion, it was coming from outside. Exchanging puzzled looks, they both dressed and headed for the door.

Garrett gently pushed Callie behind him. He cautiously opened the wooden door. Laughter rumbled through his chest as Callie tried to see around him. She quickly went around Garrett and stood on the top step, her hands on her hips.

"Nanny and Pirate, for shame," she yelled. What she witnessed shocked her.

"Now we know why she's always in his stall," Garrett said, watching the horses mate.

"She is, a hussy, a cougar, poor Pirate."

"Honey, it looks to me Pirate is enjoying himself. Nanny isn't old. She's just a year older than Pirate. She only foaled once and then she began to wander."

Callie laughed. "I guess there's no stopping true love."

Garrett turned her toward him. He leaned down and gave her a long loving kiss. "No stopping it at all, my love."

"Let's go back inside," she suggested.

"No can do. We have plans for this afternoon."

"Doing what?" she asked.

"It's a surprise."

"I don't need any more surprises in my life, thank you." Surprise or not, Callie wanted to stay in the line shack.

"I'm sorry, sweet pea," Garrett said, smiling into her eyes.

"Sweet pea? That's a new one." She playfully hit his arm. "A good name for a calf maybe."

Garrett's eyes widened in mock shock. "You wound me, sugar pie."

Callie laughed. "I do know a horse named, Sugar Pie."

"So do I." He led the horses to the barn. "Get ready to go while I saddle the horses."

Callie smiled at him. "All right you win... for now. I do intend to have my way with you later, honey bun."

Garrett's laugh was deep and loud. It made her smile while she got her things together. Garrett was right, this was the perfect place. The new memories were so important. The raw hurt of the first time at the line shack had dulled. He was a wise man.

All the way home, Callie tried to ferret out the surprise. Garrett was a hard nut to crack. She would've spilled it by now, but not him. "I think you enjoy making me mad."

"It does have a bit of fun to it," he teased. "It's not my secret or my surprise. Besides I promised on my honor."

Callie rolled her eyes. "Fine." Urging Pirate to go faster, she overtook the lead. She didn't want to ride side by side. She was sulking, but she couldn't help it.

When the ranch house came into view, she gasped. There were purple and green balloons everywhere and tables laden with food. They too were decorated in purple and green. The colors made her cringe and she held Pirate steady waiting for Garrett to catch up. "Mind explaining that?"

"Harriett called from her Yarn and Tea Shop asking what colors you prefer. I knew they planned a reception for us, but this isn't what I envisioned," he said, with a grin.

"Just don't leave me alone with those women. They're likable but..."

"Don't you worry, cupcake, I'll stand by you."

Scowling at him, Callie took off toward the house and the purple and green balloons.

*****

Garrett couldn't help laughing. It was going to be an interesting afternoon. When Harriett had called him wanting to plan a "doin" for the newlyweds, he didn't have the heart to say no. He knew it wasn't Callie's style, but heck, he wanted to celebrate their marriage. He smiled as he saw Nanny following along. He knew where she'd be today, wherever Pirate was. "Come on Tiger, let's get to the party."

It looked like half the town of Lasso Springs was there. Rows of tables had been set up, loaded with food. The grill and smoker were going, cooking brisket and ribs. The smell was smoky and mouthwatering. At the end of the tables was a wedding cake with purple and green flowers. It was the neon shade of green making it look tacky, but Garrett loved it. He was sure his bride probably wasn't as pleased.

He looked around and spotted her giving out hugs. He didn't mind the hugs from the women but the men were a different story. Walking over to her side, he staked his claim and glowered at a few of the young men. Suddenly the hugging was over and a quick polite tip of their hats accompanied their well wishes.

Callie grabbed Garrett's hand and squeezed it, painfully. He smiled down at her, not wanting anyone to know what she was doing. "Cal..."

Callie released his hand. "That's better ,cowboy. My name is Cal, not, cupcake."

Garrett loved the twinkle in her violet eyes.

"Yoo-hoo. Yoo-hoo. Garrett, Callie," Harriett yelled. She flew toward them, her long black wig once again skewed on her head. This time she was wearing fake eyelashes and one was on her cheek. "I am so happy for you."

"Thank you for doing this for us," Callie said, hugged the other woman.

Garrett was both surprised and pleased. "You sure went to a lot of trouble."

"We had such fun. Didn't we, Mable?" she asked, looking for Mable.

Mable popped right out from behind her. "We sure did. Best of all, my Bobby is here. I know you don't need any legal advice today but he is such a good lawyer."

"He sure is and he adds so much prestige to our little *sworrayy*," Harriett said smiling.

Garrett didn't have the heart to correct her. Imagine Bobby Darling bringing prestige to the soiree. "Thank you, ladies."

"Oh, oh, Cindy. Where is Cindy?" Harriett asked. "She was in charge of the balloons and decorations. She did such a good job."

Old Henry walked up trying not to laugh. "Ladies, we need to get these two on the dance floor so the rest of us can dance. I'd love to have you dance the first dance with me, Miss Harriett."

Harriett looked so happy. "Go, go you two. The rest of us want to dance." She practically pushed them away.

"Did you know about all this?" Callie asked, as Garrett whirled her around the dance floor.

"I knew about the basic concept." Looking into her eyes, he smiled. "I think the last time we danced together you wore pigtails and stood on top of my boots."

Callie smiled back. "I've always had good taste."

"I have to admit you have never made a truer statement."

"I'm having a good time," she said, her eyes twinkling. "I can't wait to eat the purple and green cake."

Before he could answer, Garrett felt a tap on his shoulder. Looking at the other man, he graciously handed his wife over.

*****

Callie smiled at Old Henry. "Had enough of Harriett?"

Henry blushed as he looked at his feet. He seemed to be counting. "I was performing a courtesy. Besides Mable told me to."

Callie felt warm inside. Old Henry wasn't a dancer but here he was dancing with her at her wedding reception. As the song ended, Callie led them off the dance floor. Turning she hugged the old cowboy. "Thank you for always being there, Henry. I love you."

"You've been the love of this old Cow poke's life, Cal girl. From the moment, I first saw you. You've always been my, special little gal."

Callie's eyes misted. "I know, Henry and it's been a great comfort to know you were always there."

"I suspect you won't need me much now you have that husband of yours," he said gruffly.

"I'll always need my first love and protector."

"Good. Enough of the mush stuff, Cal girl. Time for cake."

"My turn with the lovely bride," Stamos announced, cutting in.

Callie smiled at her handsome friend. The fact he was a fantastic dancer didn't surprise her. She'd danced with him before at the Whiskey Barrel. "So did you go back to Dallas to fight crime?"

"No. I've found what I want right here."

"What's that?"

"I've always been looking for something. Coming here to this ranch was a homecoming for me. I grew up on a ranch and couldn't wait to get away from it. Now, I feel the land, it's in my blood."

"Staying on?"

"For a bit, I have a lot of money saved and I have my eye on a piece of land next to yours."

Callie hugged him close. "It would be wonderful to have you as a neighbor."

As soon as the music stopped, Garrett was at her side. "Still trying to steal my wife?" he teased, clasping her hand.

"Always, buddy." Stamos laughed.

"Wait. I want to know who carved those dollar signs into Maggie Mae."

Stamos turned serious. "Believe it or not, it was Siggy. He's a cruel one."

Callie nodded in agreement. "Thanks for the dance and I'm glad you're staying." She kissed him on his cheek and he walked away.

"He's staying?"

"His love for the land runs deep. I know the feeling so well."

Garrett hugged her to him. "Me too, it was my greatest love, until you. You have stolen my heart, Callie."

Joy flowed into her veins and throughout her whole body. She tingled with electricity. "Cowboy, you have my heart, always have, always will."

*****

Garrett wanted to laugh when they opened the presents. They were mostly knitted. Everything from a tea cozy to a pair of scarves. Most of the items were green and purple. The most fun was watching Callie trying to look surprised and delighted. He had to bite his tongue a time or two to keep from laughing. Callie kicking him worked too.

Sitting in a chair with Callie placed firmly on his lap made it all worthwhile. They watched Harriett sing her very own rendition of Whitney Houston's song I Will Always Love You. He started to rumble with laughter, but Callie quickly put her hand over his mouth.

Callie gave him an I-don't-believe-you look as he kissed her hand. Pulling away, she tried to look serious but Harriett started singing a medley of Cher songs. "Now we know why she wears the long black wig," she whispered.

"At least she has both eyelashes on," Garrett replied, with a grin.

Mable seemed out of breath when she approached them. "There you are. I've been looking for you." She motioned to Old Henry who looked none too pleased. In his arms was a big box. "I have another gift for you."

Callie gave him a warning look. Somehow she knew he was about to groan. "Thank you kindly, Miss Mable." He tipped his Stetson at her.

"Open it," she said, turning red.

Callie stood up and reached for the box. Old Henry put it on the ground in front of her. Garrett could see she was a bit hesitant. "Open it, darlin'," he teased.

Callie pulled out a huge knitted, thing that was green, purple and orange. "Well, isn't this nice, Don't you think so, Garrett?"

"Why yes, we could use it to, umm, to."

"Don't be embarrassed. It's for your bed," Mable proudly explained. "I added the orange myself. Harriett had a big sale and it was mostly orange yarn. You do think it will fit, don't you?"

Garrett stood up and kissed the older woman's cheek. "Looks perfect to me. You have such a good eye for color and your knitting is very impressive."

"Yes Garrett is right. You have all been so generous."

"You know what I want to do, pumpkin?"

"No I couldn't even guess," she replied warily.

"Why don't you and I make sure this fits?"

Callie smiled at him. "Great idea." She grabbed Garrett's hand and dragged him toward the house.

Garrett closed the door to their bedroom and just stared at her. "It broke my heart that day when you cut your hair. I am so sorry for that day, Callie. I think about it all the time."

Callie closed the gap between them. "I cut my hair in mourning. I was mourning our love. I forgive you, Garrett. I don't even think about it anymore. We have each other now, and I have plans."

Garrett drew her into his arms, feeling the softness of her against him. "I don't deserve you," he whispered, huskily.

"I know, but I also know of a way to make you deserving," she teased, unbuttoning his top shirt button and kissing him at the base of his neck.

"I will try very hard." He trembled.

"Let's start our family," she whispered, her eyes looking so earnest.

Garrett placed his hands on her cheeks turning her head upward. He stared at her plump cherry red lips. He licked them until she opened her mouth to him. Her moan of pleasure shook him. He wanted her fast and hard. It was an urgency he had to fulfill. He undressed her kissing each new place he exposed. She was exquisite. "So beautiful," he murmured, as she squirmed under him in need. "Is it too fast?"

"No, no," she begged. "I want you now."

"Right now?" he teased.

"I want you, Garrett, this second."

Garrett entered her in one thrust, causing them both to gasp in pleasure. Her squirming was driving him mad. He could feel her heat, her sense of urgency and he moved faster. It didn't take long and they both yelled each other's name.

Garrett had thought last night was the ultimate but this was even better. He didn't think he'd ever get enough of this woman.

Callie snuggled against him, licking the crook of his neck. He smelled of leather and horses and he tasted salty, yet sweet. He was a superior specimen of a man. His whole body finely honed by hard work. Running her fingers over his chest, she played with the small amount of hair he had. Slowly she traced the hair down his abdomen until she reached the very spot she was aiming for. She wanted to explore it. It was an opportunity she never seemed to have before. Touching it she marveled at its silkiness yet, it was hard.

Before she knew it, she was being lifted by her hips until she straddled Garrett. Smiling into his eyes, she lowered herself. Her moan of pleasure seemed to echo throughout the room. "You're going to be the death of me." She began to pant.

Garrett gave her a lazy sexy grin. "You said you wanted to cowboy. Ride me, Cal. Make me explode," he said, his voice deep and husky.

Callie couldn't believe the feeling. She was so full and when he touched her breasts, she spiraled out of control. Vaguely she heard Garrett groan. Laying there sprawled on top of him; she knew her world was perfect.

Chapter Fifteen

The fall leaves were in their majestic beauty of reds, yellows, and oranges. There was a refreshing nip in the air. It was one of Garrett's favorite times of year. The coolness was such a welcoming change from the hot Texas summer. The days were growing shorter and the work was ever increasing. It was round up time, and he and Callie had been working alongside of the men from dawn to dusk. As long as there was light, they were in the saddle.

Garrett smiled as he thought of Callie. She hadn't spent so much time on a horse in a long time. Her walk had changed, and her legs wouldn't cooperate with her. He gave her nightly massages. It was something he was more than happy to do. It seemed all he had to do was touch her and she turned to molten lava. Their sex life hadn't suffered one bit. She'd get used to riding soon enough.

When he had suggested she stay home, she became a holy terror. She had even threatened to move into a different bedroom. Garrett wasn't about to let that happen. It was his favorite part of the day. Looking across the vast expanse of land, Garrett could make out Callie's silhouette. She loved ranching as much as he did.

Turning Tiger, he rode toward her. Things had been so quiet, so peaceful since the arrests had been made. They had all gotten long sentences and it was freeing to know the danger was over. He saw Callie wave, he spurred Tiger to go faster.

She was a remarkable sight. She was riding Misty and she knew how to look good in the saddle. Her short curly hair was growing out and he hoped she would grow it long again. Her violet eyes shined and her skin glowed. It made him proud to have her as his wife.

"What's an old cowpoke, like you doing out here?" he teased.

"Cowpoke, maybe but old?" she asked with a laugh.

"Are you gonna have a hissy fit cause I called you, an old bitty?"

"Have you been hanging out with Old Samuel again?"

"Maybe."

"How many words did he teach you?"

"Pert near more than you can shake a stick at, my sweet Georgia peach," Garrett said, teasing a brilliant smile from her.

"I know a few words too like polecat, horse's patooty, hill billy," she sassily told him.

Garrett let his mouth hang open, pretending outrage. "Do you know what happens to little girls that abuse their elders?" He reached out and plucked her out of her saddle. He set her in front of him. "Now tell me about those nice compliments you just gave me."

"I was kidding, Garrett. Let me down."

Garrett's laughing eyes widened as a shot vibrated through the air. He slumped in the saddle against her. Tiger started to dance around dangerously, wanting to take flight. Blood seeped out of Garrett's shoulder and onto Callie. Callie let him slip onto the ground. The resounding thump let her know he had fallen harder than she had planned. Reaching for the Remington rifle Garrett always carried, she heard another cracking noise. She clutched the rifle as she flew out of the saddle, hitting the ground hard.

Lying low, she looked around and tried to gage where the shots were coming from.

"Saddle bags," Garrett said weakly.

Shaking, she got up and grabbed the bags. Another shot rang out and both horses ran. She fervently hoped they rode for home, alerting others to trouble.

"Garrett?" she asked panicked.

Garrett looked at her.

Crawling over to him, she wanted to cry. He was losing a lot of blood, but she had to get them to cover. Glancing around again, she observed the sun reflecting off a gun barrel. She didn't even take a moment to think. She turned, looked through the scope, and fired. "Garrett, run for those rocks," she screamed, taking another shot.

Callie ran behind him, trying to get to the protection of the boulders. She felt the pain before she even heard the crack of the shot ring out. Her right arm burned but she hardly took notice. She had to care for Garrett's wound and keep them alive.

Making sure they were both behind a cropping of rocks, Callie stripped off her shirt and pressed it against Garrett's wound. It looked bad. "Is it still in?" She lifted him so she could see his back. "Through and though."

"Keep an eye out," Garrett warned, his voice conveying his pain. He cringed as she laid him back down.

Opening his shirt she looked, there was blood everywhere. She grabbed the saddlebags and took out a bottle of water and duct tape. It was nerve racking as she tried to keep an eye out for the shooter at the same time. Pouring water on his wound, she then wrapped her shirt around his shoulder securing it with duct tape.

Grabbing the rifle, she looked down its scope, aimed, and pulled the trigger. The kick from the rifle bruised her shoulder, but she didn't have a choice. A bullet had grazed her right arm and it was bleeding. "Who the hell is out there?"

"I haven't a clue, Cal. I feel so helpless. I want to be able to protect you."

Callie gazed at her husband. "I know you do, cowboy. I'll try to do my best."

Ducking as a bullet ricocheted off the rocks behind them, Callie prayed. It didn't look good unless help arrived. Another bullet and small rocks spilled down on them. Catching the glint of the shooters gun, she fired. "How you doing, Garrett?" she asked, not taking her eyes off the treed area the shooter was hiding in.

"I'm holding on. Nice work with the duct tape. I have another shirt in the other saddle bag, put it on."

She hadn't even noticed all she had on was her bra. It would have to wait. She was too busy ducking and shooting.

"He's making his way to the left, he's going to try to get behind us," Garrett called out to her.

"I'm going to be on the other side when he gets there. The sun is in his eyes now and we need to use that advantage."

"What do you propose?" Garrett asked.

"I know this particular area; I used to spy on you when you wouldn't let me go with you."

"Cal," Garrett started.

"Save it, cowboy, it was years ago. There's a trail that leads through these rocks and I know a place you can use for cover."

"I'm not letting you do this alone," Garrett protested, as Callie shot off a few more bullets.

"Let's go!" She gathered all their supplies and Garrett. He was almost dead weight. "Come on, cowboy, one more push and you can collapse."

Callie struggled to lift Garrett. He was giving it his all but it was still hard. Another bullet ricocheted and sprayed granite on them. As quickly as she could, Callie led him through a maze of boulders. Stopping at a shallow cave, she slowly released Garrett. "Be right back."

Running back to where they'd been, she shot into the woods, watching for return fire. She needed to know where he was. As predicted he was making his way, hoping to get behind them. Shooting again, she wanted him to think they hadn't moved, and then she ducked and made her way to Garrett.

To her dismay, her shirt was soaked through with blood. Cutting the duct tape away, she applied pressure on it, poured more water, and then placed his extra shirt against it. This time she bound the duct tape tight around his shoulder. She propped him up, hoping gravity would help.

Hoping to God the shooter wasn't familiar with the maze of a trail twisting through the rocks, Callie gave Garrett a lingering kiss. She didn't dare delay leaving. Keeping as low to the ground as she could, she wound her way around the dusty trail. It was a bit hard since the sun was in her eyes this time. Leaning against one of the last big boulders on the trail, Callie reached into the saddlebags and grabbed the two last rifle magazines. She prayed it would be enough.

Hearing someone cussing, Callie made herself even smaller, stepping into the shadows. She was right, whoever was trying to kill them, was climbing up the mound of boulders. If she waited, she'd be able to catch him in her sights. Perspiration rolled down her face and back. The boulders scraped at her bare skin as she stealthily moved once again.

He must be waiting for dark. There was no way to get to Garrett without exposing her position. She was worried about him. He'd looked so pale when she left him. She hoped the duct tape held out. The sun seemed to be taking it's time going down. Suddenly Callie heard horses riding close. She had prayed for help, but she hoped they didn't get hurt.

Noise had a funny way of traveling and Callie wasn't quite sure where the sound of horses was coming from. It took a lot of focus but she decided they must be on the side they went in. Rocks poured down on her as someone climbed across the boulder she was hiding behind. He was trying to get away.

Callie stood up and aimed her rifle. "Stop, or I'll shoot," she warned.

The figure stopped and turned, making Callie gasp.

Callie was too shocked to pull the trigger. She'd known him for so long. Terrified she realized he was aiming his shotgun at her. A shot rang out and seemed to echo through the air. Turning in time, Callie spotted Stamos behind her.

"That was close." He climbed over rocks to get to her. She was shaking; it was all too much for her.

"We'd better see if he's dead," she replied, her voice trembling.

Stamos nodded. "Stay here."

Staying put was not in her plans. Following close behind, she ran into Stamos when he stopped. "Where is he?"

"Looks like he's fallen into a bit of a crevice, and he's alive."

"Be careful, Stamos," she cautioned.

"Go get his gun, it fell right over there," Stamos pointed down.

"I see it." She scrambled down to retrieve it. She watched Stamos make his way to the shooter. Her mind swirled with questions. It had to be that damn oil again.

"Is he all right?" she called.

"Yes, shot in the arm is all," Stamos shouted back. "I'm bringing him up."

Callie sensed someone behind her and turned. Smiling a sad

smile, she walked into Old Henry's open arms. "Why?"

"Don't know, Cal girl. I'm just as surprised as you." He held her tight for a moment and let her go so she could face the shooter.

Immediately she checked to make sure Stamos was okay, and then she looked into Old Samuel's angry eyes. He glared at her with hate and she flinched. "Take him away. I need to get to Garrett; this piece of horse manure doesn't even deserve my consideration."

"I'll go with her if you think you can handle him alone," Old Henry said to Stamos.

Stamos already had Old Samuel handcuffed. "Go ahead, she needs you."

Henry nodded and followed Callie, finally catching up with her. "Here put this on," he said, throwing her a tee shirt.

Callie nodded and put it over her head. Getting her right arm through the sleeve was painful. She kept walking, increasing her pace.

"How'd you know about the trail?" she asked, without breaking her fast stride.

"Who do you think kept an eye on you as you kept an eye on Garrett?"

Callie stopped and turned toward him. "Oh Henry..."

"Keep walking. No mushy stuff, Cal girl," he said, his voice gruff with emotion.

Callie smiled at him and kept walking. Her need to get to Garrett outweighed all else. She knew her arm was bleeding. It must have been the adrenalin since she felt no pain. Her shoulder was bruised from the Winchester. It was a good thing it was a smaller 22 rifle, used mainly for small game, or her shoulder would be beyond pain. It almost made her smile as she thought of the much bigger rifle she owned. For such a big man he sure used a puny rifle. It did the job, that's all that mattered.

She broke into a run as she spotted Garrett and cried in relief. His eyes were open. Karl was bent over him, applying pressure to his wound. "How, how is he?"

"He's lost a good bit of blood but I think he'll be all right. We need to get him to the hospital. Nice work with the duct tape, you're good in a crisis."

Callie took a step forward and everything went black.

*****

Garrett sat in a wheelchair next to Callie's bed. He'd been sitting there for a long while waiting for her to come to. Two nurses were working their floor, a nice compassionate one named Barb and Attila the Hun named Agnes. Unfortunately, it was Agnes that kept coming in every two seconds telling him to leave.

He made it very clear he'd no intention of leaving. She gave him a superior smile and told him she had her ways to make sure the rules were followed. Two orderlies appeared and wheeled him back to his room, and put him in his bed.

Garrett didn't resist. He didn't want any of his stitches coming out. Lying there, he remembered he had been stapled together. He could have taken those orderlies on.

"Now if you follow the rules we'll get along just fine. If not, I'll have restraints put on you," Nurse Agnes said.

She looked as though it would make her day to have him restrained. "I'll rest for a while," he said.

"See that you do."

Garrett watched her leave and hoped the door hit her on the ass on her way out.

He must have dozed off. When he opened his eyes, Callie was sitting by his bed. She looked good, worried, but good. "Hi, my love," he said, his voice sounding raspy.

Callie smiled at him. "Hi yourself."

"You okay?"

"I'm better than you, cowboy. A bit sore but I'm mending."

"A lot of it is fuzzy but you were shot too, weren't you?"

Callie smiled at his concern. "Just a graze on my right arm. I'm fine really." She lifted her sleeve to expose her bandaged arm. "See no staples," she teased.

"I don't know, staples just seem so unnatural." He studied her face. She looked tired, but her color was good. "You really are okay?"

Callie got up and leaned over the hospital bed. She kissed him long and hard. Finally, she broke the kiss and stood up. "See, just fine."

Garrett laughed. "I love you, Callie."

"I know and right back atcha." Tears flowed down her cheeks. "It was a close thing, Garrett. Too close."

"Believe me, Cal, I know it. If it hadn't been for you, I'd be dead," he said solemnly, the seriousness sinking in. "I don't ever want you in danger again."

"It was old Samuel, he wanted us both dead," Callie said, her voice quivering.

"That's the damndest thing. I've gone over it, and I haven't a clue as to why."

"Me too, Garrett. He's lived on your ranch since forever. You've treated him like family."

"What did he hope to gain by killing us? I just don't get it. I've looked at it from every possible angle and I still can't come up with a valid reason."

Feeling lightheaded, Callie sat back down in the wheelchair. "The main thing is we're alive."

Garrett reached out and took her hand. He wanted contact with her. He needed to reassure himself she was fine. Staring into her violet eyes, his heart filled with love.

"Oh good you're both here," Stamos said, entering the sterile room.

"You brought me flowers?" Garrett asked.

"Hell no, these are for Callie. Here you go, darling. I even had them put in a vase for you."

Callie blushed and accepted the flowers. It was a big assortment with lilies, roses, tulips. "These are beautiful, thank you."

"You are most welcome," Stamos said, looking at her.

"Do you have to always look at my wife like that?"

"Like what?"

"Like you want to have her for your own."

Stamos smiled. "Wishing it doesn't make it true now, does it?"

Callie shook her head at the two macho men. "Any news for us?"

"Old Samuel is going to live. I just finished interrogating him. It's quite the story."

"We're not going anywhere," Garrett said sarcastically, still mad at the looks he gave his wife.

"Turns out Old Samuel is actually your uncle."

"What?" Garrett asked, in surprise.

"I hate to tell you this but it seems your granddaddy got around. Do you happen to remember a woman named Maria Clark?"

Garrett nodded. "She was the housekeeper for a long time while I was a child."

"She was Samuel's mother. Your granddaddy refused to acknowledge him. Apparently, your father knew about it and still refused to acknowledge him. He gave him a job but Samuel believed he deserved more. He wants part of the ranch."

Garrett exchanged looks with Callie. "Did you ever hear anything about this?" he asked her.

"Not a whisper."

"So what was the plan? Kill us and stake claim to the ranch?" Garrett asked.

"You got it. Especially since the oil find, he wanted his due."

Garrett shook his head. Closing his eyes, he leaned back on his pillow and ran his fingers through his hair. "Why didn't he just come to me?"

"He was sure you'd deny him like the rest of your family had. If you died, he planned to pretend to just find out the family connection and take control of both ranches."

"Why does greed rule the world?" Callie asked, in disgust.

Stamos put his large hand on Callie's left shoulder. "I'm sorry. I feel as though I should have known or seen it coming."

Callie put her hand over his. "You couldn't have known about this, Stamos. It really is shocking."

"I wish he'd just come to me. I would've worked something out. I knew my father was a hard ass but this is cruel," Garrett said angrily. "His actions almost got us killed."

"Wait one minute, Garrett. Your father was a fine man and a well respected rancher. Maybe Samuel is lying or maybe your father had his reasons. The person we should be mad at is Samuel, not your daddy."

Sighing loudly Garrett looked away. The revelations had him reeling. Turning his head, he looked into Callie's eyes. Boy she was riled up on his father's behalf. "You're right. My father was a hard ass. I guess it made him a good rancher."

"What happens to him now?" Callie asked Stamos.

"I don't know."

Chapter Sixteen

At the end of her tether, Callie sat on the living room couch and cried. It had been three months since Samuel's arrest. A long three months with Garrett at the courthouse more than at home. He insisted on sitting behind Samuel in the courtroom and Callie refused to accompany him. How could he forget the panic, and horror of the shooting? It still gave her nightmares and she would often jerk awake reaching out to Garrett to be sure he was in one piece.

He refused to stop giving Samuel his support. He was even paying for the lawyer. She didn't understand his position and it galled her to no end her labor and sweat was paying for that man's defense. They barely talked anymore.

Tears poured down her face and she didn't even wipe them away. This crying jag had been a long time coming. All of her dreams had been hers for the taking. Hell, she was living her dream before the shooting. Right now, her life had divided into two chapters, before the shooting and after the shooting. Thank God for Stamos, he was her rock out on the range. He was quite knowledgeable about ranching and it was a busy time.

Round up had been completed and they sold some cattle. The fat check they had received wouldn't go far if it was paying for Samuel too. She'd tried, Lord knows how hard she'd tried to see Garrett's point of view, but she just couldn't. Her heart was hardened against the old cowhand, and she couldn't find it within to forgive.

Sighing, she pulled a red bandana out of her jeans pocket and dried her tears. The sound of an approaching truck put her on edge. It was a tragedy really. Before, she would have been out of the front door waiting to fling herself into Garrett's arms. Now she dreaded the harried look of disappointment he gave her these days.

Nothing was ever easy. She never turned away from him at night. His need was great and she couldn't find it in her heart to deny him. Praying they would find their way back to each other, she went out on to the front porch to try to smile at her husband.

"How was court?" she asked.

Garrett scowled at her. "Fine." He brushed by her.

She watched him go inside. The hell with him. She went to the barn and saddled Pirate, and took off for the north pasture. Maybe if she stared down the section of fencing that had started this nightmare for her, she'd feel differently. She was out of ideas and this one sounded as good as any.

Her hardheaded idea wasn't the best. It was freezing out with a northern wind blowing. Despite her warm jacket and gloves, she was chilled, but she still refused to stop. Something pushed her forward, urging her to go all the way.

Her nose became cold and her eyes began to sting against the weather. Feeling foolish and half witted, she stopped Pirate and looked the land over. All the lushness of summer was gone along with the vivid colors of fall. The earth looked brown, ready for snow. The silhouette in the distance surprised her.

She urged Pirate forward. Now she knew why she had such a feeling to come here. Her heart dropped and she felt gut kicked. He wouldn't have done this. There was no denying it. There sat an oilrig on her property. Staring at it, she felt sick all over and she began to shake with rage. This was her land. No sense in approaching the men working, she already knew who was the low down snake that approved this.

Tempted to ride fast and hard, she couldn't do that to Pirate. Cantering, they headed for home.

Well, she knew where the money for Samuel's defense came from. Her land was providing him with a defense. The house was in sight but Callie halted Pirate. Jumping down she headed for the nearest bush and threw up. Her stomach was a bit better but the sickness in her soul grew bigger. Garrett knew her views on oil drilling. They fought the mob over it for God's sake. Grabbing Pirate's reins, she walked toward her house with a heavy heart.

Garrett waited on the porch but she ignored him. She needed to tend to Pirate.

*****

Garrett realized he'd been snubbed. The jig was up. Somehow, she'd been tipped off. He knew she wouldn't listen to him. He could give her a million reasons but they wouldn't matter. It seemed the answer to his problems at the time. He had wanted to right his family's wrongdoing. He wanted to be the one, who finally stood up and told the truth. He allowed his righteousness to cloud his judgment. He believed he was doing what was right, and he knew Callie wouldn't agree.

It was time to tell the truth. It frightened him. He didn't know what to say, what he could possibly say to make it right. He'd been lucky it'd taken this long for her to find out. Bracing himself, he walked into the barn.

His Callie was brushing Pirate. He smiled at the picture they made. No matter what, Callie was a rancher first and she knew the animals came before anything else. She must have heard him but she didn't look up. His heart beat erratically. It was all too much; he hadn't had a moment to relax in three months, ever since Samuel shot them.

She looked so young in her jeans and red flannel top. The silver belt buckle he'd given her glistened in the light. Her whole body seemed tensed, coiled, and ready to strike. Her voice sounded peaceful as she murmured to Pirate.

Finally, she looked up at him and the raw pain he saw in her eyes cut into his soul. What had he expected? He knew from the first phone call he had made it was wrong. Talking it out would have gotten him nowhere and at the time he'd felt justified in being selfish. Now he knew he'd made a colossal mistake.

"Callie, can we talk about it?"

Her head turned away. He knew she was gathering her thoughts. He waited for the scathing words that were sure to come his way.

"I'll be in momentarily," she said, still not looking at him.

"I'll wait for you in the study." He waited for a reply but there wasn't one. Turning away, he walked to the house. He'd ruined their lives.

*****

Callie waited for him to leave and she immediately buried her head in Pirate's neck. Her body continued to shake. It wouldn't stop. What was there to say? She really didn't want to hear his rationalizations. What he did was beyond wrong. It was a deal breaker.

Feeling at a loss, she was glad when Old Henry came into the barn. He was always in her corner and she loved him so. "You're a sight for sore eyes," she said sadly.

Old Henry looked at her. "So he finally told you, did he? Made me turn slack jawed and threatened to send me packin' if I opened my mouth. I can't abide such things."

The wind was knocked out of her. Old Henry knew. He knew. He knew. It was too much to bear. "I can't abide it either." She walked out of the barn.

Marching into the study, she gave him a long look. "It'd better be good."

Garrett stood up and started to come around the desk but Callie put her hand up. "No don't come any closer."

Garrett nodded and went back behind the desk and sat down. "Cal..."

"You had no right. How? Didn't you need my signature? For God's sake Garrett it's on my land!"

Garrett's face turned white. "It's not your land," he said, softly.

The look of regret on his face puzzled her. "It's my land."

"It hasn't been your land since before we were married."

Callie stared at him. He wasn't making any sense. "What the hell are you talking about?"

"Cal..."

"Damn it Garrett, you'd better explain."

"Your mother signed the land over to me in exchange for me marrying you."

"All this time you knew and played me for a fool? How could you? God, I hate you. Right now I hate you," she said, shakily. Giving him one more look, she raced out of the office and hopped into Garrett's truck. This wasn't her land, this wasn't her home. Her heart shattered as she drove away.

*****

Stamos stood outside of Faye's Café looking at Callie. She sat in the last booth all alone staring into her coffee. They were all responsible for her misery. It galled him at the time to go along with Garrett, but his reasons were sound. At least at the time they were sound, he wasn't so sure anymore. The pain showing on her face made him cringe. He had to help. She meant too much to him to walk away.

The bell jingled as he opened the door, but Callie didn't look up. Stamos waved to Bailey, the knock out waitress. He gave her one of his special smiles. He'd had his eye on her for a while and now that he was staying in the area. Well, who knows? He had to keep his mind on the little gal in the corner. She was in a world of hurt.

"Mind if I join you?"

Callie looked up, smiled, and then scowled. "I suppose you knew about the oil too," she accused.

"I came to see if you wanted to go home." He sat across from her.

Bailey came running with a mug and a coffee pot. "Hey sugar, haven't seen you in here lately."

Stamos grinned at her. "Been busy."

"I'm glad you're here now. It's good to see you," she said as she poured him coffee and topped off Callie's. "Did you need anything...?"

"No thanks Bailey, we have ranch business to discuss."

Bailey looked a bit disappointed but she smiled. "Let me know."

Stamos watched Bailey walk away. Her hips swiveled. He never grew tired of watching her delectable rear end. "Sorry," he said, a bit sheepishly. "You coming back?"

Callie's eyes filled with tears. "Don't see how."

Stamos reached across the table and covered her hand with his. "I have a place you can stay for a while."

"Where would that be?" she asked, her eyebrows rising.

"I own the ranch next to yours. Bought it a week ago. It's livable but I figured to wait until early spring to get things started. No sense in having to feed cattle all winter."

"You're right about that," she commented. "Are you going to be living there?"

"Hadn't planned on it, at least not yet. It's a nice livable house. I know you'll insist on working so I could use the house spruced up, and I have two horses and a few chickens I need fed. It would actually be a help to me."

"I'll take it."

They both looked at her cell phone as it vibrated across the diner table.

"Aren't you going to get that?" Stamos asked.

"No, it's Garrett. I can't talk to him just yet," Callie told him, her big eyes making her look lost and vulnerable.

"Yeah, well, let's get you settled at my place." Stamos stood up and offered her his hand.

Callie gave him a sad smile. "Yeah," was all she said.

Bailey waited near the door. She obviously wanted to talk to Stamos before he left. "See you soon?" she asked, her gaze filled with invitations.

Stamos smiled at her. She sure was sexy. "I'll be around Bailey." He winked at her.

Walking toward their trucks, Callie stopped and laughed. "What's she going to think about me shacking up at your place?"

Stamos smiled broadly. "I don't think I have to worry. She might be fun for a while but I'm not looking for long term."

"Burned were you?"

"Something like that. Let's get you to my place, it's getting late."

"I'm sorry Stamos, I forgot about your wife."

"Let's just go."

Callie nodded and got behind the wheel of Garrett's truck. "I'll follow you," she called out the window.

Callie was familiar with the property Stamos had purchased. It bordered her land. Her heart twisted. It bordered Garrett's land. She'd loved that piece of dirt all her life. It was too disillusioning to find out it wasn't even hers. What had her mother been thinking? The betrayal was beyond measure. She was glad when they drove up to Stamos' house.

It looked perfect, and she was happy for him. It could use some TLC but it looked soundly built. This land had been deserted for some time now. He's obviously cut the grass and the porch railings looked new.

"Look's great, Stamos."

"Thanks. It's not much now but it will be," he told her as he ushered her inside.

Looking around, she admired the logs. "They don't make house like this anymore. Imagine a log cabin."

Stamos smiled. "I thought so too when I first saw it. I have indoor plumbing and everything," he said, his glance dancing at her.

"That will be helpful," she said, but somehow she lost her smile. She didn't know if she'd ever find it again.

"Take the big room, it has a bed. I left some clothes here so help yourself. The kitchen has enough for a few days. I'll be by tomorrow to check on the animals and to go over things with you. Do you want me to bring your things?"

Callie didn't even hesitate. "That would be great."

Stamos kissed her on the cheek. "Good night, Callie."

"Good night," she murmured woodenly as she watched him drive away. The silence was too powerful. It reminded her how alone she really was. Running into the bathroom, she was sick again. Try as she might she couldn't get the demons out of her head. Switching on the radio, she went in search of something to eat. She wasn't really hungry though.

Peanut butter and jelly sandwiches would never be her first choice but it was the simplest. The whole burden on her shoulders weighed her down and she just wanted to curl up and forget about everything. She cleaned her dish and headed up the stairs. The house was a beautiful A-frame and the sleeping quarters were loft like. It really didn't need very much TLC but she felt glad to have somewhere to go.

Finding the only room with a bed, she entered it. There in the middle of the room was a massive sleigh bed. It was beautiful. She surmised it had come with the house; she couldn't picture Stamos picking out that bed. Walking over to the dresser, she opened a drawer and took out a tee shirt. It had been one hell of a day, and she was beyond exhausted.

She could smell Stamos' scent when she got in bed. She almost wished it made her heart beat faster but it didn't. It only made her miss Garrett. Her mind whirled but she was too tired to make sense of any of it, she went fast to sleep.

Hearing a door slam woke her up with a start sometime later. She quickly jumped out of the bed and pulled her jeans on. Hesitantly she peeked out the door and gave a big sigh of relief to see Stamos.

"Still in bed?" he asked. "Hell, I've worked almost all day."

Looking out the window, Callie could see the sun had been up for a good while. "I guess I was more tired than I thought," she said sheepishly.

"Come on down I'll make coffee," Stamos offered.

"Let me wash up, and I'll be right with you." She should've asked for her things. The white claw foot tub looked mighty tempting, but she'd already slept a lot of the day away. Dressing in yesterday's clothes, she used his brush for her hair and her finger with toothpaste on her teeth. It would have to do for now.

Stamos greeted her with a smile. She attempted to smile back but knew she failed miserably. He handed her a cup of coffee and the smell put her off. Putting it on the table, she looked at him. "What did Garrett have to say?"

"He was glad to know you were in a safe place," Stamos said.

Callie knew that was a lie. Garrett probably chewed Stamos up one side and down the other. The fact the Garrett hadn't raced over here was a good thing. Let him stew for a while.

"You know you don't look so hot. I mean, you look a bit pale," Stamos observed.

"I'm feeling a bit off."

"I'll take care of the animals, and go. You'll be okay?"

"Of course. Don't worry about me."

Stamos stared at her. "I do worry, but I know you need space. Hopefully Garrett will give you that."

It felt nice to have a friend. "Oh, I wanted to ask you about your bed. A sleigh bed for such, a hard ass cowboy?"

*****

Garrett had heard enough. How the hell did she know about Stamos' bed? He was seeing red by the time he yanked the door open and barged into the kitchen. "What's this about Stamos' bed?"

Stamos jerked around. "Didn't hear you, buddy."

He wanted to plant his fist in his face. "Obviously. You two were too busy talking about your bed. You told me you'd keep your hands off her. I never should have taken you at your word."

The air stood still. A man's word was his bond and it should never be in question without good reason. Garrett knew that and from the look on his face, Stamos did too.

"Wait you two logger heads. Just stop it," Callie yelled, getting between them. "How dare you?" she screamed at Garrett. "How dare you even think I would cheat on you? Stamos' word is more reliable than yours."

Garrett felt his throat tighten with his Adam's apple lodged in it. What had he done? Good God, what had he said? Callie looked madder than a wet hen. "Stamos, I'm sorry. I don't know what got into me. I apologize."

Stamos nodded. "I think I know what got into you. She's worth the fight." He turned toward Callie. "You'll be okay?"

Callie just nodded.

"Well then, I'll be by tomorrow."

Garrett stared into Callie's eyes, not even blinking when Stamos left. "I'm sorry," he said softly. He could feel the massive wall between them and it tore at him that he was responsible for it. He knew at the time it was wrong, and he sure as hell knew it now. "I'm hoping you'll come home with me."

Callie's eyes flashed in anger. "You're sorry? Well, you know what, I'm sorry too. I'm sorry I ever believed you. I thought the sun rose and set on you. I thought we loved each other. I thought we were going to make our ranch into something to be proud of, but I thought wrong." Tears streamed down her face. "I don't know what is true anymore. I've been thrown off my foundation and I don't know how to get back, so, no, I won't be going home with you."

Garrett closed the gap between them and took her into his arms. He held her as she sobbed, feeling worse than he ever had. He didn't say a word to her. He just held her and rubbed her back.

Callie quieted and pulled away. "I just can't talk to you right now."

Garrett studied her tear ravaged face, this time he didn't see hate in her eyes, he just glimpsed sorrow. "I understand. Can I come by tomorrow?"

Callie shook her head. "I need a few days, please."

"Whatever you want. Call if you need me." He walked out the door.

Standing outside of the log cabin, Garrett was reluctant to go. He'd have to do things her way, he realized with a heavy heart. He loved her whole heartedly and there was no way he was going to let her go. But for now, the ball was in her court.

*****

"You two sure eat a lot," Callie said to Lucy and Desi, Stamos' two paints. She'd grown attached to them but she had called Stamos to see it he'd bring Pirate over. Hearing the trucks pull up. she hurried outside to help unload her baby.

"How many horses did you bring me?" she asked Stamos, as she eyed two trailers.

"Funny thing. Garrett told me to bring Misty over and the next thing I knew Nanny and Billy insisted on going too."

Callie laughed. "Billy goat?"

"You had to be there. It was a mutiny. They were all going or none."

"As long as Garrett doesn't mind," she said, chewing the bottom of her lip.

"Ask him, he drove the other truck."

Butterflies filled her stomach, hundreds of them flying around. She was anxious to see him, but at the same time, she wished he hadn't come.

"Cal, come give me a hand, will you?" Garrett called to her.

Callie hurried over and laughed. "Nanny, you get out of there. You too, Billy. You wanted to come so stay a while."

Nanny turned and looked at her. She seemed to be studying her. With a nod of her head, she backed out of the trailer with Billy right beside her.

"Is she?"

Garrett smiled brightly. "She sure is, and she's as proud as can be."

"No doubt it's Pirate's," she commented.

"No doubt," Garrett answered, his eyes never leaving her face.

Her face grew warm, and she knew she was turning red under his intense perusal. Her anger had abated a bit but the hurt was too fresh, too raw.

"Nanny, I'm so happy for you." Callie hugged the grey horse.

"Pirate, you are quite the rascal, old boy."

Billy stood next to Callie and head butted her enough to make her scramble to keep her feet under her. "Manners, Billy, manners."

Callie experienced a bit of happiness to have her animals around her. "Thanks," she said to Garrett and Stamos.

"We'll be back this afternoon," Stamos called, as he got into one of the trucks and drove away.

"Why?"

"Stamos got a great deal on cattle from a foreclosure. Plenty of cows and heifers included. It's a great opportunity for him."

"Too good to pass up," Callie agreed, looking at his face hungrily. A wave of despair washed over her and she looked away. "I'll get these horses settled. See you later." She walked toward the barn, not even looking back when he called her name.

The afternoon came quickly. It was a remarkable sight. Truck after truck was unloaded, bringing the cattle to their new home. There was something majestic about a Texas long horn. Every hand from their place was there on horseback, helping to herd the cattle into a nearby pasture. The sight filled Callie's heart. She was a rancher through and through. Stamos had made a great deal. The cattle were in prime shape. Her heart was glad for him. He was on his way to realizing his dream.

Stamos rode up to the front porch. "Want to help?"

"Been waiting for the invite," she said smiling.

"I have someone from the diner bringing food for the men; could you wait for her and then saddle up?"

His excitement was contagious. "You bet, go on, and inspect your cattle."

Stamos barely tipped his hat before he rode for the pasture. It looked to her they'd need to open a few pastures, the cattle just seemed to keep coming. Callie felt happy for him. Watching as a van drove up, she hoped it was the person from the diner; she was itching to get into the saddle and help.

Bailey jumping out of the van surprised her. She looked full of sunshine from her long blond hair to her sparkling blue eyes to her bright smile. "Hi," Callie said.

"Hey. Where's Stamos? I thought for sure he'd be here waiting."

"Nope, he's rounding up his cattle," Callie told her. "Do you need help unloading the van?"

Bailey's smile faded. "You're living out here, aren't you?"

"Yes," Callie answered, watching as Baileys' eyes narrowed a bit.

"Garrett's been in to see me the last few days. He needed consoling. It seems to me you have one cowboy too many," she said, with a fake smile.

Callie wanted to smack the smug look off Bailey's face. Jealously did have an ugly head. "I'm off to help with the cattle." She brushed past Bailey.

"You do that man thing. I'll be here waiting, looking pretty," Bailey said.

Callie kept walking. Bailey had some problem with her. It was too bad, she'd always liked Bailey. Guess she had her eyes on Stamos. Using Garrett to get under her skin was a low blow. She shook it off as she entered the barn. She'd always been better with animals than humans.

The cowboys on their horses yelling," Yah, Yah," sounded like a symphony to Callie. This was what she wanted to do with her life. She wanted to get up every morning, put on her chaps and her Stetson, and ride. Pirate was a first rate cow horse. No horse chased down errant cattle better than Pirate did. He could stop on a dime and turn quickly. It was pure magic rounding up cattle with him. It didn't hurt Callie was the number one roper in the county.

The lulling and mooing made her smile. The cattle were in great condition. Stamos was going to be a first rate rancher. Seeing a heifer make a break for it, Callie and Pirate were right on it, cutting her off and guiding her back to the herd. If she didn't think about her personal life, then she couldn't be any happier. Unfortunately, Garrett was in her sight at every turn. He smiled at her often in what looked to be admiration. She hoped it was. A couple times, she caught herself returning his smile and she stopped herself. She could tell by the way his lips twitched he knew.

The pain in her heart hadn't lessened any. In fact, it only intensified as the day went on. Stamos called everyone in for lunch. Callie slowly headed in. She wasn't in the mood for Bailey and whatever her problem seemed to be. Hanging back, she could see Bailey playing it up to Garrett. Callie walked nearer and she heard Bailey ask Garrett if she would see him later. The smile he gave Bailey shattered her. Quietly she turned and walked away. No one had noticed her, and she just wanted to be alone to lick her wounds.

The loneliness she bore was stupendous. It shot through her body and she couldn't shake it. Brushing tears away, she got on Pirate and rode away. There was only one place she wanted to be right now. She needed to be with Maggie Mae and Honey Bun. It didn't matter her only friends were animals. As she rode on, she recognized it did matter. It mattered a lot.

It took a long while twisting and turning though pastures and gates. Finally, she found them, her babies, not so little anymore. It was a band-aid to her heart when they both came running over to her. It was a beautifully cool day. Callie reached down and yanked off one boot then the other. Soon her socks joined her boots. Sinking her bare feet into the cold earth, she wiggled her toes. This land, this piece of earth had been in her family for generations. The soil ran through her blood. It belonged to her.

How dare her mother sign it away. Signing away the land just so Garrett would marry her, what had her mother been thinking? She looked around and sighed. It wasn't hers, and it hadn't been for a very long time. Why all the illusion on Garrett's part? Why did he even bother? She always knew she was no prize. She'd been so blind. Looking at Maggie Mae and Honey Bun, she realized they didn't belong to her either. Sitting down on the land she had so loved, she raised her knees and leaned her forehead against them. Tears spilled onto the ground and were absorbed by the rich soil.

Wishing it all away was a waste of time, with each breath, each heartbeat, the pain of her loss renewed itself, never ending. Turning her tear ravaged eyes toward the heavens she beseeched God for understanding, for a healing of her pain. There wasn't an answer. She was on her own. She sought comfort within, but sadly, there was none. Her heart, her soul, her mind and body were so tired. The sun would be setting in a couple hours, she should be on her way to Stamos' ranch, but it was beyond her to move. The air grew colder and still she didn't care.

It was all too much. She felt overwhelmed. Finally, her senses started to come back to her. Self preservation kicked in, not for her but for the baby she suspected she was carrying.

It was too cold to be sitting outside. Putting on her socks and boots, Callie told the animals to be good and that she'd be back soon. Mounting up on Pirate, she rode back to Stamos' ranch. As much as she wanted time alone, she hadn't gotten much thinking done. At least not the right type of thinking. Knowing she couldn't stay at Stamos' forever made her anxious. Fatigue took over. Her thoughts were jumbled. The harder she tried to think, the worse it got.

It was a great relief to see Corky standing in front of the barn. He helped her down and took Pirate's reins. "They went looking for you," he said with a shy smile.

"Thanks for taking Pirate. I appreciate it," she told him.

Walking toward the house, she couldn't wait for a hot bath. The need to calm both body and spirit grew. She hoped Stamos had packed her Japanese cherry blossom bubble bath. Its scent revived and comforted her.

It was a surprise to find Bailey pacing the kitchen looking all kinds of angry. Callie could just imagine her with steam pouring out of her ears. Callie nodded and walked by her only to have her arm grabbed. "What the hell?"

Bailey spun Callie around until they were face to face. "Oh no, you're not going anywhere until I've had my say."

Callie just stared at her. A mad Bailey was not a pretty Bailey. "What do you want?" She pulled out of Bailey's grip.

"For starters how about an apology for running off? You created all kinds of havoc here. You spoiled my lunch. And to top it off you have two, not one, but two cowboys out looking for you."

Callie wanted to laugh, but by the strange facial contortions Bailey made she decided against it. "Only two? Huh, two is not havoc."

"It sure is when they are the best two," Bailey shouted.

"Listen Bailey, I don't know what your problem is but it has nothing to do with me."

"You're so selfish and spoiled. You've both Garrett and Stamos at your disposal and you seem to think it's your due. Well. let me tell you something, Garrett and I were making plans for tonight when they noticed you were gone. You might not want that handsome husband of yours but I do."

Callie was shocked. "You'd go after a married man?" she asked in disgust.

"Hell, as far as I'm concerned, Garrett is fair game."

Callie was too tired for this. "Listen do what you want, I'm going to bed."

Callie went up the stairs and locked herself in Stamos' room. She decided to forego the bath; she didn't want Bailey getting any ideas about drowning her. That girl had a loose screw. It took ever once of energy to get undressed. Putting on her flannel nightgown, seemed heavenly. Looking out the window she saw Bailey drive off, she was about to turn away when she saw Garrett in front of the house. He looked up at her and his stare was intense and soul piercing. Callie had to pull away from it. She was too tired. She climbed into bed and nodded off.

*****

The scent of cinnamon in the air put a smile on Callie's lips as she woke. She hoped the cinnamon rolls had lots and lots of icing. Her heart slammed into her throat, she was supposed to be alone. Panic went through her before she shrugged it off. It had to be Stamos in the kitchen. Putting her hand on her abdomen, she chuckled. "I don't think we have to worry. Cinnamon rolls are not the sign of the devil."

After a quick shower, Callie got dressed and bounded down the stairs, expecting to see Stamos. Seeing Garrett in the kitchen shocked her. All the joy drained out of her and her smile dissipated. Anger would have been a good thing, but all she had was sadness. He'd turned when she entered the kitchen, looking at her with big blue eyes.

Ducking her head a bit so she wasn't looking at his face, she said hi. It sounded pitiful to her ears. She felt pitiful, so very pitiful.

"I made you breakfast," he said.

Nodding, Callie sat at the table. She couldn't look at him. Instead, she watched as her finger traced an ancient circle on the table.

"I was hoping we could talk," Garrett continued.

She must have worn out what little patience he had. He strode over to her, grabbed her upper arms, and lifted her to a standing position. He lifted her chin until she met his look. "Callie, I can't go on like this. I need you home with me. I expect you to be home with me."

Callie put her hands on his broad chest and pushed for all she was worth. He went flying to the ground, he still had a hold of her, and she went tumbling too. A sharp cry echoed through the kitchen, it had come from her.

Garrett quickly got to a kneeling position and looked her over. "Where does it hurt?"

"I'm not sure. Give me a minute," she whispered as she placed her hands protectively over her stomach.

Garrett looked at her hands and then at her face. "Cal?"

"What?"

"Are you in pain? Should I call the doctor?"

Callie shook her head.

"Is there something you want to tell me?"

Callie could see the confusion in his eyes. She wanted to tell him she thought she was pregnant, she wanted to share the joyous news with him, but fear held her back. She shook her head. "No, I'm fine. The fall frightened me, that's all."

She accepted his help getting up. Giving him a weak smile, she walked up the stairs. She couldn't face him. The sound of footsteps echoed up the stairs as she settled into the bed.

He knew. Somehow, he knew. Hell, she barely knew, and somehow he knew. He looked good she had to admit that. Her emotions were so jumbled. She sensed a certain homecoming, whenever she looked at him. She also felt hurt and betrayed. Loving him had always been the easy part. It was a life-giving breath. Now she just didn't know.

Of course, he didn't knock. Callie hadn't imagined he would. His wide eyes sought hers and pinned her in place. The look of compassion and confusion on his face pained her. Her emotions had been so unbalanced lately. Crying had become second nature to her.

"I don't know why I'm crying," she said, giving him a wobbly smile. "I've turned into a watering can."

"You never looked more beautiful," he said softly. He took a few slow steps toward her. It reminded her of the way he approached skittish horses.

"I hurt," she cried.

Garrett made tracks to her bed. "So you did hurt yourself."

Shaking her head, she looked at him. "I hurt. My heart and head both hurt. I can't think anymore I hurt so much."

Garrett edged himself onto the bed and pulled Callie into his arms.

"No," she protested. "I'm mad at you."

"Believe me, sweetheart I know. Just let me hold you until you feel a bit calmer?"

Callie couldn't speak. Her throat clogged. She simply relaxed against him, taking in his wonderful scent and feeling his hands rubbing up and down her back. It felt close to pure heaven to be in his arms. As long as he knew she was still mad, she rationalized as she sighed. It had never been easy with Garrett. It probably never would be but she knew one thing to be true, she loved him.

"Can I make you something to eat?"

"No," she managed to squeak.

"Sit up for a moment. I want to take off our boots."

Callie did as she was told; she didn't want to fight with him. She smiled as he got one of her granny nightgowns out of her dresser drawer.

"Should I help you? Or..."

Callie took the gown from his big hands. "I can manage." He turned his back and let her change. He was giving her respect by turning away. It made her soften toward him even more.

The creaking of the bed as she got into it, caused Garrett to turn around. "This is the bed Stamos and I were talking about. See it's shaped like a big sleigh."

Garrett smiled at her. "It's certainly worth remarking on. I'm always saying or doing the wrong thing."

Callie opened her arms. "I don't want to talk about that now. Just get that big hard bod of yours in bed so I can snuggle and get some more sleep."

Garrett's lips twitched at her bossiness. "Yes, ma'am."

Garrett's body ached. Lying next to Callie had not been easy. She had meant just snuggle and his hardness began to be painful. His body didn't want to be a gentleman. It wanted to be satisfied, and damn the consequences. The cooler head prevailed.

Resembling an angel, Callie moved slightly and emitted a sigh. Garrett couldn't get enough of looking at her. He'd watched her all day long, viewing her in all the different lighting from the earth's majestic colors. So far, he liked her best at twilight. Her beautiful tresses were growing longer and her skin looked so creamy. Her lips were ripe cherries. Garrett closed his eyes. Who was that man with the poetic thoughts?

He wondered when she planned to tell him about the baby. One thing at a time. Holding her was a good start, being in her bed was one too. For so long he considered himself a failure. He hadn't been able to protect Callie. That was supposed to be his first priority and it didn't happen that way. He failed her. Good God she ended up scarred by barbed wire and she'd been shot, all on his watch. He didn't deserve her.

Impossibly hard. That's what the last few days had been. Knowing she'd rather be alone than with him, hurt. The afternoon was approaching and he knew his peaceful time with Callie would soon end. Upsetting her at this point wouldn't be right. Pregnant women needed calmness.

Reluctantly he eased out of the big sleigh bed. Walking to the door, he turned and looked at her. What a beautiful sight. Garrett's heart expanded with all the love he had for her. Carrying his boots, so not to make noise, he left.

*****

Callie absently thanked the nurse and she put the next appointment card in her purse. She sat down in the waiting room, trying to absorb her news. She felt giddy and at the same time, tears pricked at the back of her eyes. Her chaotic life was just about to become more chaotic, but in a good way. Fancifully, she pictured a baby boy with dark hair and the blue O'Neill eyes.

She had a lot to do. The Texas sun seemed to be shining brighter, just for her. The smile on her face wouldn't go away. It didn't even dim when she saw Garrett sitting on the bumper of her truck. He looked so handsome. The look of worry on his face made her heart thaw toward him. He still had a lot of explaining to do, but this was their moment.

Garrett took off his Stetson and stood up as she approached. His eyes seemed to bore into her, trying to read her mind. He must have seen her smile because he smiled back.

"Everything all right?" He took a step toward her.

"More than all right." Callie took a step toward him. He opened his arms and she went flying into them. Only in his arms did she feel whole. She relished the feeling, and then pulled back. "I have news."

The look in his eyes was so hopeful, so filled with love. "Do you want to sit down? It's kind of big news," she cautioned.

"Just tell me, woman. Please I need to hear it from you."

"We're pregnant," she said, softly.

"We are?" he asked, hopefully.

"Yes Garrett, you and I. The two of us."

Garrett took her into his arms and kissed her cheek.

"I have a surprise for you, but first we need to talk. I have a lot of explaining to do."

Callie pulled back and looked at him. He looked serious, pensive even. "Okay."

"Get in the truck; I have a place we can go."

Callie nodded and got in. She didn't ask where they were going. It didn't matter. The man she loved was beside her, and it sounded as though he intended to make things right between them.

Soon enough Callie knew where they were heading. Garrett was taking her to her favorite place along the Lasso Springs Creek. "You remembered," she murmured.

"I remember everything about you. From your bight sexy smile to the little moans you make when we make love."

A warm glow coursed through her body. "It looks like this is it," she said as they pulled up to her spot.

Garrett got out, grabbed a blanket from the back, and opened Callie's door for her. Helping her out, he held her for a long time.

Callie felt cherished in that moment.

"Let's sit," he suggested. He took her hand and led her to the river's edge. He laid out the blanket, and then he shrugged out of his coat and put it on Callie. "It's a bit colder than I thought."

Callie smiled at his thoughtfulness. "You wanted to talk?" she prodded.

Garrett looked at her and nodded. "Callie, I love you and I don't want to lose you."

When Callie started to open her mouth, Garrett put his finger over her lips. "Let me finish." Callie nodded. "I need to explain why I did the things I did. I need you to understand. First, I should've told you the land had been signed over to me. I should've signed it back over to you long ago, but I was afraid you'd meet someone else at college and it seemed my only connection to you."

Garrett took Callie's hand in his and caressed the back of it with his thumb. "I honestly thought I was doing the right thing by trying to put distance between us. Foolishly, I thought our age difference was too much. I was wrong about that too. For the record, I didn't receive the invitation to your graduation. I'd have never missed your big day."

"Garrett," Callie whispered.

"No, let me get this all out. To my utter shame, I couldn't protect you. The barbed wire, the shooting, the threats, I should've been able to spare you that. I feel responsible for all of it. Maybe I shouldn't but I do. I also feel responsible for my father and grandfather's mistreatment of Old Samuel. I wouldn't be much of a man if I didn't right the wrong my family did to him. Yes, I should've talked to you about it, but I was worried out of my mind. I couldn't lose you too. I figured if I sold the oil all the danger would go away, and you'd be free to ride the range again."

Reaching toward her, he cupped her face with his hands, looking into her eyes. "I love you, Callie O'Neill, with all of my heart and soul. I never meant to hurt you."

Callie gazed at him. "So much has happened. You broke my heart, Garrett. I don't think I'm the woman for you. I'm still that hick tomboy who wants to cowboy with the men. I want to round up cattle, rope them, brand them, and feed them. I'm not wife material," she said sadly, as she hiccupped.

Garrett put his Stetson on her head. After all these years, it still made her smile. "You're everything I ever wanted."

"What about Sylvie? It looked to me you wanted her, and she was so beautiful."

"She'd been rubbing up against me for so long, and I already decided I couldn't hold you to our marriage vows. It wasn't fair you were too young to know your mind when we got married. I regret kissing her. I regret hurting you more. You are the most beautiful person in the world to me. I can't believe I hurt you the way I did."

Garrett stood up and walked closer to the creek. Callie's hesitation was killing him. Would he only see his child during visitations? The thought became intolerable. Bowing his head in defeat, he felt lost. He could hear her walking toward him but he didn't look at her. He couldn't. He'd let her have her say, and then he'd drive her home. Stamos' house, this couldn't be happening.

Callie put her hand on Garrett's shoulder. He didn't turn. He didn't acknowledge her. "Garrett?" Still no answer. She wrapped her arms around his middle and pressed her face into his back.

Garrett could feel the strength of her sobs go through him. Instantly he turned and took his weeping wife in his arms. Kissing the top of her head, he held her. He hoped to God it wasn't for the last time. He wanted to weep too. He'd had it all and now he was lonely and heartbroken. He felt like such an ass for making Callie cry, once again.

"I'll take you back to Stamos'," he murmured.

Callie pulled away. She looked fiercely angry. "Oh no you don't, cowboy. You're not getting rid of me so fast." Turning she began to stalk away.

Garrett's jaw dropped. Hope filled his being as he ran toward her. Sweeping her up into his arms, he kissed her. He continued to kiss her until he realized she had her hands on his chest, pushing him away.

Pulling his head away, he looked into her eyes. He spotted love, and hoped he wasn't mistaken.

Callie smiled at him and put her arms around his neck. "You literally took my breath away."

"What?"

"I pulled away because I couldn't breathe," she explained, her lips twitching.

"You are my whole world, Callie O'Neill."

"Let me down. I have a few things I need to say to you."

Garrett put her down but he didn't let go. He took her hand and entwined his fingers with hers. Leaning over he gave her a searing kiss. He loved how red and swollen her lips looked when he pulled away.

"Don't kiss me. I can't think when you kiss me," Callie protested, letting go of his hand.

Taking a deep breath, Callie stared straight into his eyes. "First of all, I have loved you heart and soul since forever. When I said our marriage vows I meant them even though the marriage was a sham."

Garrett began to protest but Callie shook her head at him. "It's my turn, cowboy. It killed me to be away from the ranch and from you when I went to college. I didn't have a single friend, I didn't belong. I know where I belong. I belong on this land. I belong in your arms, but mostly I belong in your heart."

Garrett wanted to take her into his arms but she had that look. She wasn't done.

"Second of all, I'm a grown woman and while I enjoy your protection, it's ultimately my job to keep me safe. You never failed me that way. You have hurt me, stripped my heart and soul that you did do. I'm disappointed you didn't tell me you owned my land, but now I'm glad I didn't know. It would've been too devastating after mama's death. You are a hardheaded man, Garrett O'Neill. I know working a ranch requires quick decisions and I understand we won't be able to confer on all things, but I expect to be part of all major decisions. As far as Old Samuel, I admire your loyalty and integrity."

Garrett stared into her eyes, seeing all the love she held there. He let out the breath he wasn't aware he's been holding.

"And another thing, cowboy, I expect you to change diapers." She walked into Garrett's waiting arms.

*****

Callie snuggled her face against his neck. Every nerve in her body was on fire for him, but first she needed to know he understood she expected to be a partner in running the ranch. Callie kissed his neck, wishing she had the nerve to give him a hickey. She'd never done that. Pulling away while she could still think, disappointed them both.

Garrett wouldn't let her go completely. Standing in the circle of his brawny arms, she smiled. "Well?"

Garrett's smile lit up her soul. "I promise to hold your heart next to mine and treat it as a precious gift. I promise to try, really try to make decisions jointly. I promise to be a hands on father, and I promise to love you with all of my being."

Awestruck, Callie stared at him. His words became a song in her heart. They brought tears to her eyes and they soothed her being. Callie could see his sincerity and his love. She bit hard on her lip not wanting to cry. "Well you better, cowboy." She stood on her toes to kiss him.

It was reminiscent of a first kiss, filled with wonder and excitement. He tasted of mint and coffee. His tongue darted into her mouth making her sigh. Wrapping her arms around his neck, she pulled him closer. The hardness of his body excited her. Reaching down she pulled the snaps of his western shirt. One by one, they opened. This time she heard him sigh as she stroked his naked chest. Muscles rippled under her hands. Reaching down further she grabbed at his belt. Garret's hand stopped her.

"I need to show you something first."

"Show me later. I have something right here I want to see, touch."

Garrett groaned.

"As much as I want this to happen, I need to show you something."

Callie frowned. "What could be so important?"

Garrett grabbed her hand and led her away from the creek, toward a hill. Callie kept looking at his face for clues but to her chagrin, he didn't give anything away. The hill wasn't even very big and in short order they stood at the top. Callie smiled at the view. She was familiar with this piece of land. She often rode out to the valley to see the wildflowers.

"Give me a clue, what am I looking for?" she asked eagerly.

Garrett chuckled. "Look closer."

Callie scanned the valley slowly and that was when she saw them, stakes in the ground with red tape on the top of them. "I don't understand."

Garrett put his arms around her and gave her a gentle squeeze. "You are looking at our future."

Callie turned toward him, feeling puzzled. "I don't understand."

Garrett took her hand and led her down into the valley. They stood among the land markers and she gasped. "A house. You're building a new house?"

"I hope I am," he said looking at her face. "It's in your hands now."

"I don't understand."

Garrett smiled at her and picked her up into his arms. "Let me give you a tour and then you can decide." Garrett carried her to a staked out room that seemed massive. "This, my love, will be the bedroom."

"Put me down, I want to walk it." Callie walked the perimeter of the room. "It's twice the size of your room now."

"I wanted us to have plenty of room. I didn't know if you wanted to put the crib in here at first or what."

Tears poured down Callie's face. "You, stupid, stupid man." She sniffled.

Garrett's eyebrows shot up as he frowned. "What's that supposed to mean? I didn't start building because I wanted you to have input. I planned to share the decision making with you."

Callie smiled brightly through her tears. "I called you stupid because you-- we could have avoided so much discord if you had thought this way before. Garrett, I love you."

Garrett's eyes misted as he drew Callie into the circle of his arms. "You are my heart, my soul, my best friend. I've been lost without you." He kissed her forehead and pulled her tight against him. "I'm never letting you go again."

Callie snaked her arms around his neck and looked up into his blue eyes. "I'm not going anywhere. We are building a future, together. You and me and our children." She kissed him deeply and then let go, hearing Garrett groan in protest.

"Show me where the bed is going to be."

Garrett gave her an odd look and walked over to a spot in the massive staked out area. "I was thinking right here would be good."

Callie laughed a long earthy laugh. "Well, cowboy, what are you waiting for? Go get the blanket. I feel the need for some cowboy loving only you can provide."

Garrett ran up the hill. Callie sighed; he sure did fill out those wranglers. Joy filled her being. Happiness was hers for the taking and she intended to be greedy, very greedy. Looking around the valley, she felt a sense of homecoming. Together they would have a wonderful life. Garrett was her life and he was her heart.

Callie laughed as Garrett practically fell, running back to her. Her body tingled, the passion she felt for her husband ran through her. There was nothing like a little cowboy lovin' in the afternoon.

Epilogue

Callie smiled as she realized she'd finally gotten more than three hours of sleep. It had been a hectic last few months. The house, now completed, was a dream. Updated kitchen, wrap around porches upper and lower, and a Master suite. She'd never seen one before but now she wouldn't be without it. The jetted tub was plenty big for the two of them. The only problem was finding a quiet moment.

Speaking of quiet, she wondered where everyone was. Garrett had gotten her to use a breast pump so he could bottle feed while she got some sleep. Callie smiled. Garrett was such a big man yet he was the gentlest loving man she knew. A blessing, that's what she had. Many blessings. Good health, wonderful love, and her heart filled with joy.

Callie had finally found solace in her family. She still enjoyed riding through the tall Texas grass with her hair blowing in the wind, but her soul was happiest with her family.

Making her way down the stairs, she looked in the kitchen. No Garrett. Actually, it was a little too quiet. Looking throughout the house, she grew a bit concerned. He couldn't handle an outing by himself yet. Finally looking out the front window, she spotted him.

Her heart smiled as she gazed at him. He was sitting in one of the Adirondack chairs, asleep with their son Aidan in the crook of his left arm. Aidan looked content just to lay there, his big blue eyes looking at Garrett in hero worship. He loved his daddy. Aidan's curly brown hair looked identical to Garrett's. It was uncanny how much they looked alike.

In the crook of his right arm was Rose. She was named after Callie's mother. Rose was the more vocal of the two. Once she started, Aidan seemed honor bound to join in. This moment of quiet was a rarity. Rose took after Callie. She had blue eyes the same as her daddy but her blond curls were all Callie. She even had the same heart shaped face. She loved her daddy. Rose already had Garrett wrapped around her finger. She too just stared at Garrett.

The contentment and love Callie felt was beyond anything she'd ever imagined. They had finished the house in the nick of time. They were able to bring the twins home to their new house straight from the hospital.

Garrett's head dropped to his chest, he snored slightly and jerked his head back to lay it against the chair. The twins both waved their little hands. So that was it. Garrett provided them with entertainment.

Whatever worked. Garrett had them both bundled up but it was a chilly morning. Callie stopped herself, before she went out there and fussed over them.

Callie knew how comforting Garrett's arms could be. Looking out on the horizon, the beauty of nature filled her soul. She didn't care what the future held, as long as she had her family, she'd be happy. Rose began to stir and Callie went to make coffee. Garrett would need some after wrangling with his two little cowpokes all night.

Visit Lasso Springs Again
Lasso Springs Book Two: Lone Star Joy

About Kathleen Ball

A voracious reader, Kathleen quickly discovered the world of romance novels and she knew she was home. At the encouragement of her sister Tricia, she decided to try writing. Kathleen wrote her first book two years ago. She was shocked to find out that people loved what she wrote. All of Kathleen's novels are award winners. Callie's Heart is her first published novel. It is the first book in The Lasso Springs Series. Kathleen lives in Texas. She moved there from Rochester, New York and is having the time of her life exploring Texas culture. Kathleen is married to her wonderful husband Bruce and they have one son, Steven. They just welcomed new additions to their family, a new daughter in law, Brittany and her cute as a button son, Colt.

She feels blessed to be supported in her writing by her family and friends.